A VAMPIRE'S BANE

RAVEN STEELE
AVA MASON

A ROUEN NOVEL

CHAPTER 1

Thick and muscular but lithe as a jaguar, the vampire strode down the street with the confidence of a lion. His hurried, lengthy steps echoed off the dilapidated buildings around him and rats scrambled to clear the area or faced the unfortunate squish under his unruly shoe. From where I stood, perched on the rooftop above him, I could see the glow of his silver eyes.

He yanked open the door of the large warehouse across the street. It squealed in protest and banged against the back wall as he disappeared inside. I refrained from rolling my eyes at his unnecessary clamor; vampires were only noisy like that when they wanted to feel important.

Briar and I were following the same vamp I'd seen at Sinsual the night I met her. I'd kept an eye on him after that night, never finding anything too interesting except that he distastefully drank from humans in a more public manner than I was comfortable with. After Silas died, the vamp had disappeared, only to reappear again nearly a week ago at the same club. This time, something about him had set off my radar like a demon rising from the grave. He was trouble and now, I was determined to find out what kind.

A slight breath of wind, cold and invading, brushed the base of my neck. The temperature of its invisible touch was too cold for this time of night. I glanced behind me and surveyed the dark rooftops in the distance. Someone was watching us. I was as sure of it as I was the number of times Briar had adjusted her bra.

"Why do you keep looking behind us, Sammie?" Briar whispered. "The action's down there."

Her gaze dropped to the parking lot thirty feet below us. The sliver of a moon barely illuminated the large moving truck as it rumbled toward the big warehouse. We had been perched on this small spot of roof across the street for nearly two hours. The vampire had come here every day this week. Tonight, we were going to find out why.

Briar shifted her position against the hard bricks for the tenth time, but I had barely moved. I enjoyed the stillness and the feeling of being at one with the darkness.

"It's nothing," I finally answered, not wanting to worry her. The vamp led us to discover that Bodian Dynamics was back in business. We thought we had beat them back out at Evergreen swamps, but they'd returned only a few weeks later in a different location. And not just any location. The exact warehouse where Dominic and Vincent had kept the drugged-up shifters. I still hadn't figured out how they gained ownership. One day it belonged to the Silver Claws, the next it belonged to the large research organization. "And don't call me Sammie, Briarpatch."

She groaned. "That is the worst nickname ever."

"That's why I say it."

"No, I mean, literally. It's dumb. Why not call me Badass Briar or Briar Big Bush or—"

I silenced her before she could say something else stupid and pointed below us. The truck had come to a stop and the back door had opened into an empty bay. Two men and one woman, vampires, waited expectantly at the edge. I expected to see workers unload boxes or crates from the back of the truck, but instead, a dozen people were rushed out, their hands bound. Briar and I glanced at each other. Moonlight captured a speckle of gold in her brown eyes.

"Human?" She raised her eyebrows.

I looked back at them and focused my vampire senses. Their chests rose and fell in a regular pattern, which meant they weren't vampires. I sniffed the air, sorting out Briar's shifter scent, and even Luke's still clinging to her. He was hanging out with Briar every day now.

I zeroed in on the people being held captive. A faint aroma of shifters, magic and chemicals reached me. I'd smelled the chemical scent before. The mutated creatures Briar called Hydes. It was a name I thought was ridiculous at first, but the more I witnessed their strange conversion from human-like to monster, the more I saw the similarities between Dr. Jekyll and Mr. Hyde's transformation.

"I believe they are shifters, human and a witch or two."

Briar cursed. I resisted the urge to scold her for her foul mouth. I had always been taught to choose my words carefully. Words were important and conveyed different messages. Cursing was reserved for extreme moments. Briar seemed to have a lot of those.

Briar shook her head and adjusted her bra for the seventh time. "I can't believe they are still at it. We're going to have to do something drastic so our message is more clear. Can we burn the place down?"

"Not yet." She adjusted her bra again. "And quit playing with your brassiere."

"I can't help it." She tugged at it, grunting. "I put my booby knife in wrong, and it keeps poking me. And don't say the word brassiere. It shows your age."

I motioned to the twin blades warming my back. "You could carry a blade like a normal person."

She scoffed and turned back toward the warehouse. "Nothing about that is normal."

I watched her for a moment, my dead heart tightening. Briar had been through so much this last year, her whole life really. She had learned the hard way that seeking revenge created jagged scars on our minds that never quite healed right. But she tried. Every day she woke up and pushed through the darkness I felt inside her. It mirrored my own. Maybe that's why I felt a connection to her the first day we met, despite her abrasive language and uncouth behavior.

After the prisoners below us were ushered into the warehouse, the boxes I had been expecting to see came next. Large ones stamped with Bodian Dynamic's logo. "Let's get closer."

I didn't wait for her to respond. By the way she was tapping obsessively against the bricks with her fingers, she was just as anxious as I was to pick a fight.

Leaping from the rooftop, I landed in a crouch on the sidewalk below. Briar joined me a second later. We darted behind another truck that had been there all night and peered around the side. Beside the dozen or so captives, there were at least six Hydes and a few vampires. I sucked in a quiet breath when I recognized one of them worked for Mateo.

I leaned back into the truck, thinking hard. He must be working against Mateo. He had to be. Mateo couldn't be working with Bodian. He had helped us destroy one of their facilities only weeks ago.

"What's the plan?" Briar turned to me.

I looked around the side again, a familiar hunger racing though my veins, and took off my glasses. I folded them up and placed them on the bumper of the truck. "Kill and destroy."

A slow smile spread up her face. "Just what I was hoping you would say."

Briar darted out of our hiding place first and leapt into the open bay of the building, holding a dagger she'd snatched from her boot. It wouldn't be very effective against the vampires, but that wasn't who she was aiming for. I was right behind her when she slashed the throat of a Hyde so deep his head lobbed to his shoulder, attached only by a small flap of skin. She kicked him to the concrete floor and leapt over the body. That got everyone's attention.

Almost everyone. The vampire I recognized lunged for me. I shoved him to the side, sending him flying across the room. I didn't want to kill him just yet. There were some questions I needed answered.

Two Hydes attacked me at once. They were strong, far stronger than a regular human, and fast, too. I swung my blade forward, but the first one dodged just as the other rammed his fist into my spine.

4

Pain shot through my body, but, like I was taught so many years ago, I compartmentalized the heat.

Relying more on instinct, I swung around, my blade slicing through the air so fast, I could barely track it. It met its mark, decapitating the Hyde behind me. A thrill raced through me at the sight and sound of the blood misting the air in front of me. For a split second, I moved to partake of the crimson liquid, desperate to feel it coat my throat and stomach, but the better half of me, the part I had trained and honed over the last several hundred years, held back.

For the next few minutes, Briar and I made quick work of killing the Hydes and vampires. There was only one left—Mateo's man. I stalked toward him as he scrambled across the floor away from me, blood smearing the floor from a wound in his leg. Briar had almost killed him, but I had stopped her just in time. Behind me, Briar was freeing the prisoners.

"Why are you here?" I said to the vampire on the floor. His back hit a concrete wall, leaving him nowhere to run.

He didn't look at me. His gaze was darting to the space above me, as if expecting help. This gave me pause.

Keeping my blade fixed in his direction, I slowly looked up and focused my senses. I could hear nothing, smell nothing, but my sixth sense ... "Briar!"

I slowly backed up toward her. She cut the ropes from the last of the prisoners, saying, "All of you get out of here."

"No one's going anywhere," a deep and familiar voice said from up above.

"Well, shit," Briar said.

Above us, slowly approaching the railing, was Mateo, followed by the rest of the Sangre Nocturnas, at least three dozen of them.

"Angel?" Briar said, sounding as confused as I felt. "What the hell are you doing here?"

Angel's expression was unreadable as he stared down at us. Mateo's was the same.

I clutched the blade tightly in my hands. "What is the meaning of this, Mateo? When did you start working with Bodian Dynamics?"

His jaw muscles bulged, and he curled his fingers around the railing. "You shouldn't be here, Samira. You and Briar need to leave. Now."

"Answer me!" The sting I felt from his betrayal reached a place in my heart I thought I'd buried. This wound couldn't surface again. I'd barely survived it the first time.

"Samira, please," he said, his voice softening. "You must leave. None of this concerns you."

"Like hell!" Briar snapped. She kicked at a nearby box. "I know first-hand how horrible these drugs are. I won't allow you to infect these people," she motioned to the group of people cowering near the truck, "or anyone else."

"Stay out of it, Briar," Angel said, his voice a warning, but there was a look in his eye, a warmth directed in Briar's direction.

"You stay out of it," she retorted. "I thought you were better than this."

"Enough!" I let out an exasperated sigh and met Mateo's gaze. "We fought side by side with you, with all of you, to stop Bodian. How can you now be working with them?"

"There are things you don't understand. So I'll say it again, leave now before we make you leave."

I sized up their numbers, their strengths and skills. One of them, a vampire on the end, stood out. The one we followed here. It took me only a second to place his dark hair and silver eyes. What was Mateo's relationship with him? Had Mateo been working with him all along?

Briar and I couldn't win a battle against them. I glanced back at the fearful group of supernaturals. At least four of them were human from what I could tell. "Let us take them, at least. Whatever you're involved with, don't harm others, especially our own kind. That can't be what you want."

He closed his eyes briefly, then stared with that fiery gaze that still burned a line of heat straight through me. "Take them, but, Samira, I warn you. Don't get involved again. There may be consequences I can't stop next time."

I didn't acknowledge him as I ushered the group of people away from there, but Briar pointed at Angel. "You and I are going to have words later, back-stabbing asshat."

After grabbing my glasses, we left the warehouse, hurrying quietly away, in case anyone changed their minds. I could barely put two thoughts together from the shock at seeing Mateo there. It didn't make sense. He had always been against harming supernaturals without cause. So what would prompt him to work with Bodian Dynamics? Money? He had plenty. And money had never been a motivator in the past.

We reached the van a few blocks away. By the way Briar was pacing in front of it, she was still pissed. I turned to the nearest person, a shifter by the smell of it. "Who did this to you?"

He shook his head, his eyes downcast. "I don't know. One minute I was sitting at the bar, the next I was in the back of a truck tied up with rope. The others are all the same."

Briar had stopped to listen. "Where are you from?"

"Wildemoor."

"That's hundreds of miles away!" she gasped.

"Take everyone to the bus stop and leave the keys in the visor." I said, handing him the keys in my pocket. "Get home and make sure the others do, too."

He nodded and thanked us.

I addressed the rest of them. "There's money in the glove box. Divide it up and return home."

No one argued as they climbed in, many of them in shock. None of them looked harmed, which was something. As soon as they were gone, Briar cursed a string of words, half I didn't recognize. I began to walk home. She fell in step next to me.

"I just don't get it," she complained. "I thought they were on our side. Hell, we killed the smoke monster together!"

I didn't say anything. Pain was leaking out of the scar on my heart, making it difficult to breathe. Somehow, Mateo had found a way to betray me again. I was a fool for letting him back into my life, even as a business acquaintance and nothing more.

"Why aren't you more upset?" Briar said, eyeing me sideways. "The dude you like to blink at just betrayed us. Don't you ever feel anything?"

Anger surged through me, touching the dark places in my mind, the place where ancient rage festered and burned. I stopped and inhaled a breath, careful to calm the beast inside me. "It doesn't matter what I feel. I can only go forward, only do what has to be done."

"Bullshit. March your skinny ass back there and give him a piece of your mind! What he did was so messed up and you know it!"

I tried to block out her words, to not give in to the emotions tugging at my heart. It was dangerous to pull those strings. "You don't know what you're asking."

She shoved me, not hard, but enough to make the fangs grow long in my mouth.

"Feel something, Samira," she said. "Let loose so we can finally—"

I slammed into her, lifting her by the collar, and raced across the road in a blink of an eye until we slammed into the side of a building. Inches from her face, I hissed, "Do you want to see what happens when I let loose, Briar Big Bush? There is a monster inside me you don't want to poke. The beast is real and it is hungry for blood and violence."

She searched my eyes, her brows furrowed. "I have so many jokes going through my head right now, I don't know which one to say first."

I let her go and turned away. I shouldn't have expected her to be serious.

"Oh, come on, Samira. You think you're the only one who tries not to feel? I did it for years and look where that got me! Sure, it hurts like hell, but you need to show emotions or you're going to end up alone in a very dark place."

"I've managed this long."

She touched me lightly on the arm. "But you don't have to. You were there for me when I needed someone the most. Let me be there for you. I can tell you're hurting. What Mateo did, it had to have pissed you off."

"I am really…pissed off." I let myself say the words, let myself feel this one emotion.

She smiled. "There you go. It's a start. Let's see what else you got in you."

Her words struck a chord, rattling me to the core. "No one, especially my friends, can see what's inside me. If you did, you'd run away screaming."

Before she could respond, I disappeared into the night.

CHAPTER 2

*S*tars kissed the night above me. Their light was a constant assurance that I didn't have to give into the darkness. No matter how black or suffocating, there would always be light. Even if it was only a pinpoint. I thought of this as I walked back to Lynx's house. Briar didn't understand, nor would she unless I told her the truth about my past. But if she, if any of them, knew... I couldn't think about the consequences.

Instead, my thoughts turned to the house at the end of the street. Lynx's home. I hadn't meant to invite myself to stay. I could've remained at my hotel and immersed myself into their lives that way, but there was something about Briar and Lynx that night at the club that made me act impulsively. Maybe it was the way Briar had fearlessly fought those shifters, despite the odds, and how Lynx had appeared so timid and sweet. I hadn't been around people for a long time. In the moment, the idea of having roommates, friends, had struck me so hard I didn't look back.

And I haven't regretted it since.

As long as they didn't discover the truth about me. But my secrets would remain safe because I would be careful.

I was almost to the house when I caught movement on the porch, a slight variation in the shadows. I stopped and waited for the threat to reveal itself.

"Samira," a soft voice carried on the wind. It's one I'd heard a thousand times before. It was also a voice that used to strike lightning straight into my heart, but now it only reminded me of betrayal and heartbreak.

Mateo slid out of the shadows to greet me. I tensed at the sight of him and strode past the home and around the side. I pretended I didn't notice his golden eyes, the color of warm honey, burn into me or the way his chest muscles rippled when our eyes met. I had to pretend. He meant nothing to me.

He appeared next to me, walking as quietly and gracefully as a jungle cat. Once we were well into the woods, he stopped. "We need to talk."

I kept on going. "There is nothing to say. You chose a different side the first chance you got."

"It's not like that. Would you stop walking, please?"

I turned to him, despite my brain telling me to keep moving. Being near Mateo was like standing on the edge of a cliff with a storm at my back: surrounded by danger on all sides. It was too much of a temptation to jump in with both feet. Except, if I did, there was no doubt I would end up hurt. "Speak quickly."

His mouth opened then closed again. His brows furrowed. "It's hard to explain."

"Only if you make it so."

"My actions are not my own." He gave me a meaningful look. "I have to do what's best for my coven."

"You are their leader, are you not?"

"Yes, but—" His mouth closed again. He groaned and raked his fingers through his hair. I tracked the movements with my eyes, remembering how I used to do the same thing but in a very different setting.

I cleared my throat. "You say you want to talk to me, then you don't speak. Why did you really come here?"

His eyes hardened, and he straightened his shoulders. "I came to tell you to stay away from the warehouse."

I froze, my blood turning to ice in my veins. "Excuse me?"

"Stay out of Bodian Dynamic's business. I mean it, Samira."

"Are you threatening me?"

"There are things beyond my control. I cannot always protect you, especially if you insist on getting involved."

"You stopped protecting me long ago."

He growled, his fangs sliding out to pierce his bottom lip. "That's where you're wrong."

I looked into his eyes, remembering how they used to make me melt. My heart skipped a beat, the sharp sensation scratching at the jagged scar on my heart. "You will never know, or understand, the way you broke my heart that night. You made your choice. Now you think you can tell me what to do? Never again, Mateo."

"Maybe you should try to understand that choice I made so long ago."

I turned to leave, tired of this game, but he gripped my arm, pulling me to him. This time his eyes were soft, and he cupped my face with his hand. "I'm trying to keep you safe, Samira. Can you not find a sliver of trust in that heart for me, *mia anima gemella?*"

I melted at his words. *My soulmate.* The name he used to call me, so long ago. Heat and desire pulsed into my body, every inch of my flesh tingled as if I'd walked through an electrical field. That's how it was with him. The feeling hot and addictive. I met his eyes.

"Why are you working with them, Mateo?" I didn't hide the desperation in my voice. "This isn't you. At least not the you I remember. Have you changed so much over the years?"

"There are reasons why I do the things I do."

"Tell me then. Explain it to me."

"I cannot. You have to trust me. Please."

I hardened my face, just as my heart broke all over again. Every single time I had seen him since that fateful night in the swamps, my body, my heart, my mind longed to be with him again. But, no matter what he said or did, I hardened myself against it. I couldn't let him hurt me again.

I yanked my arm out of his hold. "You lost that right a long time ago."

I stepped back so he could no longer touch me. "If you cannot tell me, then I suggest you go. Leave this city with your men and your drugs. Sever your ties with Bodian. Walk away and leave us all alone."

He gave me a pained expression. "I can't do that."

I sucked up close to him and twisted the front of his shirt in my fist. "Then you stay out of my way."

I shoved him backwards and walked back toward the house, anger swelling inside me.

"Don't do it, Samira," he called after me. "Your life is in danger."

The smarter, wiser part of me wanted to stop and ask him what he meant, but I gave in to the more emotional part of me, as small as it was, and kept walking. I rubbed at my chest, wishing it didn't hurt so much.

"You can fix that," the ancient darkness inside me whispered. It spoke to me often, but I rarely indulged it anymore. This time, however, I pondered its words, remembering my vow to never feel the kind of heartache that shatters the soul ever again.

* * *

THE SUN SET. I couldn't see it from the confines of my coffin stuck in the basement, but I could feel it, much the same way a human feels coldness slowly seep into their bones as the flames of a fire sputters out.

I lifted the coffin's lid and inhaled the darkness, the smell of rusty pipes and moldy water stinging my nose. I could've taken one of the rooms upstairs, but, no matter how many curtains or drapes, darkness up there would never feel complete. Not like it was down here. Plus the basement had a newer shower.

It didn't take me long to get ready. After showering, I pulled on my favorite black leather pants and paired it with a gray tank top. I had plenty of clothes, but very few of them were part of my go-to wardrobe. I combed through my long hair and reached for my glasses on the counter. My hand hesitated over them, remembering the day I'd chosen to wear glasses.

"You need to find something to tie you to your humanity," Detrand, my old mentor and friend, had told me once when I found myself in a very dark place. I think he thought I had misunderstood him the first time I'd worn the spectacles, but I hadn't.

I slid the glasses onto my face. As long as I wore them, they reminded me how I needed to see through the eyes of those with less power, whether human or supernatural. I had been gifted with something terrible, yet powerful. I could use it for good if I learned to control it.

And I had.

Lynx greeted me in the kitchen. She must've heard me coming, which meant I was tired, because she handed me my thermos of blood.

"Do you want me to heat it up for you?"

I shook my head. Drinking warm blood reminded me too much of drinking from the vein, something I never wanted to do again. "But thank you." I leaned against the counter and drank slowly, still stewing over last night.

"You look a thousand miles away," Lynx said. "How did last night go at the warehouse?"

"Did Briar not tell you?"

"She didn't stay long last night, but she was mad about something. Said there was someone she had to see."

"Angel." The word left my mouth before I could stop it.

"Why would she see him?"

"Probably because she's mad at him for betraying us." When she bombarded me with questions, I held up my hand to quiet her, then told her what had happened.

"Those dirty snakes," she said, smacking the towel on the table. "I knew I should've gone with you guys. I would've slapped some magic so hard on them, their heads would've spun."

A smile tugged at the corners of my mouth. "I would've liked to have seen that."

"Maybe you still can."

I glanced up at her; her green eyes shined bright like that of a predator. It wasn't a look I saw often, but whenever I did, it gave me chills. Lynx had no idea the strength of her power or the darkness it contained. I hoped when she did, she would be in a good place, because otherwise it might sweep her into the shadows. "What do you mean?"

"Let's go back there. All three of us, but this time we'll be ready."

"It's not wise."

"It is if we're prepared."

"I don't know." I said the words, but deep down, I wanted to return and show Mateo I wasn't going to back down.

"I insist." She gripped my arm. The touch was hot, almost scolding. "We can't let those drugs into our city, especially if they're going to use them to turn supernaturals into Hydes. Plus, we can't just let people go around kidnapping others. They need to pay."

"Fine. We can try again, but we need a solid plan."

She squeezed and let go of me, spinning on her heel. Before she left the room, she added, "I'll take care of everything!"

I glanced down at my arm where she had been gripping me. My flesh was burned in the shape of a hand. Power, indeed.

I left the house, noting the time. Almost seven. Sersi would only be up for a couple of more hours. The President of the Ames de la Terra was well known for needing her sleep. A thousand-year-old fae, Sersi was my oldest friend. She knew me before I had met Mateo. Our friendship had been a rocky one, but it was as sure as the ground beneath my feet.

An hour later, I pulled up to the Blutel Estate thirty minutes outside of Rouen.

This place was the reason I was in Rouen. Blutel Estate was a large structure made of stone and iron, built over three hundred years ago. It had been destroyed in the late eighteenth century when a war broke out among supernaturals and humans, a war no one remembered now.

In time, Blutel Estate was built back up into something better and stronger. This was where a few powerful supernaturals joined together to create the Ames de la Terra, a group dedicated to keeping supernaturals' existence hidden to mankind while also protecting them in the process. They turned Blutel Estate into a respite for all the otherly creatures of the world. A place where we could heal from the darkness that so often infected us. Here, in this grand place, they also taught us another way to live. To find and embrace the light within us, for we all have it. Darkness cannot exist without the light.

It had also been my own home for several years and had helped me harness the demons within me. After I joined them, their vision grew to encompass humans as well, any who had been harmed by supernaturals or needed assistance. The Ames de la Terra became a governing body for the world to ensure there was balance between good and evil. I wished I'd had the sense to join them sooner, but I never believed I needed their help.

Not until I'd hit what humans call rock bottom.

I walked up the stone steps and pushed open a heavy wooden door. A blast of air ruffled my hair, smelling of spice and cedar. Turning to my left, I walked past the grand entryway, the walls lined with dark wooden wainscoting and floral wallpaper not made in this century. Flecks of real gold still lay embedded within its many colors.

Two females, a young vampire and even younger shifter walked past me, giggling to each other. Orphans, no doubt. Those lost in a world that otherwise would've abandoned them. They were probably heading to the estate's movie theater, built in the last ten years off the back of the building. Every Friday night, a movie was shown. I had seen many here.

Sersi was right where I thought she'd be—in her office finishing up for the day. Her blond hair, the color of wheat on a summer day, was swept up into a loose bun, stray tendrils falling to her chin. Her gray eyes looked up at me as I walked through the open door. Her gaze used to unnerve me, the sheer intensity of her attention, and the way her eyes penetrated into my soul, as if she could see every secret, every dirty thing I'd ever done. I used to shy away from that stare, but I'd since learned her prying eyes were those of concern and love. She didn't know how to do anything else. She was a rare gem in this world, and I was glad she was at Blutel, safe and protected from the darkness.

"You look especially bothered today," she said to me in that soft voice as sweet as the song of a morning dove. People would come from all over the world to hear her lectures. She thought it was for their uplifting messages, but I'd never tell her it was because the mere sound of her voice soothed the hardest soul.

"Life has been challenging lately." I didn't bother sitting down. I wished I had time, but there was much to do.

She smiled kindly, those gray eyes twinkling. "But it's also been fun, too. Wouldn't you say?"

Once again, she had looked inside me and seen something I didn't know was there. "It has been nice to have roommates. Friends. They make my challenges easier."

"As it should be." She came to her feet, the blue material of her long gown whispering against the back of the chair. "You came to check on the Abydos?"

"Yes, if you don't mind."

"Not at all. It is yours to keep safe. We only provide the walls." She turned around and pressed a button on a wall panel behind her. Two doors spread open, revealing a small elevator. She motioned me through first.

I stood next to her as the elevator doors closed. Sersi blew on her palm, captured the invisible air, then released it near a small black pad next to the elevator buttons. Wisps of blues and purples swirled into the air and was sucked into the blackness. The elevator jerked to a start and moved down deep within the bowels of the old mansion. Every President had expanded its floors, using not only modern methods, but magical ones too, to go over eight stories below the surface. The floors were used for different reasons—classrooms, dorm rooms, even a second banquet room—but the lowest of the floors was reserved for the oldest and most sacred artifacts. Only a few chosen people even knew of its location or had access to it. I happened to be one of them, given the right when Sersi discovered I had been given the Abydos to protect.

The doors slid open and lights came on. I followed Sersi into the giant, open room. Rows and rows of counter-height glass containers filled the space, each holding something of value. One day soon, I would like to spend days in this room studying all of its artifacts. I walked by a familiar-looking sword from the twelfth century and moaned at its exquisiteness. I imagined being there as men tried to pull it from its stone.

"You are welcome to come here any time," Sersi said over her shoulder. "It's a shame more of these items can't be appreciated."

My gaze slid over a long, oval mirror resting on its back and protected by glass. A single apple engraved into the gold frame adorned its top. Tingles exploded across my skin as I realized what it could be. These objects weren't just from our realm. "I would love to."

"Anytime." She stopped at a glass enclosure at the back. It appeared empty, but I knew otherwise. She turned to me. "Would you like to unlock it? Just like we practiced."

I nodded and closed my eyes, whispering the words: *"Per sol, luna et sidera, resera hoc secretum locum."*

I breathed into the pocket of my closed hand, then released it over the enclosure. The glass case slid open. At first nothing happened, but after a few seconds, the small chest that held the Abydos appeared. I reached in and carefully lifted the lid. The small vial of dark blood rested on plush velvet.

"Of all the items in this sacred place," Sersi said, "this could be the most important. Silly, for such a small thing."

My gaze slid over to the enclosure next to it. It contained the only other item I brought to Sersi at the same time I delivered the Abydos.

She followed my gaze. "You are still worried about the prophecy."

"I admit, I am a little." Detrand was the one who had given me the prophecy, believing it to be about me. "I thought it could be prevented if I stayed close to Briar, but then she killed the third Alpha."

I swallowed despite the dryness in my throat. That night at Fire Ridge, when we had come under attack, I had tried to stay close to

Briar. She had just discovered that Vincent, her uncle, was working with the strange and powerful being that both Dominic and Vincent worshiped. Up until that point, I never believed Briar could ever harm her last surviving family member, but then he'd betrayed her. I tried to go after her when the smoke being carried her into the woods, but that would've left Mateo, Lynx and so many others at the mercy of rival shifters and Hydes.

In the end, I could not stop Briar, and the first part of the prophecy had been fulfilled. At least she had killed the smoke monster, that terrible, seemingly unstoppable creature whose identity we had yet to uncover. Our only theory was that Vincent must've summoned it from another realm or maybe even created it using magic.

"There is still a long way to go before the prophecy comes to fruition," Sersi offered. "If it ever does."

I nodded and closed the lid. When I withdrew my hand, the box disappeared and the glass slid back into place over it. I approached the next case and peered inside. A rolled up, faded parchment paper tied off with a leather string laid inside.

"Do you want to look at it?" she asked me.

"No. I have it memorized." More for myself than for her, I quoted it out loud:

"When the crimson moon rises on the eve of Litha, three dark souls will give their blood to bring forth the great Trianus, Lord of the Underworld, from the dark abyss. A Komira, sealed by the blood of three Alphas, a vampire who abandoned the Kiss of the Eternal Night, and a witch blessed by the sun and the moon. Bonded by fire and ice, the three will bend a knee and bow to the new Prince of Darkness, true and faithful servants, as he takes his place as ruler over mortal lands once again."

I met Sersie's penetrating gaze, as deep and endless as an ocean's storm. "This prophecy will never come to pass."

"How can you be so sure?"

"Because I would never give up the Kiss of Eternal Night. I earned it, and it will always be mine."

CHAPTER 3

*S*ersi followed me outside. Moonlight, more than the night before, cast a silvery glow across the well-groomed landscape. A large stone fountain sprayed water into the night air, creating a fractured rainbow of dark purples, blues, and greens just above it. Only magic could've made that happen, but it was breathtaking nevertheless.

The weight I always felt whenever I thought about the prophecy squeezed my chest, making it harder to remember to breathe.

It had taken me many years of waiting and watching for clues about who these other two people could be. It wasn't until I began to research the Morgan family line that I found the connection. It was through Cassandra, Lynx's mother, who married a Morgan. Cassandra was born a Trite and came from a long line of witches who drew their powers from the moon, or so the rumors said. It was one reason I stayed in Rouen. I had to know if the prophecy was referring to a Morgan witch. So far, only one gave any indication she could be kissed by the sun—Lynx. I wasn't sure what that meant yet, but sunlight poured from that woman.

"Samira," Sersi said, stopping me before I reached the bottom of the steps. "There is someone I want you to talk to. I believe he might be able to shed some light on recent developments, specifically the creature who recently terrorized the Silver Claws, the one Briar vanquished."

My eyebrows lifted, genuinely surprised. I had asked everyone I knew about this creature and, other than old tales, I had found nothing. But the way that it had disappeared had felt too easy. Briar disagreed. "Who? I haven't been able to find any leads."

She laughed a sweet sound that eased the pressure on my chest. "I know something you don't? I think I can die happy now."

"You know more about humanity than I ever will." It was the biggest compliment I could ever give.

Those gray eyes stared into mine until I looked away. "You know more than you think you do, Samira Chevoky."

I warmed at the sound of my birth name, a name I hadn't heard from someone else's lips in decades. "Who is this person?"

"His fae name is Triandal Genlynn, but in the human world he goes by Eddie. Eddie …" She frowned. "I don't know his human last name."

"Eddie who owns the club Sinsual?"

"That's the one."

"He's fae?" I swallowed down my surprise. "I mean, I knew he was a supernatural, but I never paid much attention to him."

"You never had a reason to before. Now you do. Work with him."

"I will. Thank you." I gave her a hug of farewell, one of the few people I ever touched, considering her words. I was surprised Eddie had information I did not. He seemed too distracted with his mortal world to be useful in the supernatural one. He was always at the club, and I'd never seen him at the usual supernatural haunts. I licked my lips, eager to find out what information he could give me.

* * *

I PARKED a few blocks from Sinsual, away from the normal lot. I was always afraid my car would get scratched by the hordes of drunk people who left there each night. This club wasn't one I liked to go to.

It was always too crowded, filled way past the allotted occupancy limit. But I didn't have a choice.

Circling around the back to avoid the long line in front, I leapt up to the roof. There I found an access door to inside. The thirty-year-old locked door didn't hold when I jerked it wide open. Once inside, I pressed it back into place. By the layer of dust just inside the door, this exit hadn't been used in months. Good. It could be my personal entrance from now on should I need it.

I maneuvered my way down a set of stairs and a metal walkway until I was overlooking the club from the back wall. It was almost eleven and mostly packed. Eddie's office was just across from me. I sighed a breath of relief. I didn't want to have to navigate through those crowds.

The music changed just then. Deep bass slammed through the club, making the crowds bounce up and down, but it made me plug my ears to prevent a headache. Even the scent of sweat and pheromones made me ill.

When I reached Eddie's office, I pounded on the door to be heard over the music. A second later the door opened. Eddie's violet eyes, contrasting with his green button-up dress shirt, widened at my presence. They were so vibrant, I wondered how I hadn't noticed before.

His expression quickly slackened. "You're Briar's friend, right?"

By his reaction, he recognized I was a vampire, or at the very least, a supernatural. "My name is Samira."

"What can I do for you?" He peeked over my shoulder, scanning the area below.

"Can we speak in private?"

"Sure." He ushered me inside and closed the door. He circled around back to his desk, keeping a watchful eye on my movements. I reminded myself to breathe, to touch my face, shift my position. All the things that put others at ease. Vampires' unnatural stillness could be terrifying, something I hadn't really realized until Briar had pointed it out.

When we were both sitting, I said, "You and I share a mutual acquaintance."

"Do we?"

"Yes. Sersi."

His pupils dilated briefly. "The name doesn't sound familiar."

I sighed. "I don't have the time to do this. I know you're fae. I know your real name is Triandal Genlynn."

His mouth fell open, and his eyes lightened again. "How do you know that?"

"Sersi. And she would have only told me if I could be trusted. She said you could help me."

He leaned back into the chair and ran his fingers through the back of his sandy blond hair. "You're a vampire."

"Yes."

"You live with Briar, who is a shifter. Your other roommate is a Morgan witch."

"Correct."

"That's a deadly combination."

I leaned forward and rested my hand on the desk, tapping my fingernails. "It can be. Are you able to help me or not?"

"It depends. What do you need?"

"I'm searching for information about someone. Someone of great power who had a connection to Trianus."

The color drained from his face, and he glanced around as if someone might be watching us, even in this small room. "We don't talk about him."

"We?"

"Fae. His name is a forbidden word."

"So you do know about this demon?"

He nodded his head, the knot in his throat bobbing up and down. "Demons can gain power just by the mention of their name, by the stirring of belief." His eyes darkened, and I captured a glimpse of his true power. "That is why we don't speak of him." He stood. "And why I cannot help you."

"I fear someone may still try to summon him again by using the Abydos. Have you heard of this sacred blood?"

He sat back down, his face paling further. Silence descended over us, thick and dense. I let it settle. Long silences didn't bother me, but they did others.

Finally he spoke. "I can't discuss this here. Too many prying eyes and ears, but come back tomorrow night. I will take you somewhere where we can talk privately."

Just then the club beyond the door exploded in cheers. Eddie smiled. "Briar must be here."

"She's working tonight?"

"Surprised? It's been a few weeks since she came in. Something must be bothering her."

"What do you mean?"

He rose from his desk again. "Briar only works when she needs to release some pent up anger. It's like she goes to another place when she's performing. I don't mind, though. She brings in some serious cash. Have you ever seen her perform?"

"I don't like the crowds."

"They can be a bit rowdy, but you should stick around. There's a spot on the balcony that's not too crowded. And since you're a friend of Sersi's, I'll make you a special drink." He winked at me.

I checked the time. It wasn't even midnight yet. "Perhaps I will."

Eddie opened the door and pointed to a small table on the other side. It was tucked around the corner where most wouldn't notice. "Have a seat over there. I'll bring you a drink soon."

I thanked him and circled around the balcony until I reached the table. Down below, Briar stood on the bar, laughing and shouting into the hordes of people who had all surged forward to get a better view. I spotted a familiar looking shifter in the crowd; she was grinning and holding up a wine cooler in Briar's direction. I thought her name was Loxley. Briar mentioned she'd been coming to Fire Ridge more often, offering help. I guess now she was showing up at Sinsual, too.

This wasn't the first time I'd seen someone attach themselves to Briar. With her powerful presence and desire to help others, a more recent development, people flocked to her like devoted worshipping groupies.

Briar's movement caught my eye. She only wore a sports bra and a pair of short jean shorts with tall boots. She juggled bottles of Jack Daniels in the air, bouncing them off her shoulder, her forearm, and buttocks to keep them from falling. It was entrancing and almost unbelievable. She even managed to sling one off her foot, catching it gracefully before she poured them in seven shot glasses, lined up across the bar. A group of guys surged forward, throwing their cash into her outstretched hand before grabbing them up.

I hated to admit it, but she did put on a good show, although some of it was because of her shifter influence. I could feel her power pulsing outward, blanketing everyone with a thin layer of fevered energy and influence. I admit, it also affected me.

Snatching a lone straw on the table, I slid the straw from its paper covering. I looked at it and then at Briar, an idea coming to my mind. She always said I needed to let loose.

Balling the paper up, I stuck into my mouth and began to chew. I'd seen this same move on one of the movies I'd seen at Blutel Estate. Once the paper was sufficiently wet, I attached it into the end of the straw and lifted it to my puckered lips.

When Briar stilled to let a man tuck a five-dollar bill in her boot, I blew hard. The wad of paper met its mark and smacked Briar in the forehead. She froze, scowling, reached up and grabbed it, then scanned the crowd for the offender. Her gaze moved upward and stopped when she saw me. Shock crossed her face. I saluted her.

A smile teased the corners of her mouth. She raised the bottle of Jack in her hand and mocked a toast before downing a long swig. With the music still blaring, she continued to dance, even motioning for me to join her at one point. Of course, I declined. I wasn't that ready to let loose.

Without warning, the hair on my arms lifted. I sucked in a slow breath through my teeth at the unseen threat and casually glanced around. All the people, humans and the occasional shifter, appeared disinterested in me and instead were focused on Briar.

Again, I felt the needle pricking of cold eyes on me. I scanned the club, stopping when I met the gaze of an abnormally tall and thin bald man. He stood out from the crowd, so much so I wondered how I had missed him on my first sweep. His eyes were dark pits, nearly black as he stared up at me, his expression void of any emotions. He didn't look angry and yet, everything about him screamed aggression.

Eddie appeared at my table and set down a tall, thin glass full of red liquid. I glanced away for just a moment to tell Eddie thank you, and when I looked back the bald man was gone. I searched all around, but it was like he had never existed.

I remained on alert for several minutes, enjoying Eddie's special drink of whiskey and cow's blood, but when I didn't see the man again, I decided to leave via the roof exit. I moved to stand but stopped when I saw Lynx. She was shoving her way to the bar to get to Briar. Briar noticed her and leaned over to hear what Lynx was saying. Briar looked up at me, then said something back to Lynx.

A moment later, Lynx worked her way up to my table carrying a duffle bag. Her red hair had been braided loosely and hung off to one shoulder. The deep red color stood out against her white dress. She pulled out a chair and dropped next to me. "I'm so glad you're here. Didn't you get my texts?"

"I only check them once a day at sunset."

She stared at me as if I'd eaten a baby. "There are so many things wrong with that statement, but whatever. I have something to show you."

"What?"

"Not until Briar gets here." Even as she said it, Briar was finishing up the show that ended with blowing fire from her mouth. Lynx looked at her wistfully. "She is so good."

Shortly after, Briar arrived at our table, wiping her forehead with a towel. She collapsed into a chair. "I am beat."

"Work off your anger?" I asked.

She shrugged, her eyes dropping to my drink. Her nose wrinkled. "Where did you get that?"

"Eddie."

"Eddie?" She swiveled her head toward his office. "He knows you're a vampire? How? What else does he know? Does he know about me?"

I hesitated, wondering how much to tell her. I didn't like telling other people's stories. "You'll have to ask him."

Lynx dropped the bag onto the center of the table. "No more talking. There's something we have to do. Tonight we're taking out the Nocs."

Briar and I looked at each other.

"You want to kill the vampires?" Briar asked.

Her eyebrows lifted. "What? No! No one's going to die. I just meant we're going to destroy that warehouse."

Briar slumped into her seat. "They'll just go somewhere else."

"Then we'll destroy that one too."

"Where's this sudden aggression coming from?" I asked her. I'd only seen hints of her darkness, but this was something new. This was her seeking it out, actually wanting to take part of something destructive and harmful. Could this be the beginning of Lynx seeking out the power of the moon that ran through her blood? If so, I needed to stop it before it grew too big, which could potentially fulfill the prophecy.

Lynx squirmed in her seat and lowered her gaze. "I'm just tired of bad things happening and not being able to do anything about it." She looked up at each of us. "We are strong. All three of us. We can do this, together."

Briar thumped the table. "Damn straight."

Lynx was right. We were stronger together, but did that come with a cost? I studied Lynx, the worry in her eyes, the determination of her chin. Maybe she just wanted to do something good. Maybe this had nothing to do with the prophecy.

I motioned toward the bag. "What's in there? And what's your plan?"

"Well," she rested her hand on the black canvas. "This is my first mission as leader."

"Leader?" I looked at Briar. "We have a leader?"

Briar chuckled. "Just go with it. This is great. Please continue, Lynx."

Lynx unzipped the bag and reached her hand inside. She paused and said, "I want you each to wear these. It's important we blend in."

She handed us each a pile of clothes. Briar burst out laughing. "You got us matching outfits! This is the best!"

I unfolded them and held up the black shirt. "I don't wear long sleeves."

"You are tonight, Samira," Lynx ordered.

Briar was stretching out the shirt. "Will my boobs fit in this?"

"Honestly, I'm not sure," Lynx said. "But we'll tape them up if we have to."

I set the clothes down. "What's the second part of your plan?"

She opened the bag to show us several bottles of lighter fluid. She pulled out a lighter and flicked it on. "Simple. We're going to burn the whole thing down."

CHAPTER 4

"This isn't a good idea," I said for the fourth time. I was driving across town with Lynx and Briar in the back seat changing into their clothes. Turns out the shirt Lynx got Briar fit, just barely; it showed a bit of her stomach. "Back me up, Briar."

"Sorry, Sis, but I can't," she said. "I talked to Angel about it last night. He practically begged me to stay out of it and wouldn't say anything else. It's like he forgot who he was talking to. If they aren't going to stop, then we got to do what we got to do."

I eyed her in the rearview mirror. "Does Luke know?"

"No, and we're not going to tell him. He'll give me a lecture about playing with fire, then he'll make out with me to distract me. And it will work, so best not to tell him just yet."

Mumbling under my breath, I turned onto the street leading to the warehouse. It wasn't a horrible idea, per se, burning down the building. It was a quick way to take care of a big problem, but I couldn't ignore the nagging questions at the back of my mind. Mateo had been absolutely against working with Bodian, even to the point of fighting against them. Why would he suddenly switch sides? And kidnapping supernaturals? This was something he had always been against.

I couldn't shake the feeling that I was missing a critical piece to an abstract puzzle. Sure, burning down their building would make a big statement, but there was something more important at play. I needed more information to understand the whole picture.

"Pull over next to the coffee house on the left," Lynx said, pointing ahead. She held a paper in her hand and kept glancing down at it.

"What's in your hand?" I asked.

"It's the plan."

Briar snatched it out of her hands. "Step one. Get dressed. Step two. Go to warehouse. Aww, you even drew pictures!"

Lynx snatched it back from her. "Leave me alone. I know I got a little carried away, but I was super bored today. And this was a lot of fun."

I parked the car.

"You're turn to get dressed," Lynx said. "We'll wait for you outside."

I grabbed the shirt off the seat next to me. "I'm just going to wear this. My pants are already black."

Lynx pouted, but didn't argue.

A few minutes later, we were standing behind the warehouse, my senses tuned in to what was going on inside. I could hear movement, but not much. The air smelled of chemicals, which probably meant Hydes were nearby.

Briar pointed up. "There's a window up there. I'm going to take a peek."

Before we could stop her, she leapt into the air and caught her hands on the lip of a window. She hauled herself up, balancing precariously on the edge until she had lifted the window. She disappeared.

I groaned. Leave it to her to take unnecessary risks.

"Should we follow after her?" Lynx asked, as she pulled her ponytail tight. There was an anxiousness to her movements that made me nervous. Something about all of this felt wrong.

"We wait."

It wasn't long before Briar returned. "Only half a dozen Hydes. I didn't see any vampires."

I looked around the corner. "Are you sure?"

"I walked all over upstairs. It's pretty dead. There's lots of crates in there."

"Next part of the plan," Lynx began glancing down at her paper. "Disarm all the guards. If they try to hurt us, we can kill them."

"We'll do the killing," Briar said before I could.

Even though I could sense darkness inside of Lynx, there was also an innocence I wanted to protect. She represented the best part of me, the part I wanted to become, and I suspected Briar felt the same way.

Briar led the way. I took up the rear, keeping a look out. The last time we were here I had a strange feeling we were being watched. I didn't feel that now, but that didn't stop me from being careful.

As soon as we stepped inside the warehouse, Lynx surprised Briar and I by announcing our arrival.

"Hello? Could everyone please come join us in the ... great room with all the boxes?" She looked at us and shrugged.

"What are you doing?" Briar hissed. "Wasn't the point of the outfits to be all sneaky and shit?"

She snorted. "I just wanted us to look good."

The Hydes began to gather, appearing like simple humans but that would soon change. Four moved into the room and five more crowded above us and stared over the railing. Even though their expressions were emotionless, their eyes bled fire and rage. Briar had counted wrong, of course. What else could she have missed? I should be in charge of counting from here on out.

"Quiet," I snapped at Briar and Lynx who were still arguing. "We have company."

Lynx cleared her throat and stepped forward. "Hi. We haven't met. My name—"

"You've entered an unauthorized space," the largest of them said. His human features began to sharpen and the joints in his body popped and snapped into something greater, stronger and faster. He tightened his fists, sending a ripple across his massive chest.

"Yes, well—"

"We must kill you now," he interrupted again.

Lynx grunted in frustration. "I wanted to say that first."

Briar reached down and removed the blade from her boot. "I'd say that constitutes a threat on our lives, right Lynx?"

One of the Hydes nearest me lunged fast and hard. One second I was reaching for the blade on my back, the next Lynx was standing in front of me, the Hyde frozen mid-lunge. She had stopped time. "You have forty-five seconds."

Behind her was the Hyde, his face twisted into a deathly scowl, and his eyes full of animalistic rage. Both of his hands were curled into claws aimed for my throat. I stepped past Lynx and sliced his head off. Briar had already leapt to the balcony and was making quick work of the Hydes upstairs.

"You guys are doing great!" Lynx called up.

Out of the corner of my eye, I noticed her hands were shaking. Her arms were twitching and sweat poured down her flushed face. She looked like she was about to faint. Another head fell victim to my sword. "Are you okay, Lynx?"

"Twenty seconds!" she called.

I raised my blade and was about to swing it against another Hyde, but just before it made contact, a hand shot up and snatched it. Caught unaware, I didn't move back fast enough before the Hyde's fist crashed into my face. He wasn't frozen any more. By the sound of Briar's grunt above me, she had also been taken off guard.

"What the hell, Lynx?" Briar yelled.

Lynx stumbled back, her legs weak. "Sorry. Too many of them. Besides, it's not rocket science! I can't tell you the exact time I'll be able to hold it."

Three Hydes attacked me at once. I ducked as a dagger swung across my head, but I failed to miss the end of a broomstick crash against my back. Pain shattered into my spine, dropping me to my knees. Giving up that precious second had all three of them kicking and punching at my body.

"Samira!" Lynx cried, but I heard the exhaustion in her voice.

I grabbed a foot just before it hit my face and twisted hard. The crack of bone echoed off the concrete walls. Something hard rammed into my head, making my vision blur. I rolled out of the way when I felt something rushing at my face.

This wasn't working. I needed more power.

I scrambled away and concentrated hard on the ancient power that mostly lay dormant inside me. It surged forward at my request and darkness filled my mind and body with new power. The Kiss of Eternal Night. The dark gift I had nearly lost my life to obtain.

With its presence overwhelming me, all other feelings were shoved aside. I felt nothing. No pain. No sadness. No joy. It simply took over and did what it did best: kill.

One by one, I dispatched the remaining Hydes, oblivious to the blood spraying my face, the sounds of flesh tearing, bone crunching. I grabbed the hair of a Hyde who had Briar pinned to the ground, while another held her arms. I jerked him so hard, he flew over the railing and all the way to the concrete floor.

"Briar! Quit playing around."

"Yeah. That's what I'm doing." She jerked her arms out from under the Hyde pinning her down.

I leapt over the rail to go after the one I'd just tossed; she could finish this one off.

The Hyde on the floor, his eyes empty as if he held no soul, attempted to stand, but both his legs were broken. I stalked toward him, sliding the tip of my blade across the floor. The high-pitched screeching might've bothered me before, but the Kiss inside me smiled at the melody. It was the song of death.

The Hyde kicked his leg out; the motion snapped his bones back into place. Before he could do the same with his other leg, I drove my sword into his heart over and over, puncturing that sensitive organ. Blood and tissue polluted the air.

"Samira!"

I spun around, my blade raised.

Lynx cowered, and Briar jumped between us as if to shield Lynx from me. I breathed heavily, taking in the scene. Lynx's frightened green eyes, as timid and fragile as a newborn doe. Briar's dark gaze, ready to defend Lynx from my blade.

I blinked and stumbled back. I sheathed my blade and began to count silently.

Briar was saying something to me, her expression a mess of anger and worry.

Each number forced the Kiss back into the shadows of my mind where it belonged. When I reached twenty-one, I finally looked up. "I am better."

"What the hell was that?" Briar asked, her weapon still trained in my direction.

"You are not the only one to hold something dark and ancient inside you."

"Let's hurry," Lynx said, unable to look at me. She held a gas can in her shaky hands and hurried over to the nearest crates. She dumped the fuming liquids on top.

Briar finally turned away from me and moved to join her. I remained where I was, still counting and breathing. Even though the Kiss had retreated, I still felt its icy breath racing through my veins.

I had lost control. I don't know what would've happened had Briar not intervened. I'd like to think I would've stopped myself, but I wasn't so sure. I had been using the Kiss too much. In the past few months, I'd used it more than I had in decades. But the evil in Rouen was growing, causing me to rely on it more and more.

Briar and Lynx returned to me. Briar slapped my shoulder. "You good?"

I nodded.

Lynx stood back, resting her hands on her hips, as she scanned the warehouse. "I think we doused it good enough. Who wants the honors?"

I held out my hand, wanting to make up for earlier. "I'll do it."

Lynx placed the lighter in my hand. I flicked it on and tossed it into the nearest crates. Flames ignited and quickly spread in waves of yellows and reds. All three of us stepped back as heat warmed our skin.

Lynx brushed her hands together with a satisfied smile. "Mission accomplished."

"Should we go get a drink to celebrate?" Briar asked. "Maybe come up with a team name? I was thinking Briar's Bitches or Briar's Bad-asses."

While Briar and Lynx discussed names, I watched the flames licking at the floor and the walls. Something still didn't feel right. Like the thin strand of spider's silk tickling my skin. I couldn't see it, but I could feel it.

"Let's go, Samira," Lynx said as the flames grew unbearably hot.

We were about to turn away when something inexplicable happened. The flames, once wild and free, began to recede.

"Stop," I ordered to the other two.

The flames continued to die down as if an invisible heavy blanket was smothering the fire.

Both Briar and Lynx froze, their faces a mask of surprise. I had seen this once before, centuries ago.

My body stiffened, and my blood chilled.

The missing piece of the puzzle snapped into place.

My insides shook and fear gripped my heart, dumping adrenaline through my veins. I scrambled to consider my options. Fight and die. Run and live another day, even if my friends were trapped behind me. Warn them, and stay to protect them by playing the game, and possibly lose it, and thus, my life. There were no good options.

In a split second decision, I turned to them, growling, "Get out. Now."

"What's going on?" Lynx asked, the confidence gone from her voice.

"Run. Now! Before it's too late," I commanded them, rage searing through my heart. I had to make them understand. I should run, too. Run far and fast, but I couldn't be sure that Briar and Lynx would get away in time.

I pulled on Lynx's arm, grabbing for Briar's but she slipped out of my grip. "You have to go. Now! I don't have time to explain."

"Samira," a voice hissed, the sound curling around me in a cold embrace.

"Who is that?" Briar asked, her head swiveling and blades drawn.

I froze. They couldn't run now. It was too late. We were all caught in the web, and I doubted we would untangle ourselves alive.

Doors at the back of the room flew open, stirring up the last of the smoke in the room. A figure emerged. Tall and broad. Commanding and bold.

I spun and grabbed Briar by the shirt, pleading with them one more time. They might make it, if they ran as fast as possible. "Take Lynx and go! Now!"

She stared over her shoulder, her mouth open. Then she looked back at me, resolve in her eyes. "We're not leaving you."

"Fool," I grumbled and turned back around, gathering strength and determination inside me. I would need all I could muster to face the monster who had just entered the warehouse.

My maker.

CHAPTER 5

*H*e looked the same as when I last saw him. Long, ink-black hair that was as shiny as an ocean eel. His high cheekbones and long straight nose had always reminded me of Egyptian royalty seen in history books and old paintings. He'd admitted to me once that he used to be royalty thousands of years ago. The way he carried himself, graceful and lithe, yet with a viper's glare, backed up his claim.

He came toward me, stopping ten feet away, but his presence expanded much further. I could feel the power of it pressing against me, as strong and unbreakable as gravity. It threatened to swallow me under, pulling memories from my mind that had long been forgotten. Memories of the old me, who used to believe that vampires were better than humans and who used to kill on command for the very master before me. I had been brutal, ruthless, and unforgiving. A vampire I now abhorred.

My old master stood before me, a stark reminder of that life I left behind. He was time himself: there when Spartacus and his warriors finally fell against Crassus' line, who manipulated the collapse of the Han Dynasty, and also played his part in Prince Ivan's brutal reign of terror in Russia. Wherever there was death and destruction, my maker Korin Khalid had been there to play a part in it.

"Samira." The word fell from his thin lips, a foul, dirty thing I wanted no part of. Not from him. Not ever. "It's so good to see you again. And even better seeing you covered in blood, just the way I remember you."

I blinked, wondering if this was some horrible nightmare. Korin couldn't be here. He was supposed to be fighting shifter wolves in Europe, a war that had been quietly raging for nearly five decades.

Briar stepped forward, ever the aggressor, but I snapped my hand out to stop her from getting closer. She huffed. "I don't know who you are, nor do I care, but you look like an asshat, so listen up, asshat. Rouen is our city, and we don't like what you're doing in it. So pack up your shit and get the hell out!"

His eyes, a faded light blue like that of a human's who had been dead for several days, shifted to Briar.

"Don't look at him," I warned her, already knowing it was too late.

"Close your mouth," he said to Briar.

Her jaw snapped close. Her eyes widened in alarm, and she clawed at her face.

"Hold still," he compelled again.

The muscles in her body became rigid and by her grimace, the tension was painful. Lynx moved as if to help, but I quickly shook my head. She remained back.

Korin calmly turned to me. "I've missed you, Samira. I've always known you were here, and I respected your desire to stay away from the coven." He said this last word with a possessive hiss. "But you insisted on getting involved, even though Mateo requested you stay away."

The realization that Mateo's words were not a threat but a warning, washed over me like a tidal wave. I'd grown too careless over the years, mistakenly content that Korin would leave me alone. Why didn't Mateo just tell me our sire was here?

Korin continued. "And so, I've changed my mind about leaving you to your business. I've decided that I've put up with your little rebellion long enough. It's time for you to return to your family."

I stared him in the eyes. Unlike everyone else, I was immune to his compulsion. His ability to compel was unparalleled among vampires and made him highly feared. That used to be me too until I fought, nearly dying, to obtain the Kiss of Eternal Night. He held no power over me any longer.

"What are you doing here?" I kept my voice even, fighting the familiar urge to cower. I wasn't that same woman anymore.

"I received word that you and some filthy trash were trying to destroy what I've built here. When I heard it was you, I had to see it for myself."

"You are working with Bodian?"

"Not with. I am Bodian. The special divisions department, anyway. I have great things planned for Rouen. And if they work, which they will, we will expand to other cities across the country. Wonderful things are in store, and I'm not going to let anything stop it." He paused to lift his lip in a sneer. "Least of all you."

My stomach revolted, twisting and turning. This was so much worse than I could imagine. Maybe he was here to finish the prophecy.

He moved closer, practically gliding across the floor. "Things are going to change, whether you like it or not. Starting with my returning to town, along with your old coven, Buio Sangre. Do you remember them, your old friends?" He paused. "I'm not the only one who misses you."

I was too stunned to answer. The Buio Sangre coven. My old vampire family whom I had abandoned over three hundred years ago. Back in Rouen.

"We don't have to be enemies, Samira," he cooed and sucked up even closer to me, staring at me with his penetrating eyes. I could feel him attempt his compulsion against my mind, but the barrier I'd put in place was too strong. "We can start over, you and I, forget the past. If I'm willing to forget your ruthless betrayal, surely you can forget my wrongdoings."

I still couldn't speak, too shocked at what was happening. Maybe this was all a dream, a terrible nightmare. But Briar's frustrated grunting told me it wasn't.

"Maybe I have something that will help change your mind." Korin glanced over his shoulder. "Faithe, come here."

Blood drained from my face, and my legs weakened. Crushing weight pressed on my chest, and I struggled to breathe. "No..."

And then I saw her. The person I loved most in the world. The one I'd give anything for, including my life.

And my only child.

The only human I'd ever turned.

Memories flooded my mind and I drowned in them, pulled under by their indomitable current. The first time I saw Faithe.

She moved waist-deep in a lake surrounded by a wall of great pines in an area untouched by man's hands. Silence was complete, broken up by the occasional howl of a distant wolf. Moonlight cascaded down from the dark sky in silver ribbons, and one of them captured the woman in its grasp, electrifying her already stark-white hair. Her white dress floated around her, moving up higher with every step she made toward the center of the inky water.

I watched her from across the lake, fascinated by her pink, nearly red eyes. Not because of their odd color but because of the utter despair they reflected. Life hadn't just beaten this woman; it had decimated her. She did not intend to return to the shore alive.

In that moment, my soul wept for her.

It was a rare feeling; humans died all the time. Some even violently by mine own hand. But this woman... I saw myself in her. I used to be a shadow of a woman, barely able to speak without fear of being beaten by my husband. I was lost, alone, afraid, and my daily life was filled with pain and agony. I had no other family, no other obligation. And, also like her, I had the same determination to end my own life.

But Korin had found me just in time and had offered me a new life. He only had to ask once. "Say the word, and I will make you a ruler over man, untouchable and powerful. Never again will you ever have to suffer by a human's hands."

And in that moment at the lake, watching Faithe, I realized I could offer her the same thing. It tugged on my heart, a yearning so strong I couldn't ignore it. It only took me a second to decide to give this pitiful creature the choice he'd given me.

I had never considered turning a human, but then again, I had never met someone who reminded me so much of myself.

And like me, she didn't need to be asked twice. She accepted easily with a plea. "Please. I can't hurt anymore."

Her simple words seared my heart and ignited something foreign within me. A deep love I had never felt for anyone, different from even Mateo. More possessive, almost maternal. And so, that night, with the stars as my only witness, I made a vow to protect her. No matter what happened, she would never suffer again.

But now, the very woman I had vowed to protect, was walking through the door to the warehouse. She was still slender and stoic, the perfect picture of beauty and grace. Her long, wavy white hair, partially pulled up, was as striking as her light pink eyes and ghostly pale skin.

She came forward, staring with her eerie eyes only at Korin. She stopped next to him and slid her hand up his arm. "You called, Master?"

He lowered his gaze to her. "Yes, pet. I want you to see whom I found."

She slowly turned to me. There was no startled reaction, no change in her expression giving away how she felt about seeing her maker after all these years.

"Faithe," I moaned, unable to keep the desperation from my voice. A thought flashed through my mind, one I regretted but felt all the same. It would have been better to have let her die that day in the lake, than for her to live at Korin's side. Shame and rage flooded me. I hadn't kept my promise. Korin was preying on her, as he had done with so many others, myself included.

I bit my tongue, forcing my emotions in check, and straightened my shoulders. I could not let Korin see how her presence affected me. I held my hand out to her, clearing my throat. "Hello, Faithe."

She let go of Korin and came toward me, stopping just in front of me. She slowly looked up at me and linked her hand through mine.

"What are you doing here?" I had to ask it.

She gave me a cold smile. "Sweet Samira. Always trying to do the right thing."

"And yet, you are with him again." I couldn't contain the horror I felt inside.

"You abandoned me. I was all alone." Her words held bite, her eyes, angry.

"I put you in a place where you could be safe!"

She bared her fangs and hissed in my face, spittle wetting my cheek. "You left me to die. You didn't care for me. You wanted to live your life, free from a burden like me."

"No, I didn't." I held her shoulders, needing her to understand. "Listen to me—"

She gripped my chin, her long nails cutting into my flesh. "You listen to me. You are like all the others, Mother. And because of that, you are dead to me. Korin found me when you left. He has never abandoned me, like you. He has taken care of me more than any other person."

She shoved me away, and Korin held his hand out to her. She didn't hesitate to accept it or recoil when he pulled her to him. He kissed her, long and deep, his tongue flicking at her lips. Seeing him taste her, making a spectacle out of her, made blood come up my throat. I barely managed to stop it before it spewed past my lips.

I wanted to crumple to the floor, to beg her for forgiveness. I thought if I left her with the Madabbe Tribe, she would be safe from the constant running I'd done at the beginning or from the evil that I'd eventually become. I thought if I left her, Korin would forget about her. I had checked up on her at first, but in the last couple of centuries had been afraid to. I'd sensed Korin's watchful eye and never wanted to lead him to her.

But I had underestimated Korin. By leaving her, it only left her vulnerable to him. It was a stupid decision and, seeing how he had turned her against me, one I would probably regret for the rest of my life.

I had half a mind to grab her, throw her over my shoulder and run away with her. Take her to the safest place I could find and live forever keeping her protected. But I had to keep my emotions in check, keep a cool head, otherwise we would all die this day.

Korin separated from her. "Ah, they're here."

I drew my brows together, as did Briar and Lynx. Korin looked over our shoulders just as Mateo, Angel and the rest of the Sangre Nocturnas filed into the warehouse. My blood chilled. What were they doing here?

Briar made a muted breathing noise, and Lynx grabbed Briar's arm, squeezing it tightly.

I stared at the Nocturnas in shock, willing Mateo to look at me, to give me some kind of explanation. But he wouldn't look at me. Briar was making all sorts of sounds beneath her closed jaw. Angel's jaw was clenched as tightly as the muscles on his body at the sight of her, and yet, he did nothing. I looked again, closer this time. From Angel, to Mateo, and the way Mateo's dark gaze was lit with fire, and that's when I knew.

I couldn't believe I didn't recognize it as soon as Korin had compelled Briar to be quiet. Korin had always had the power to compel his own children, but never outside of that.

But now... No, no, this was not possible.

They were all compelled. He could compel Briar, who was a Komira, for heaven's sake. Angel was also compelled, who was not one of Korin's children. Were all of the Nocturnas compelled?

A twisted feeling in my gut told me they were. I stared at Korin in dread, wondering how he'd gained so much powerful magic.

"I meant what I said earlier." Korin approached me and towered tall over my smaller frame, but I didn't flinch. The back of his knuckles brushed over my stomach and moved up over my breast and to my throat, where his fingers played with my flesh, teasing the space just above my artery. "I've missed you."

He lowered his mouth to my throat, and his lips hovered over that fragile vein. Disgust rolled through me. In one bite, he could rip open my throat. I couldn't fight him. I wasn't strong enough. Not when I was so emotionally disarmed.

"Come back to us." Korin struck forward, his lips lapping my neck in a sloppy kiss, and his eyeteeth grazed my flesh. I glanced at Mateo, shame marking my face. Korin was playing with me now, showing me how he could touch me, come so close to killing me. But he kept me alive for now.

Briar growled, low and loud, breaking the moment. Korin leaned back and turned his attention to her. "You are a feisty creature for a shifter. Are you something more?"

"What are you planning?" I said, trying to bring his attention back to me. Briar had no idea who she was dealing with.

Korin ignored me and touched Briar on the forehead with his thumb. Her wide eyes vibrated with rage. His thumb dragged down her face, grazing over the skin on her cheek. Then he pierced her with his nail and brought her blood to his mouth, tasting it. His silver eyes lit up as bright as a full moon. "An Alpha stands before me! And something else. What is that?"

He looked back at Mateo. "What is she?"

"Alpha of the Silver Claws," Mateo said, his expression flat.

"She's something more."

I closed my eyes, hoping he didn't demand Mateo tell him more. Mateo would have no choice but to tell the truth.

"Play with her, Master," Faithe said. "She needs to learn respect." She looked up at Korin with eager eyes, hopeful for his approval.

Korin looked from Faithe to Briar. "You're right, pet. I'm new in town, so it's best I set expectations now."

Briar growled again. I wish she'd learn to shut up.

Lynx moved as if to step forward, but I shook my head, a desperate warning. Anguish filled me as I realized Korin could do whatever he wanted to them, and I would be powerless to stop it, not while Faithe was within his grasp. Whatever Korin did, Briar could handle it, but Lynx ... she didn't have the ability to heal like we did.

"You don't have to do this, Korin," I said. "Any issues you have are with me."

"That's true, but this Alpha could cause problems for me later. Especially since the Silver Claws are no longer working with us, a fact I'm still not happy about." He looked back at Faithe. "Give me your hair pin, will you?"

She complied and removed it from her snow-colored hair.

He took it from her open palm. "Thank you, pet."

Facing Briar, he held up the long pin and stared into her eyes. She tried to avoid the heavy gaze, but she was up against something she'd never faced before.

"Take this from me," he ordered Briar.

Her hand shot forward, and she gripped it between her thumb and forefinger.

"Master," Angel said, his voice deep and gravely, as if even speaking the words took great effort.

"Silence!" Korin commanded.

Silence became a living thing as it twisted and knotted around everyone in the room. My mind raced. What could I do? If I attacked him, he would order Mateo's coven to kill me. Probably Briar, too. And Lynx.

Korin leaned toward Briar and whispered, his words razorblades. "Shove it in your ear and pop your eardrum."

CHAPTER 6

*T*ry as she might, Briar couldn't stop her hand from turning the hairpin toward her ear. I could see her Komira powers try to surface, her eyes flickering a deep yellow, but Korin's compulsion was too strong. Her eyes faded back to their soft brown color. As long as I'd known him, his gift of compulsion had not been this strong. Something had changed. He'd grown significantly more powerful.

"Stop, please," I begged. "This isn't necessary."

The pin drew closer. Angel made a slight strangling noise, and I stepped forward to cover it up. "Master, please..."

The words soured on my tongue. In only a few minutes of seeing Korin again, I was already cowering.

"Faster," he ordered Briar.

"Yes," Faithe hissed, "teach her a lesson."

In one quick motion, Briar's hand struck forward into her ear. Red flushed her face and she squeezed her eyes, tears slipping through them. She moaned loud and long through her closed mouth. The smell of her blood perfumed the air.

"Now do it to your other ear."

"Stop!" I tried again, hitching a breath. I could see Lynx mumbling under her breath, the beginning of a spell that would only get her hurt, if not killed. "I'll return to the coven, Korin. We'll start anew."

"Hold," he said to Briar and slowly turned to me. He grabbed my face, grinning, then softly patted my cheek. "That's my girl. We've returned to Winter's Cove. I expect you to stop by tomorrow night to reintroduce yourself to the newer members of the coven."

"Winter's Cove was destroyed in a fire hundreds of years ago." I'd been the one to set match to the flame.

"You know how sentimental I can be. It has been fully rebuilt to the exact specifications as before." He gave me a sly grin. "I ensured your favorite room was decorated just how you like it, in case you decided to return for good."

I knew then he never really intended to leave me alone. He'd planned this all along.

"I expect you to fully integrate yourself into the coven. You are to be present when I entertain and to make yourself available when I need you."

I had no intention of doing that, but I nodded, playing the role, for now.

Satisfied, he looked back at Faithe. "Ready?"

"Always." She sucked up to him again, linking her arm through his. She turned to me and for a brief heartbeat I saw the old Faithe lingering in her eyes. The young woman who collected caterpillars just to watch them bloom into butterflies. The woman who spent years learning to play the piano as well as the greatest pianists in the world. Faithe was a fighter, not this submissive shell of a woman in front of me. Korin must've compelled her like he had the others.

"See you soon." She smiled before she turned away, following alongside Korin. Before he left, he released the hold he had on Mateo and the others.

Briar fell to her knees, grimacing and cupping her ear. "Son of a bitch, that hurt."

Angel was there in an instant, as was Lynx. I stared down at them, horrified. I couldn't help feeling this was somehow my fault. I shouldn't have gotten so close to them. Just like Faithe, Korin would use them against me. I resisted the desire to run away; it was too late for that.

"Samira," Mateo said and rested a gentle hand on my arm. His glossy amber eyes were like hot embers, ready to explode into raging flames.

I averted my eyes, unable to look at him right now. Too many emotions too close to the surface. I didn't know how to process them all and feared if I did, it would feed the Kiss. "When did you know about Korin?"

He shook his head in frustration.

"Answer me!" My voice was louder than I intended.

"He can't," Lynx said and stood. "None of them can. I can sense old magic. Korin's compulsion."

I looked back at Mateo, wondering what information he could share. "Is it safe to say you've been ordered to not say anything about Korin?"

He nodded, his jaw clenched tight. "I am bound to him."

"I'm so sorry, Briar," Angel was saying, smoothing back her hair. His whole body was rigid, his jaw clenched. He looked like he wanted to rip everything around us to shreds. "I couldn't stop him."

Briar looked up at me. "So he's your maker? How are you semi-normal?"

I was staring right through her, my mind reeling. "This changes everything."

"Can we please go?" Lynx rubbed at her arms. Most of Mateo's men had already exited, but a few remained behind, standing as guards.

Angel helped Briar to her feet. "I'll take you home."

"It's okay. I came with Samira." She still held her ear, unable to look at him. A small trickle of blood ran down her neck. "And Luke is waiting for me at the house. We have pack business tonight."

Angel's expression darkened, and he stepped back.

"Lynx," I said, an idea coming to me. "Do you think there's a spell that might break Korin's compulsion?"

She glanced behind her toward the door, looking like she wanted to bolt but trying very hard to stay with us. What Korin had done was horrifying, but I sensed something else going on with Lynx. Her heart was pounding so hard it was hard to filter out the noise.

"There could be," she answered as she began to back up toward the open bay door. "I'll look the first chance I get."

I followed after her, Mateo by my side closer than he'd ever been before. Angel didn't give us a second look as he walked around the corner of the building. A few seconds later, I heard his motorcycle fire up.

"Why does he seem so upset?" I asked, eyeing Briar.

"I don't know. I don't have him figured out yet." She watched where he'd disappeared almost as if she was waiting for him to return, then sighed. Turning to us, a look of resignation on her face, she tapped on her ear. "Sucker still hurts. I think it's healing, though."

"You know Angel better than you think you do," Mateo said to her.

She wrinkled her nose. "What's that supposed to mean? You're the one who knows him best. He never explains anything to me."

Mateo studied her. "He has told me nothing as well. But I have never seen Angel take such care of a woman in at least four hundred years, or longer." He turned to me, dismissing her. "I will walk you to your car. We must go now."

Mateo followed us to my vehicle. He was still seething. Though he tried to conceal it, I could feel his rage just under the surface.

There were bigger things for me to worry about. "Tell me, Mateo. Who is the silver-eyed vampire? I saw him before with Silas."

His expression hardened. "He is a parasite. Korin has forced him upon me, yet he doesn't have to follow any of my commands. He comes and goes as he pleases, and he won't even give me his name. I think Korin sent him to watch me."

"We need to find out more about him."

"I've tried," he scowled. "There's nothing."

I pursed my lips together. I didn't like unknown variables.

"I need to speak with you alone, Samira," Mateo said, his pleading voice a vice on my most fragile organ.

"I'm going home." I opened the driver's side door just as Lynx scurried into the back.

"Then I will meet you there."

I met his eyes and could see a thousand things in that gaze. Moonlit walks through the gardens of Paris, our many nights of being pursued by vampire hunters and having to sleep in some unusual places, one of them included sharing the coffin of a recently deceased human. Sharing blood in the most intimate ways possible. Those nights were full of unbridled passion, drinking freely from humans, indulging our every whim.

It was freedom I had not allowed myself in centuries, nor would I again, now that I'd found a better way to live. One that brought peace instead of chaos. I may have lost some things in the process, but I no longer hated myself for my actions.

I glanced away, shoving the memories aside. "That's not a good idea."

"I'm coming anyway."

Briar was on the other side of the car removing her bloody shirt. "I don't want to mess up your car with Hyde blood."

"That's why I have leather seats. Besides, I have no aversion to blood."

"I can tell. You're caked in it." Briar snickered, as I subconsciously swiped at my forehead. I didn't want to look like the old me.

Briar opened the car door. "I'm leaving my pants on, though, but don't worry. I'll clean up any blood I leave. I don't want to catch you licking it up later."

She laughed, then grimaced, tilting her head as if in pain.

I cast Mateo one final look before I slid behind the wheel. Once everyone was inside, I drove away, watching him in my rearview mirror, a dark prince of the night. Lynx sat in the back, her head resting against the glass. Briar settled next to her, hitting at her ear.

I peered at her in the rearview mirror. "How does it feel?"

"Slowly getting better. Hey, Sammie, tell me something. Who is Faithe?"

The car was silent for a moment as I processed my feelings. What to tell them? The truth seemed the easiest. "She is my daughter."

Both Lynx and Briar gasped.

"Like, daughter, daughter?" Briar asked.

I shook my head. "I turned her centuries ago."

"So weird," Briar responded.

"That I turned someone?"

"Nah, not that. I just have a hard time wrapping my head around your life spans."

"Oh." I thought about that. "Would it help if I used other terms? Maybe decades?"

"No, that's still weird."

"Have you turned anyone else?" Lynx asked.

"No." The word escaped quickly.

"Was she always like…" Lynx paused. "That?"

"Not at all." My voice was quiet. "Korin has changed her."

"What did she used to be like?" Lynx leaned forward, resting her arms on the back of the seat.

I rubbed at the back of my neck, exhausted from the mental battle of keeping my emotions in check. "I found her one day wading into a lake trying to commit suicide. Back then, albinos were seen as bad omens. She had been a freak in her time, abandoned by her parents when she came into the world. Her family and the village believed she was the spawn of the devil and brought a curse to them. As a baby, she was left in the woods to die, but a Romanian woman heard her cries in passing and cared for Faithe into her teens. But when a terrible fire destroyed their village, the people believed it was punishment for taking in the ghost of the forest. They killed her adopted mother. Faithe managed to escape before they killed her, too.

"Once again, she had no home, wandering village to village to beg for food, but her unearthly appearance inevitably forced her to move on when she would be beaten and tortured.

"This is when I discovered her. Her soul and mind broken. Halfway into the lake. She'd had enough of a world that had treated her so harshly."

"That's terrible," Lynx whispered.

Briar also leaned forward, still rubbing at her ear. "Then what happened?"

"After turning her, I took her far away from those people who tortured her to a place in Africa, where the climate was warmer, the skies more clear, and the people more open minded to someone like Faithe. I had heard of a tribe there, the Madabbe Tribe, who accepted those who were different. They believed people like us were gifts to mankind." I inhaled a hitched breath. To be a vampire and to be considered a gift was not something I believed.

I continued. "It took some time to find the remote village deep inside the Congo, and I almost gave up, but then I'd see that forlorn look in Faithe's eyes again. I was determined to find the tribe, to find a place where she felt valued. I considered returning to my coven, but a part of me knew she wasn't ready for that environment. She needed to find her inner strength first. Vampires could sense weakness and might torture her mercilessly.

"Eventually, we found it and, like I'd heard, the Madabbe people took us in. They embraced Faithe fully, even giving her a name: Specter. With her white hair and skin and reddish eyes, they didn't treat her like a monster, not like the rest of the world had. They treated her as if she were a god, something to be in awe of, something to be respected."

"Whoa, that's awesome." Briar leaned back and rested her feet on the back of my seat. "Bet they loved you, too."

"Actually, they feared me at first. Apparently, they had heard my name whispered among their visitors and none of it was good. This was the first time I realized what kind of monster I had become. The realization was eye-opening and made me decide to stay longer than expected. After a long period of time, we finally returned to my coven with Korin."

"So you used to be kind of wicked?" Briar asked.

Briar's hopeful voice made my stomach clench. She was looking for solidarity, but if only she knew. Wicked was a tame word for what I'd once been.

To ease the sudden tension in the air, Lynx quickly asked, "Briar, how's your ear?"

"Meh, burns a little." She lowered her feet and leaned forward. "I still can't believe Korin did that to me. It was the strangest sensation, feeling my body move even though I was screaming at it to stop." She met my eyes in the mirror. "If Korin wanted you to go see his coven, why didn't he just compel you like everyone else?"

"Because I can't be compelled anymore."

"How? And can you share whatever it is with the rest of us?"

I tightened my grip on the steering wheel. My roommates didn't know my history. I had deliberately kept it from them for a number of reasons. A lot of my past was violent and bloody, especially when I was a full member of my old coven. For some strange reason, their opinion of me mattered, and I didn't know how they would react if they knew what sort of person I used to be. Keeping my past to myself also helped me keep my roommates at arm's length. And yet, as I looked at both of them, I couldn't deny the unlikely friendships that had developed, despite my best intentions.

Maybe it was time to let them know the real me. Parts of me, anyway. It would help in this situation. "I fought and earned the Kiss of Eternal Night."

"Sounds sexy," Briar said. "I'll fight to get it."

"It wasn't. It was pain and torment, the worst kind you could imagine. I had to pass three trials. The first tested my body, the second my mind, the third my soul. I wouldn't wish it on anyone."

"Why did you do it?" Lynx asked, her voice soft.

"One reason was to break the hold Korin had over me. If he couldn't compel me, I wouldn't have to do his bidding."

Briar smoothed her hair back into a ponytail. "What were the other reasons?"

"Nothing that matters right now." The words escaped faster than I intended. "We need to talk about what this means. If Korin is working with Bodian Dynamics, or is Bodian, that means he might also try to bring Trianus back."

"Trianus?" Briar scowled. "I thought we eliminated that problem.

Don't tell me you think someone still wants to bring that demon back?"

"We can't rule it out." I almost told her about the prophecy, but the timing felt wrong.

Briar folded her arms and mumbled, "I think we can. I kicked that incorporeal thing's ass to pieces. At least it felt like an ass I was kicking."

"How do we get rid of Korin?" Lynx interrupted, her heart pounding.

I adjusted my weight on the seat, considering her uneasiness. She seemed to be more nervous than usual lately. "I don't know. Many have tried to kill him, and just as many have died."

"He's got to have a weakness," Briar said. "Like a mind nut sack we can punch repeatedly."

Lynx leaned forward, her eyes hopeful. "Could you beat him? This Kiss thing makes you fight better than anyone I've ever seen before."

"I wouldn't say that," Briar said, "but Lynx has a point. Your fighting skills are insane when you beast out."

I frowned, not understanding the term. "Beast out?"

"You know, go all crazy-eyed monster killer. Do that on Korin."

"The Kiss of Eternal Night is not to be used lightly. It has consequences, severe ones I didn't know about when I went through the trials. I don't know if I would have fought so hard to obtain the Kiss had I known about them."

Lynx tilted her head. "What kind?"

"The Kiss of Eternal Night is pure darkness said to have been stolen from the blackest pit in Hell. Light has never touched it. Its power is rooted in rage and violence. I left Korin with the desire to escape the violence, and instead I ran right into its arms."

Silence crowded the small space. Briar broke it. "What are our other options?"

"Could we drive him out of town?" Lynx asked. "We almost burned down the warehouse. If we can somehow try again and be successful, maybe he'll leave."

"First, we have to find a way to un-compel everyone," I said. "We need the Nocs working with us again."

"I agree," Briar added. "It was weird seeing Angel so submissive. And yet, there was something appealing about it, too." She touched her lips, her eyes distant. I didn't want to know what she was thinking about.

Lynx leaned back into her seat. "I'll find something. I promise."

No one said anything else the rest of the way home. Lynx was lost in her thoughts, Briar was probably thinking about how to make Angel submissive to her, and I couldn't stop thinking about how we could stop Korin. Once Korin made a plan, he didn't give up on it. And anyone who stood in his way was destroyed.

I knew that because I used to be his destroyer.

CHAPTER 7

I drove past Lynx's house and into the driveway behind it, passing Luke on the way. He was leaning against his bike looking anything but happy.

"Someone's in trouble," Lynx muttered.

Briar groaned and smoothed back her tangled hair. Parts of it were matted with blood. "I should've brought a change of clothes. How bad do I look?"

I opened the car door, pausing. "Like you've returned from a date with Michael Myers."

Both Lynx and Briar turned to me, mouths agape.

"Was that a pop culture reference?" Briar asked. "Fist bump, girl." She held her fist for me to tap.

I ignored it and exited the car. I may not keep up on the latest celebrity gossip or popular music, but I knew some things. Human's version of horror intrigued me. Plus, part of me enjoyed the banter between us. It had been centuries since I'd had friends like them. I didn't realize how much I'd missed it.

Luke rounded the corner and came straight for the car. When Briar exited and he saw her in a bra and bloody jeans, hair matted, the color drained from his face. He hurried to her and touched under her ear, the blood already dried. "What happened? Are you okay?"

While they spoke, I walked inside with Lynx. She crossed through the kitchen but stopped at the doorjamb. She looked back at me over her shoulder. "I'm sorry about tonight."

"Why would you be sorry? You did nothing wrong."

"If I wouldn't have been so anxious to storm in there, Briar wouldn't have been hurt, and you wouldn't have met your maker. I can tell he terrifies you."

"None of this is—"

"It's just that sometimes, I get this hunger for danger. Like there's this darkness inside me wanting to come out, wanting to hurt others." She looked up at me with glossy eyes. "It scares me."

I went to her and lightly placed my hand on her arm. "I won't pretend to know what you're going through, but I know I have my own darkness I have to fight, sometimes daily. It can be so hard not to give into it, if only to silence the constant whisperings."

"How do you do it?"

It took a single beat of my heart to answer. "I only have to remember the monster I once was to know I never want to become that again. But you need to find what works for you."

She nodded her head, her gaze returning to the window.

"You should sleep. It will be dawn in a couple of hours."

"Maybe. Thanks, Samira." She walked towards her room and closed the door softly.

Outside, Luke's bike fired up. When Briar didn't come back in, I assumed she left with him. I vaguely thought of the blood in my car and wondered if she, indeed, had wiped it up.

Alone, I inhaled a shaky breath and fell into a chair by the kitchen table, the realization of what had happened finally hitting me. I'd faced Korin, the vampire who made me all those centuries ago. Once I was free from him, I never thought I'd see him again.

There was a time I thought I'd never leave his side. He was my father, the person I turned to if I ever needed advice or help. I gripped the table in front of me, my breath heaving as memories threatened to pull me under. All the terrible things I'd done for him. I was a different person then, far removed from who I was now.

Closing my eyes, I focused on my breathing, trying to calm my emotions. Seeing Korin again also brought out the dangerous side of me, the kind that liked to maim and kill. Trying to calm the monster, I thought of my favorite spot in this world, a place I hadn't been to in a long time. I pictured the lush forest, hidden by a veil of mist with its gnarled roots and twisted branches grown rugged as if to protect its heart. Its heart being a series of lakes and dozens of cascading water-falls, the color of rare emeralds shining in the moonlight.

"Are you thinking of Croatia?" a voice said. I opened my eyes. Mateo stood in front of me, only a table between us. "One of the last times we were together was at the Plitvice Lakes."

"I remember."

Silence pressed between us, something that didn't used to exist. Not between us. And yet, the pull to him was undeniable. I felt it with every beat of my heart: the need to touch him, even just a simple caress. I pushed the craving away.

"Whatever you think you need to say, don't. I understand that you must do things for Korin. There is no need to explain." I stood and stepped away from him, trying to resist the yearning he had awakened in me.

His lips tightened as he watched me move back from him, then he hitched in a breath. "There is so much I want to tell you."

I shook my head. "It doesn't matter anymore. Things are different."

"I thought so too, but when I saw you in the swamps with Silas that night, I realized that nothing's changed." His body moved around the table so fluidly, I don't think he even knew he was moving toward me. "I tried to pretend my feelings weren't real, that I was only feeling the way I do because you brought back the only fond memo-ries I have ever had, but I can't do that anymore. Not when you are so close." He reached up and palmed my cheek, his thumb brushing across my skin. He moaned, a tortured sound. "Oh, Samira. All my feelings for you, they never left me, they are only buried here." He touched his chest where his dead heart thundered. "It is so hard to see you, smell you, to be near you without touching you the way I want."

I closed my eyes. "Stop, Mateo. We can't do this." I tried to convince him, and myself, that I didn't love him anymore.

"There is fire between us, Samira, and though it may have died down, there are still embers that burn hot. We just need to find our way to each other again." He slid his hand behind my neck just like he used to, and his touch ignited every part of my flesh. I sucked in a breath through my teeth.

"Do it," he ordered.

His command struck a nerve. The most sensitive one that sent waves of heat through my abdomen. I knew exactly what he was talking about. In the past, whenever he had touched me in this way, I would tilt my head to the side, offering my life blood to him. Then we would make love for hours, just taking and giving to each other. In that world, he was the only being that existed for me, and I him.

And it had almost killed me.

"We can't do this." I stepped away from him.

His hand fell to his side, but he closed the distance between us again. Fangs grew in his mouth at my refusal. "Now that you know the truth about Korin I can tell you my true feelings. I've come for you, Samira. I cannot stay away any longer. I tried to resist. I swear I tried."

He gripped my hips, yanking me to him, allowing me to see the torture it had cost him in his eyes. "But I cannot ignore your call to me any longer. It has not abated over the centuries. No, it has grown. You are the only woman for me, Samira. *Mi completi. Senza di te la mia vita non ha senso.*"

You complete me. Without you, my life has no meaning.

I clung to him, fighting against the desire to let him press me against the kitchen wall and bite into my flesh. I was the same as him. Distance, time, or even the tearing of my heart from my chest had not lessened my feelings for this man. I wanted to tilt my head to the side and give in to my hunger. Lust and longing surged through me, overpowering my control.

Yesss, the dark voice inside me crowed, begging to be released. To feed on my emotions, to take control of my body and release a wave of blood lust no one could stop. I sucked in several shaking breaths, trying to control my feelings. If I gave in to them, it could release the Kiss. I needed to be in control of myself now more so than ever before.

And so, I slowly released him and moved away. I did not miss the disappointment in his eyes. But I wrapped myself up in courage and strength, something I'd worked hard to acquire over the centuries, and said the words I thought would push him away.

"I do not love you anymore, Mateo."

He drew his brows together. "I do not believe you. I feel it from you, just as I know you can feel my passion, my love, for you."

I released a trace of venom into my words. "It is too late for your exclamations of love. I waited three nights for you, even though I put both myself and Faithe in danger to do so."

He stepped closer. "You were never in any danger."

I pushed him back, trying to put some distance between us. "I was in danger. I had to kill Henrik, who had been compelled to find me and cut off my head. He was a good friend and it pained me to kill him." Grief clutched my pounding heart, thinking of that night. Of my helplessness, my pain in killing my dear friend.

His face darkened. "That should not have happened."

"But it did." I felt the cold and dark tendrils of the Kiss begin to seep from its cage deep inside me. I needed to get Mateo out of here and out of my life. "You must leave, now."

"I can never leave you, Samira. Not again."

Anger swelled within me, raced through my blood. "You are the one who rejected me, remember? Or have you forgotten?"

"I didn't reject you."

"You never came for me. Even though I know you could've found me after Faithe and I fled the coven."

"I'm here now."

I laughed out loud, a sound foreign to my ears. "It's too late! I'm not the same woman anymore."

He growled at my laughter. "And I'm not the same man, and yet, I am still consumed with my desire for you."

"Stop this. Right now." I backed away, afraid if he said one more word, I'd return to his arms, releasing a torrid of emotions that could break carefully placed mental barriers. I couldn't become that person again. Too many had been hurt by our union, especially myself. And if the Kiss took over my life again, I would hurt much more than just myself. My roommates, the friends I had grown to love. "Leave."

"I will do as you ask, but know this." He drew close again leaving no air between us. "You were gifted the Kiss of Eternal Night, a feat no one else has survived. I can't imagine how it changed you, but I sense so much of you is blocked. In that fact, you are right. You're not the same woman I fell madly in love with all those years ago, and yet, I still see fire in your eyes that ignites when you look at me."

He palmed my heart, just above my breast. "You're still in there, and somehow, I'm going to smash through those walls you think you need to control the Kiss." He leaned toward me, just a breath away from my lips. "Love and passion are powerful weapons against darkness."

He brushed his lips against mine and turned, disappearing into the night, leaving as soundlessly as he'd arrived. My body melted, and I slumped to the floor, too overwhelmed by everything that had happened tonight.

Mateo was wrong. He had no idea how powerful the Kiss was. He hadn't seen my rampage across all of Asia and Europe for over a hundred years. The destruction I had caused when I had released the Kiss.

My mind numb, I dragged myself down the stairs and into my coffin where I let darkness bathe me in a warm cocoon. Tomorrow would be better.

I whispered the lie over and over until I let the first of the sun's rays pull me under.

CHAPTER 8

The house was empty when I woke exactly as the sun set for the day. It had been a long time since I'd slept all day, but my mind, battered with old memories and emotions, needed the respite.

A note from Lynx on the refrigerator said she was away doing research. Probably something to do with a cure for compulsion. There was nothing from Briar, but that didn't surprise me.

After showering and dressing, I cleaned and polished my weapons. My fingers slid across the cool metal with a soft cloth in gentle strokes. I often found this nightly ritual to be therapeutic. A cleansing of blood to erase my sins. I could clean these blades for a thousand years and not come close to atoning for all I'd done.

My mind raged as my fingers worked calmly; I only wished it could be as composed as what I portrayed to the rest of the world. Keeping my emotions in check was essential to their survival. And tonight, returning to my old coven, it was even more important to stay in control and keep my mind sharp. I cleaned and whetted my tools until I felt balance settle within me. I sheathed my swords and prepared to leave, a nervous flutter in my stomach the only sign of the fervor I'd felt earlier.

I left the house and drove to the east side of town where the wealthiest people in the city lived. I knew exactly where Winter's Cove was. It was the oldest mansion in all of Rouen, built in the seventeen-hundreds. On and off throughout history, the Buio Sangre coven had split their time between it and another mansion, an exact replica, in Croatia. I used to love that mansion in Europe up until the day I abandoned it and my coven. When I returned, I'd burned it to the ground in an attempt to erase my past and all the horrible acts committed in that place. I would've done the same to Winter's Cove, but Korin had it spelled against anyone who dared harm it in his absence. I know, because I tried. Nearly burned all the hair off my body trying to bring Winter's Cove to ashes.

And now it loomed before me, a reminder that I would never be able to erase that part of my history.

The grand structure made of iron and stone sat on forty acres surrounded by a dense forest just as old as the mansion. The long lane leading to it was barred by a black metal gate bearing the symbol of a half-moon with a sword through it. A memory of me killing someone on the tip of that sword flashed in my mind. I pulled my car up to the gate and peered into the security camera. This was new. A moment later, the gates creaked open.

Dread clenched my gut as I drove down the dark lane beneath a canopy of tangled tree limbs. Those long, spiny branches seemed to recoil when my headlights touched them. Part of me believed what I was seeing. I had no idea how much evil had taken hold of this property, making it a living and breathing entity.

I parked in front of stone steps and removed my glasses. Inside this place, I needed to remember my vampire side. I exited the vehicle. The mansion looked as I remembered it. Dark stones, the lower ones covered in dull, thick moss, piled on top of each and ended in iron spirals clawing at the darkness. A gross intrusion into an otherwise beautiful night.

Sliding my swords into the sheaths on my back, I made my way up the stone steps, my legs heavy, until I reached two large wooden doors. My reception would not be well received. Not with how I left things. I shoved the doors open; they groaned in protest.

The entryway looked the same. A massive iron chandelier hanging from the high ceiling had been lit with a thousand candles. Flat stone floors with thick blood-red veins fractured the dull surface. On the wooden paneled walls hung paintings older than the mansion, depicting images of angels and demons, wars, death and destruction. I hated it all.

A human servant dressed in a tuxedo of the highest quality hurried toward me. The gray pallor of his cheeks contrasted with his yellowed eyes. Life was nearly vacant in those glossy orbs. This is what it looked like when humans worked for vampires. He had either been compelled or made some deal with one of them in exchange for riches for family members.

He bowed in front of me. "My name is Branson. How may I serve you, Samira?"

Someone had told him about me. This worried me. Who else knew I was coming? "I do not require your assistance. I know my way around."

"Thank you, miss. Your bedroom has already been prepared for you."

I shivered, as memories of that bedroom assaulted me. Long nights of drinking after restraining a human on the bed, then making passionate love to Mateo on every inch in that bedroom while the human bled out. Or Edward's shocked face as I sliced his head off, all because he'd dared talk back to Korin. It didn't matter that he was once my friend. Korin laughing gleefully.

I held back the bile threatening to lurch up my throat. All disgusting acts, once considered normal to my warped mind. Something I'd long since overcome.

I held my hand out firmly. "Not necessary. I won't be staying."

"Nevertheless, it is ready."

I lowered my head, dismissing him. I wasn't staying any longer than necessary in this dark pit of memories.

Before I could look for Faithe or those who might still have a small fondness for me, I had to follow protocol and check in with Naburus, Korin's firstborn and self-appointed Prince of our coven. He was just as bad as Korin, maybe even worse. His thirst for knowledge had crossed over into something grotesque, rivaling the worst ethical offenders since the beginning of time. There was no line he wouldn't cross in the name of science, no code he lived by, save that of furthering his understanding of life and death.

I turned to my left and toward a stairway leading into the basement. I had yet to cross paths with another vampire, but it didn't surprise me. No one ever headed in the direction of Naburus's private lab.

The temperature dropped as I descended the stairs to the next floor. I walked down a cold and dark hallway, the sound of my steps echoing against stone walls. The bitter smell of chemicals and blood stung my nose the closer I came. An ice-cold chill clawed up my spine at the familiar scent that always followed Naburus wherever he went.

Reaching the metal door at the end, I knocked on the door, softer than I intended.

"Enter."

His voice made my stomach tighten. I placed my hand over the sensation, hoping to calm it, then pushed open the door.

The lab was as I remembered. Long rows of counters topped with beakers, centrifuges, burners, incubators; anything he might need to conduct his latest experiment. The florescent lights flickering above were an improvement over the old torches. Naburus stood beneath one, his pale skin looking sickly under its illumination. His stringy hair, missing on some parts of his scalp, was tied back in a loose ponytail with a string. His face, long and straight, was all angles and sharp lines made worse by his sunken countenance. In the crook of his left arm, where the skin was mottled and discolored, an IV had been placed. Long tubing ran from it up to an IV pole where two bags of blood hung.

Naburus had been Korin's first attempt at making a vampire. Korin had had no one to teach him the complicated process, plus it didn't help that he had chosen a man who had just fallen victim to the

Plague of Justinian, a disease that had killed more than ten thousand people daily in the Roman Empire. Something about this combination left Naburus in constant need of blood.

"It's been a long time, Samira," he said and moved toward me, his IV pole squeaking behind him. The heavy material of his long dark robe swished. "Korin said you would be coming."

"I'm just letting you know I may be by to visit now and then, while the coven resides at Winter's Cove."

"Come here," he ordered, curling his long finger into a hook. "I want to show you my latest experiment."

I reluctantly followed after him. There had been so many times I'd thought about killing him. Chopping that long, blood-filled tube in half, leaving him to wither and die, but Korin's fury would be violent and swift. It wouldn't be just me he hurt, it would be everyone I ever knew and loved.

Naburus turned a corner into another section of the lab. Pressed against the wall in a handstand position were two naked humans. Blood ran from their noses where Naburus had fashioned tubing to collect the crimson liquid. By the looks of their pale legs, they had been in that position for some time. Both their eyes were closed. I might've thought they were dead since I heard no heartbeat, but the beats must've been faint because blood still flowed.

As for their odd positioning, stiff handstands maintained with no devices, this was Naburus' gift. He could control living tissue, but only to the extent of making it rigid and unmovable. This was a small extension of Korin's power passed through to Naburus. Very few of us, as Korin's offspring, were given these powers. No one really knew how or why some vampires were gifted with more abilities than others, like Angel's gift for healing, for example. Sometimes they were gifts, other times they were curses. I had earned mine. And in this moment, I was glad I had it because it made it possible for me to withstand Naburus's control over my own body should he attempt it.

"What is this?" I asked, not attempting to hide the revulsion in my voice.

He walked over to them, his robe whispering along the stone floor followed by his IV pole, and stared down. "Just before all their blood is drained, I'm going to fill their veins with shifter blood."

I glanced around for shifters, but didn't see any. He probably had some stashed away in the dungeon. "Why would you do that?"

"To see if I can. Maybe if we can make our own shifters, they can become our guardians during the day."

"You're insane." The words left my mouth before I could stop them.

His head jerked my direction, and his pale eyes flashed a vibrant yellow. My muscles snapped into a tight contraction, making it so I couldn't move. This is what he did—trapped his prey like a snake coiled around a rat.

And he had me.

CHAPTER 9

*N*aburus moved in front of me, his mouth a straight line. "I told Korin it was a mistake to let you live all those years ago. You were too wild, too reckless."

He lifted his bony hand and ran the back of his fingers across my cheek, down my neck. "But I'm glad you're alive. For now I have full authority to do whatever I want with you."

His fingers traveled lower to my breasts. Enough of this.

Easily breaking his hold on my body, I snatched his hand and twisted hard. "Don't touch me."

His eyes lit up with wonder, obvious to the pain his arm must be feeling. "Then it's true! You do have the Kiss of Eternal Night inside you."

I shoved him away. "I will follow the rules of this coven, but nothing more. I've made myself known to you. Goodbye."

Turning on my heel, I resisted the urge to run and walked instead. He may have held power over me before, but no more. I would not be afraid of him. That's what I told myself, but I could still feel the ice in my veins from his touch.

As I made my way across the mansion to search for Faithe, I tried not to think about the humans or shifters trapped in Naburus' lab.

Saving them would be near impossible. But could I still be who I was if I didn't at least try?

"Samira!" a voice called.

I stopped just as I was about to walk into a formal living room and turned around. A boy who looked barely eighteen, yet carried himself as someone much older, hurried toward me, confidence in each step. His brown hair held blond highlights as if it had been kissed by the sun. His light complexion and light blue eyes were familiar. So was his broad smile, a single dimple on his right cheek.

"Teddy?" I asked, the heaviness in my chest lifting.

His grin widened. "Yup!"

"You look so different!"

He threw his arms around me in a tight hug. "I've missed you! I can't tell you how many times I searched for you."

We let each other go, and I stared at the boy who had once followed me around like a lost puppy for years. He was turned by one of our sentries in the late seventeenth century, shortly before I left the coven, but that sentry was killed and wasn't able to teach him how to live as a vampire. And out of everyone he could've learned from, he had latched onto me.

I squeezed the muscles on his arms. "You've grown yourself."

"Easy to do when you're a vampire. All of it comes from training. You should see me fight!"

The way he was talking to me, so carefree, made guilt eat at my heart. "You're not mad at me for leaving?"

His smile disappeared, and he leaned forward conspiratorially. "I'm glad you did. All those things Korin made you do. I only wish I could've gone with you."

"About that, I'm sorry."

"Don't be. You would never have made it far with me by your side. I was so young and careless." He searched my eyes, and his smile returned. "Come on. Let me show you around."

For the next little while, he gave me a tour as if I didn't remember what the original mansion looked like. It was unsettling how he had managed to replicate every detail down to the lace mantel scarves. All he added was modern conveniences like electricity and outlets for cable and internet.

Like I expected, few vampires acknowledged my presence. I recognized many, but there were several I didn't know. I froze when I spotted the silver-eyed vampire from Sinsual, the one Briar and I had been tracking when we went to the warehouse. He seemed at complete ease here, which meant he'd been here for some time.

Teddy stopped in the library and motioned toward the back of a woman with long blond hair. I'd recognize it anywhere. "You remember Kristina?"

She slowly turned around. Where her hair was shiny and vibrant, her eyes were sullen and gray, a mere shadow of the blue they used to be. "Kristina?"

"Samira." She smiled but the motion took great effort. "You're back."

"I'm visiting," I clarified and hurried to her side. I bent down next to her and rested my palm over her cold, small hand. "You're ill. What's wrong?"

"Do I look that bad?" She attempted to smooth her hair back, but her hands shook.

I glanced up at Teddy. His eyes were sad as he stared down at her.

"You don't look bad," I said to her. "Just sick. Has something happened?"

She tapped her forehead with her finger. "There's only so much this can handle."

"I don't understand."

Teddy cleared his throat. "Mind control. After you left, she became Korin's enforcer. She tried fighting him, so now he just compels her to do everything. Doesn't even give her a chance to disobey now."

I sucked in a breath. Long term compulsion was known to have serious side effects on humans and vampires. A brain locked in a mental prison could only withstand so much. By the looks of Kristina, she was close to breaking. No wonder, since he'd have been compelling her for over three hundred years.

I'd seen a few crazy vampires in my time, ones whose minds had fractured from either too much compulsion or magical spells. They were dangerous and reckless, often exposing themselves inadvertently to sunlight or going on a nighttime rampage, slaughtering anyone in their path. Very few bothered to lock up vampires like that. Since there was no cure, they were eliminated. Permanently.

"What can I do?" I asked, desperate to help my old friend. We had been turned around the same time. Her father used to be Korin's closest friend before he was killed in the vampire-witch wars over four hundred years ago, but we had been friends for even longer. That changed when I told her I was leaving. She swore she'd never speak to me again if I left, but I don't think she ever understood how bad things had gotten for me. By the looks of her now, she understood.

"I'm trapped, Samira," she said, staring down at her hands. "Nothing can be done."

"That's not true. I found a way out."

Her gaze slowly moved up to mine. "And yet you're back."

"It's temporary."

She shook her head sadly. "It's never temporary with Korin. He will find a way to keep you here."

"It's different this time," I assured her, keeping a mask of calm on my face. She couldn't see the weakness I felt inside, the doubt I held.

She didn't say anything and even Teddy averted his gaze. Could they see right through me? I set my mouth in a firm line, determined to keep my emotions from showing. I pulled out a chair and sat with her at the table. Teddy did the same, sitting opposite of me.

"Tell me," I said, "what happened to Faithe?"

Teddy's face darkened, anger filling his countenance. "She became Korin's plaything."

"She did what she had to do to survive," Kristina clarified.

"Is she compelled?"

Teddy rubbed at the back of his neck. "She could be. I rarely see her away from him. I've tried talking to her, but she always has this distant look in her eyes, almost as if she's somewhere else."

I nodded. I knew the look. I'd seen the same thing when I found her half way submerged in the lake. I'd saved her then, I could save her again.

"What do you know about Trianus?" I asked.

Both their mouths tightened as if invisible strings had pulled them tight. I groaned. "You've been compelled not to say anything, correct?"

They stared at me, but Teddy was blinking furiously, which told me Korin must have said something to them about Trianus.

"Somehow, I'm going to find a way to break his hold over you. Over all of you. His reign of violence and terror must end. It's gone on too long."

Teddy's eyes widened. "You'll get yourself killed."

"Things are different now. I'm different."

"And that makes you stronger than Korin?"

I bit my lip, something I hadn't done since I left the coven, and thought about his words. I might be stronger with the Kiss, but did I dare unleash its full power? I'd used just a small portion of it the other night and almost didn't stop myself before running my sword through Lynx.

I answered honestly. "I don't know."

He leaned toward me, his eyes serious. "Then you better get sure, because if you go against Korin with any hesitation, he'll kill you."

I LEFT Winter's Cove feeling no better than when I arrived. Since I was forced to return, I had hoped to learn something that could help me against Korin, but instead, I only discovered how much my old friends were suffering. Something had to be done.

Parking again a few blocks from Sinsual, I snuck through the roof access again and into Eddie's office. Now that I knew he was fae, I was surprised I hadn't noticed before. The signs were all there: small, yet quick movements, a slight sheen in his eyes when he got angry, a musical tone to his voice.

When I walked through the door, Eddie barely looked up at me from his computer, his hands flying across the keyboard. "Welcome back, Samira. Give me a second, would you? And could you close the door?"

"I can wait outside, if you'd like."

"No, no. I'm about ready, just close the door."

I complied and stepped to the side, settling into the room as if I was a part of it. Eddie tapped away a few more minutes, his eyes darting from a paper on his desk and to the computer screen. He stopped, pushed away from the desk, and closed his eyes. I was about to ask him if he was all right, when his body began to shimmer, then separate. Much the same way a tarantula sheds its skin, Eddie became a duplicate copy of himself. My lips parted, and a breath escaped. I'd only ever seen that one other time, and it was just as shocking as it had been the first time I saw it.

Standing, Eddie stared down at himself. "I have a stain on my shirt."

The duplicate version of him looked down and shrugged.

"Is your duplicate body corporeal?" I asked.

"That would be impossible." He swiped at the copy, his hand going right through his head, a swirl of blue magic twisting into the air. "As long as I avoid contact with anyone or anything, no one will ever know."

He crossed the room and opened the door, motioning me through first. The copy of Eddie turned and stared out the office window to the club below.

"Does anyone know?"

"Only my kind, and now you. Please keep it secret."

Outside the club, I turned toward my car, but Eddie jerked his head another direction. "This way. Black Glen isn't far."

I raised an eyebrow. "How big is this place?"

He looked back and grinned. "Huge."

I didn't waste words asking what he meant. I'd know soon enough. I hadn't spent much time with fae in my long lifetime. Their numbers were by far the fewest among supernaturals, so they tended to keep to themselves. They also wielded powerful magic, which made a lot of the other species fear them, but I found them to be quite agreeable.

Maybe it's because I felt a kinship to them, being so different from everyone else.

Eddie turned left down Central Avenue. Streetlights lit up red hues in his hair, and when moonlight hit him just right, his skin almost looked incandescent.

"How long have you known Sersi?" he asked.

"Centuries."

He nodded, thinking.

"You?"

"I met her a few decades back," he said. "About the same time I opened the club. Well, shortly after. I was a mess when I first came to Rouen."

"Most are."

He eyed me sideways, then glanced around to make sure we weren't being listened to. "Our kind knows something is changing in Rouen. We've felt the shift in the wind, a darkness blowing in from the East."

"The East?"

"We noticed it over a decade ago, but in the past few months it has been growing."

"What does it want?"

"What everyone in this city who desires power wants lately." He met my gaze. "The Abydos."

I kept my face even, not wanting to reveal anything. Briar had put me in charge of it, and I would protect it with my life, if necessary. "What is the fae's interest in the sacred blood?"

He let out a long, weighted breath. "Depends upon who you ask. Some want it to increase our wealth and power. Some want it because they think it will help us reproduce easier. Then there are others, like me, who want nothing to do with it. That kind of power shouldn't be allowed in anyone's hands. Plus, it would put a target on our back, and our population is already small. We couldn't defend ourselves against an attack, if someone decided to fight us for it."

He stopped walking. "We're here."

We still stood on the street. A line of shops were on my left, but on

74

my right was Rouen's biggest city park: Emerald Park. The wide expanse of manicured green lawn with strategically placed trees and walking paths held farmer's markets in the summer, music festivals every few months, and even a yearly Renaissance fair.

I peered into the empty park using my night vision. "There's nothing here."

He grinned. "Not yet."

CHAPTER 10

*U*nder his breath, Eddie said, in a language he probably thought I didn't know, "By the moon's light upon the floor, reveal the secret, open the door."

But I did speak Fae, and I spoke it well, having learned it centuries ago. I had always made it a point to speak every language possible. This had helped me on countless occasions.

I pretended I didn't understand him, but when the park and all its trees began to dissipate in front of me, I gasped. In its place was a city from another time.

"Come on," Eddie said and urged me forward.

Small thatched-roof homes and shops crowded the space, the walkways between them narrow and tight. Lit sconces adorned each door, casting warm light in all directions. And it was busy. So many people, fae, bustled about in clothing reminiscent of a Scottish village in the sixteen-hundreds. They carried baskets of food, pelts from animals, and books wrapped in ribbons. The crowded shops sold all manner of food and clothing. Some sold magical objects, while others looked like small pubs.

More than all the sights and sounds of talking and the clanking of objects, were the smells that filled the air. Plum pudding, sweet rolls, and candied apples. It was as if I could taste each one on my tongue, the scents alive and vibrant. I rarely ate human food, but suddenly I wanted to taste it all.

"Why is this place so different?" I asked.

"Different?" Eddie nudged aside a plump man carrying a bag of grain. No one paid us any attention. It was as if they were used to visitors from the outside world.

I fumbled to find the right words. "So old fashioned. Quaint. And the smells…" It reminded me of my youth.

He chuckled. "The smells are the best part of this place. We plant most of our food in soil that's over a thousand years old. It holds magical properties that grows with the food. As for the odd time period you see, Fae folk like to stick to tradition, but if you look closely, hidden within all their folds of clothing, you'll find modern cell phones. They are the kings and queens of hypocrisy." He stopped abruptly and turned to me, his expression serious. "Remember that."

I nodded and moved out of the way of a man pushing a cart full of hay. This one did look at me and frowned as he eyed me up and down. My black attire must look terribly depressing to him.

"This way," Eddie said, guiding me down a narrow alley, then cutting over to another street. He stopped suddenly. "One second. Briar is at the office trying to talk to the other me."

He turned toward a bare wall, and a white film came over his eyes. "You know you can take whatever time you need, Briar. Just show up whenever."

He paused, then, "Don't feel bad. Go. You have a busy life and a lot of people depend upon you."

Another several seconds passed.

"I just mean you have a boyfriend now and roommates. That's a lot of responsibility. Now leave, please. I have a lot to do."

A moment later, his eyes returned to normal, and he turned to me. "That was close. It's hard to remember that she doesn't know about me, and I'm not supposed to know about her."

"I'm sure that will have to change soon."

"Yes, I'm sure it will."

We continued to zigzag our way through the maze of crowded homes and shops until we reached a tall iron fence. Beyond it, across an expansive lawn full of flowered gardens and shrubs, was a mansion, more like a castle by the look of its spirals and fluted columns, rivaling Winter's Cove.

"This is Warwick Castle, where our King and Queen live," Eddie said and walked past the open gates. There were no guards posted, no sign of security. Apparently, they didn't live in fear of their lives like many supernaturals outside of Black Glen had to.

"Will we be meeting with them?"

He shook his head. "Not today, but we will be meeting with their lieutenant, Folas Valxina. He has information you might find helpful."

"Why have a lieutenant when I see no soldiers or security?"

He turned right down a path, past several rose bushes that were a shade of blue I hadn't seen before. "Oh, it's here. You just can't see it. Our security is probably the best in the world. We don't take our safety lightly, not when there are so few of us. However, they know who I am, so we can move about as we wish."

I didn't ask any more questions, but instead took in every detail of the castle. Anything that might be useful later. I noted the oddly placed dead flowers tied with ribbons at each crossroads, and the eerie gargoyle statues resting in the center of each small garden. If Eddie was right about fae's hypocrisy, then I would not let my eyes tell me the truth about this place. I would have to rely on my other senses, and right now they were screaming we weren't alone, that powerful magic lay in traps around us. Even though I might appear safe here, I was far from it.

Eddie walked beneath an arched stone tunnel lined with torches until we reached a thick, iron door. This seemed to be a back entrance into the castle. He knocked in a pattern, three hard raps of his knuckles followed by two softer ones.

The door creaked open. A small fae woman with narrow eyes and pointy ears motioned us in, her mouth a straight line. Eddie said nothing to her as we passed and descended a long set of stairs. With all this rock and moving down, the temperature should be cool, but it was pleasantly warm.

At the bottom of the steps, the space opened up into an archaic library with thick wooden shelves and straight tables with no curves or beveled edges. Even the chairs were wooden and hard-backed. In one of them, a tall thin man wearing a red robe pored over several books sprawled out in front of him. His clothes underneath his robe were rumpled, and his shaggy blond hair hung over his eyes. He looked up at us, his cold dark eyes boring into me.

"Folas," Eddie began, "this is Samira, the vampire I told you about, the same one Sersi vouched for. She is looking for information about Trianus."

"Sit," he ordered. Two chairs across from him pulled away from the table on their own accord.

"Thank you for seeing me, Folas," I said and lowered into the chair, staying just on the edge should I need to bolt quickly. There was something about this man that made me not trust him. Maybe it was because of the wooden stake tucked under a book to the side of him, or the tip of a silver dagger peaking beneath the folds of his robe.

"You want information on Trianus," he said, leaning forward, his hands resting only an inch from the stake. "May I ask why?"

"I believe someone is still trying to bring him back into our realm. I want to stop this from happening. As we both know, Trianus has the power to destroy our world."

"Yes, he does. We also want to stop him." He reached with his long arm for a book near the corner of the table. His sleeve slipped up exposing a small tattoo of what looked like a pitchfork with a circle around it on top of his wrist. He set the book in front of me and flipped it open to a page. "Do you know this tale?"

I quickly read its contents. It spoke of a powerful fae witch named Ivona. Her powers were unmatched for her time, and yet she couldn't have the one thing she wanted—a child. When she finally did have one after years of trying, the child mysteriously died shortly after. Grief stricken, Ivona turned mad and raised a demon from hell to take over the child's body, Trianus. It was a familiar tale, one Briar had retold to me after hearing it from one of Dominic's bodyguards. That was also the same night Briar had first seen the smoke creature speaking with Dominic in the graveyard.

"I've heard the story, but," I scanned the pages searching for a date, "when did Ivona raise Trianus? I don't see it here."

"Thousands of years ago in Babylon," he explained. "It took powerful supernaturals to send him back to hell. Ivona, however, escaped. She continued throughout time to try and raise him again. It was the Red Tree Witches', a coven made from twelve of the world's most powerful witches, who finally contained the immortal fae in the ninth century. They buried on her sacred land beneath one of their homes. She remained there up until about one hundred and fifty years ago." He flashed me a deadly stare, a dark glimmer in his eyes. "Ivona should never have gotten out."

I stared right through him as something dawned on me. Detrand knew about the fae witch because he'd been one of the first to discover she'd escaped. That's one of the reasons he sent me to Rouen: to watch for the fae witch who would most likely be drawn to Rouen's unique placement on the globe. Rouen had been built over a rift in the earth's magic, where power from the earth's core leaked into the world. It's why supernaturals were drawn to the area, and also made it the perfect place to raise Trianus.

I had no idea until just now that Ivona and the fae witch were one. Detrand mustn't know either. All he knew about her was that she was extremely powerful and wanted to bring Trianus into the world.

"I agree. She should've remained buried."

Nodding, he closed the book and set it down on a stack next to him. "But she did and now she's in Rouen in search of the Abydos. In fact, the Komira fought her not that long ago."

I barely managed to keep my mouth closed. They knew Briar was a Komira? I glanced at Eddie. They knew too much. "When did this supposed fight happen?"

"At Fire Ridge," Folas said. "Ivona was in smoke form then."

My head snapped back to Folas, my brain working quickly. The smoke in the graveyard with Dominic, the paintings of Vincent and

Dominic worshipping the entity, and finally the way Vincent had fought side by side with it against us all in order to get the Abydos. I was surprised and frustrated with myself that I hadn't put the pieces together sooner, but I simply hadn't put much stock in the story Briar had heard. It made more sense that someone else would try to raise Trianus.

"How do you know it was her?" I asked, still needing confirmation.

"Many of us fae lived during Ivona's reign of terror. A few of us even helped the Red Tree Witches bind her deep within the earth. We know the magic they used and how it worked. Not only did they trap her, but they also stripped her of what powers they could. That way if she ever did escape, her abilities would be limited."

"That doesn't quite answer my question."

He leaned forward. "One thing you should know about the fae is that we are incredibly intelligent and love to gather knowledge. There is very little we don't know. And because we live such long lifetimes, we are always thinking ahead, centuries even, into the future. We knew it was just a matter of time when Ivona eventually escaped, so we secretly created our own spell around the home to alert us when that time came. And it was little surprise that when she did escape, she came to Rouen. She needs the Abydos."

I swallowed through the fullness in my throat. Could they know about the Abydos' location?

Eddie answered for me, almost as if he could detect my fear. "And that's why she continues to stay in Rouen. She senses it's here like many other supernaturals, us included, but she can't pin-point its exact location. Just like we can't pin point hers, only traces of her magic."

Wanting to steer the conversation away from the Abydos, I said, "That night at Fire Ridge, we believe Briar killed the fog creature, or really I should say Ivona ."

Folas laughed a grating sound, making my muscles tense. "You think she can be killed so easily? Have you not been listening? Last time it took twelve of the world's most powerful witches to put her down and still, in the end, that did not work. All Briar did was make the fae witch stronger."

My heart skipped a beat. "How is that possible?"

"On that same night, a powerful wave of energy rushed through the city. We think this is when Briar killed the third Alpha within a three-moon cycle. Such a thing should not have been possible. This power surge made the fae witch stronger, giving her abilities to change into multiple physical forms, and not just her one human body." He paused, his expression grim. "We believe she can now be several different people within the same day."

I inhaled a hitched breath and repressed a shiver. "How can we stop her?"

"That's what we are working on, but, like I said before, it took a powerful coven of witches to trap her before. We don't have access to that power anymore, but that's not the real issue right now."

I searched his eyes, understanding dawning on me. "You don't know who she is."

"How can we when she can be anyone?"

A weighted silence filled the room. I darted my gaze to Eddie, then to Folas, dread filling my gut. I thought of Briar and the prophecy. Maybe I should've told Briar about it. Maybe it would've stopped her from killing at least one of the Alphas, maybe. But I doubted it. She was too impulsive.

Folas continued. "Our last intelligence indicated that she may be appearing as a male human and is going by the name Phoenix, but again, that could change at a moment's notice."

"Is there a way to track him?"

"Not that we've uncovered, but … we might if we had access to the Abydos. Do you know where it is?"

"No."

He studied me carefully. I glanced at Eddie who looked to the floor.

"I don't know where it is," I repeated, the lie easily slipping from my tongue.

"Are you sure? There's only one reason the Phoenix would remain in Rouen and that's because the blood is here. We need to find it first and use it against her."

"No one should use the Abydos. It's too powerful for anyone to wield."

"It's been used before." He stared at me pointedly, challenging me.

"It's too dangerous."

"In most hands, yes. But the fae only seek to use it to protect the world."

From the corner of my eye, I spotted Eddie's hands curling into fists.

"Do you have any more information for me?" I asked, realizing it was time to go.

He was silent for a long moment, then, "We have heard of you, Samira, bearer of the Kiss of Eternal Night. We know your blood is also valuable."

I came to my feet, letting a slip of my power fill the great room. "We're leaving."

He rose to meet me, standing a good head taller than me. "Not without a price. We gave you valuable information, now you must give us something in return."

"That wasn't the deal, Folas," Eddie said, pushing his chair away from the table.

Folas's eyes didn't leave mine. "Give us a drop of your blood. Do this as a sign of good faith, and we will continue to work with you. Share our information."

"I can't do that."

The doors behind us snapped close on their own accord and a powerful breeze whipped through the room, lifting papers and blowing dust into the air.

Folas stood before us, wind lifting his long blond hair. It twisted around his face and shoulders. "We do not give valuable information without a cost. It is our way."

"Why my blood?" I demanded.

"For research. We believe it may be able to stop the Phoenix. We already have the Komira's. Now we need yours."

My head snapped in Eddie's direction. Did Eddie steal her blood somehow?

As if reading my mind, Eddie gave me a pleading look, "I didn't have anything to do with it, I swear."

I looked back at Folas, wondering if it would be worth the risk trying to kill him deep within their well-fortified castle. "How did you know about Briar being the Komira?"

"Because we pay attention. The streets of Rouen are full of secrets, many of them made by blood and bones. We follow their paths, put the pieces together. It is one of the reasons why our kind has managed to stay affluent still. Without our knowledge, your kind and others would've killed us."

"That's not true." But even as I said it, I remember hearing talks of enslaving fae folk for the sole purpose of using their blood. It was rumored their blood held magical properties that made one stronger if ingested. I'd never tested the theory. But I hadn't heard that kind of talk, enslaving fae, for over five hundred years.

"We have long memories," he said. "And we will protect our kind at any cost. So please, give us just a couple of drops."

I considered my options. The wind in the room had died down, but the doors still remained closed. I could fight my way out, but if I got into an altercation in the middle of their secret city, Eddie would probably be punished for bringing me here and letting me in on their secret.

I also wanted to keep the communication open between us. I might need them later on. But ... "How do I know you won't just hand my blood over to the Phoenix?"

His lips curled up at the corners. "So you know she also wants your blood."

"Yes."

"That is why we want it, too. We believe it will help us uncover her motives. Besides, I believe she already has it."

"How?"

He scoffed. "How many scuffles have you been in? You don't think she didn't have one of her men cut you while you were fighting another? It probably happened so fast, you didn't notice."

"I would've."

He stared at me as if I was a naive child, which made me doubt myself. I would've noticed, wouldn't I? Now I wasn't so sure.

"Will you give us your blood willingly? A sign of good faith? If you do, you would be considered a friend of the fae." He looked ready to fight me for it and that worried me.

I glanced at Eddie.

"It's okay," he said, but I caught the hesitation in his voice.

I turned back to Folas, deciding I had more to gain than lose by giving him my blood. "Where?"

Folas couldn't grab a small vial from his pocket fast enough. I bit into my wrist and held it over the opening. After several drops fell, the wound healed.

"Thank you," he said and sealed the bottle. "Consider us friends and allies."

"Time will tell, but I promise you," I leaned over the table and let power surge within me. "If you betray me, I will kill you."

He didn't seem fazed by the threat. "Noted. You may go now."

The doors opened behind us.

"Let's go," Eddie said quickly.

I cast Folas one last look and followed after Eddie, a sick feeling burning my gut. Had I just made a huge mistake? But I had learned something—the Phoenix could be anyone. I glanced sideways at Eddie, realizing one terrifying thing.

I didn't know who to trust anymore.

CHAPTER 11

*W*e left Black Glen, both of us silent and thoughtful. I worried I'd made the wrong choice, and I was certain Eddie was questioning whether bringing me there had been a good idea. However, I was grateful he had. I would happily live with the repercussions of giving Folas my blood because he'd given me vital information.

When we reached the sidewalk, Eddie stopped me. "Be careful, Samira. We fae have long traditions and long memories. Vampires have betrayed us many times over the centuries."

"What are you trying to tell me?"

He flexed his jaw, his gaze shifting to the darkness over my shoulder. "Just watch your back. That's all."

He turned and walked away, leaving me to stare after him.

I decided to walk home, despite my vehicle still sitting near Sinsual. I needed time to think through everything Folas had said. They knew far more about my situation than I would've ever guessed. Could they know about the prophecy, too? Even though Sersi had been living at the Blutel Estate for the last several decades, she was still fae. Maybe her loyalties lay with her own kind and not with me.

Maybe she wasn't the Sersi I knew at all. Maybe she was something darker, something far more powerful.

I groaned, hating I was doubting her, because that meant I would doubt everyone in my life. Who was I sure about? I knew Briar was Briar. She was a Komira and that couldn't be faked. I also felt fairly certain that Lynx was who she said she was. I'd seen the way she used magic, and it wasn't in the way a fae pulled magic from within themselves. And yet, I couldn't be a hundred percent sure, and that bothered me. Lynx held a special place in my heart, and after seeing Faithe again after so long, I knew why. Lynx reminded me of Faithe in so many ways. Though Lynx had not been physically abandoned, she had been emotionally and mentally abandoned by her family. It was the sole reason she craved love, yet that didn't stop her from giving it freely.

No, Lynx had to be herself. I couldn't let myself think she was anything different.

Thinking of Faithe brought the familiar pain to my heart, the one that had been opened wide when I first saw her again. She wasn't the Faithe I remembered. The old one was kind and compassionate. Where hate and prejudice had shaped her beginnings, after I had turned her, she'd been determined to only be kind to others. I had to find out what Korin had done to her to cause such a dramatic change in her behavior. It must've been bad to make her forget the woman she used to be—strong, confident, and most importantly, a woman with love and compassion, just like Lynx.

Somehow I would free her from Korin's grasp. My only offspring would not suffer under his control any longer. I fisted my hands, digging my nails into my palms. I would make good on my promise to her, made under a moonlit night with stars as my witness.

I was three streets away from home, in a well-maintained subdivision, when the hairs on the back of my neck rose. I reached up and rubbed at them, thinking the growing feeling of dread icing my body had to do with Faithe, but then the hairs on my arm followed suit.

I stopped moving and focused. The feeling was all too familiar. I'd had it on and off again too many times these past few weeks. The knowledge that someone was indeed watching me, filled my veins with such certainty, I knew it to be true.

The moon, full and bright, hung in the sky like a giant clock pendulum ticking slowly. I heard its tick as I breathed in and out, concentrating on the sounds and smells around me. A dog barking from within a home, the scurrying of claws inside a garbage can— probably raccoons—and the faint whispering of the wind through the tops of the trees, telling me something was wrong. Hidden within that slight breeze was the smell of sulfur.

I began walking, keeping my movements even, despite how tense I was. Tick, tick, tick. Adrenaline flooded my body. I casually glanced over my shoulder. A tall shadow moved out from behind a tree. Tick, tick, tick. Ancient power as old and dark as night slid up my backside coating me with dread. Whatever it was, it was getting closer.

In one fluid motion, I spun around and slid a dagger from my jacket. A man, exceptionally tall and bald-headed, stood beneath the burned out light of a street lamp. My left eye twitched as I realized it was the same man who had been watching me at the club; the dark pits of his eyes bore into me just as they had that night, making a chill run up my back. Was he fae? Maybe one of Folas's men spying on me, and yet, why reveal himself now when they had gone undetected all this time? Could it be the Phoenix?

Tick, tick, tick.

Its darkness and power began to press against me, an invisible barrier meant to scare and intimidate.

It didn't know me very well.

I raced toward him so fast, the homes on each side of me blurred into streaks of grays and blacks. Just as I reached the lamppost I blinked, and the tall man was gone. There wasn't even a hint of his power left behind. I spent several minutes searching for him, but found no trace.

Frowning, I turned back, pondering over this turn of events. It was almost midnight when I returned home. Briar lounged on the couch, her legs draped over Luke's lap while he massaged her feet. A fire burned bright in the fireplace, casting dancing shadows across the room.

"Where have you been?" Briar asked. "I texted you."

I pulled it out of my pocket and glanced at the screen. "Yes, you did."

"I know. I just said that. You're supposed to respond."

I stared down at the simple message: *What's up?*

It was a dumb question that literally didn't make sense. I should probably ignore it, like I did most things that came out of her mouth, but something had changed ever since seeing Faithe and Mateo and confronting my past. That wound had bled open and with it had come memories of how I used to be. I knew Briar thought I was boring, but I didn't used to be. In fact, I used to be a lot like her until the conse-quences of my reckless behavior caught up with me.

But just this once, maybe I'd shock her.

Before I could second-guess myself, I typed back, *By the looks of it, Luke's cock.*

A second later her phone buzzed. She glanced at the message then at Luke's lap. She burst out laughing, holding the phone to her chest.

"What?" Luke asked. He followed her line of sight, his face redden-ing. He growled and pulled her into a kiss.

I walked past them both, smiling to myself as I pushed up my glasses, but when I walked in the kitchen and saw Lynx, it disap-peared. Her hair might've been in a bun earlier, but most of it had fallen out and parts of it stuck to sweat on her forehead. She was leaning over the kitchen table that was crowded with all sorts of objects: plants, flowers, glass jars full of sand and different colored liquids. In the center of the table sat a large bowl, smoke spiraling out its top. Parts of the metal edges had been burned.

"What's going on?" I asked.

She puffed a long breath past her lips, lifting strands of red hair in front of her face. "Don't ask."

From the living room, Briar called, "She's been working on that all day! I can't get her to stop."

"What?" I asked again.

She slumped into a chair. "I'm trying to make something to break the compulsion. I think I'm super close, but I'm missing one ingredient that's impossible to get so I'm trying other spelled objects, but nothing's working."

"What are you missing?"

She shook her head. "A petal from a rare flower grown in only a few places in the world, none of them close. Have you heard of a Corpse flower?"

"The *rafflesia arnoldii*, found in the rainforests of Indonesia."

"Exactly. But I was pronouncing it so much worse."

"Does it have to be a live sample or will a dead one do?"

She lowered onto a chair. "Dead will work, but what does it matter? It's not like one of us has the time to go traipsing through the forest to find one."

I smiled, knowing the one person who could probably help us. "No, but I know someone who could get one."

Her green eyes lit up, life returning to them. "You do?"

"I'll go call him now."

"That would be amazing! You are the best!"

I stepped outside, feeling good. I'd made Briar laugh, and I was solving a problem for Lynx. This is what my life the last hundred years had been about—helping others. My way of redeeming myself from past actions. But helping those I cared about? Somehow it felt so much more rewarding. Plus, I was anxious to speak to my old friend. He'd been there for me at a time when I was lost and still trying to determine how to live my life.

He'd accepted me as I was, grounding me to my new life. He'd also been the first man I'd grown to love, truly love, as a father figure. Not the twisted love I'd once had for Korin, but a true bond of friendship.

It had been decades since we'd last spoken to each other. Last I heard, Detrand was in Croatia; his poor wife, Adelaide, was dragging him there to help with the local fae's decrease in population, something I was certain he detested. Detrand only liked helping those he truly loved.

For them, he would tear the world apart. Otherwise, you'd better get out of his way.

I texted our code to the service that helped immortal creatures stay in touch with each other. Within five minutes, I had his new cell number. I called it. He didn't answer. I called again, then again three more times. He finally answered.

"What is it? You'd better have something important or I'll rip your throat out," a familiar deep voice growled.

A stuttered a breath as a wave of warmth washed over me, a smile splitting my face. Typical Detrand. It felt strange to smile like this after so long. "It's Samira."

Silence answered me, then a more softened but still gruff tone. "Are you smiling?"

My grin grew bigger. "How did you know?"

"I can count on one hand the times I've seen you smile. I'll never forget the way you sound when your lips turn upward."

I was quiet, pondering this.

"Are you getting married or something?" he asked.

I sucked in a surprised breath. "Of course not. Where are you?"

"Stuck in the middle of a wet forest. Indonesia, to be exact."

My heart skipped a beat. "What are you doing there?"

"Adelaide brought me here, of course. She said it was for you."

"She did?" I should've guessed Adelaide had something to do with them being in the one place I needed. She had uncanny psychic abilities.

He muffled the phone and spoke to someone, and I just barely captured Adelaide's sweet voice in the background. Then he returned. "She said you'd know why we were here. Do you require anything? You only have to ask."

"I need the petals from a Corpse flower."

He paused long. "You must be dealing with some powerful magic. Is it because of the fae witch? Is she getting closer?"

"We believe she's here and growing stronger. And her name is Ivona. She believes she's Trianus' mother."

"Are you in danger? Do you need me to join you in Rouen?"

Part of me, an older, more broken part, wanted to tell him yes, especially now that Korin had arrived. Detrand knew about my dark past serving Korin, but something stopped me from saying anything. At one point in time, I had relied on Detrand for everything, and not in a healthy way. I needed to see if I could do this without him, which led to the other reason he sent me to Rouen. He wanted me to work with the Ames de la Terra because he knew I needed something to assuage my consciousness for all the bad things I'd done. Resisting Korin all on my own would be a good test.

"I like the sound of 'we'," he continued. "You were not meant to be alone, Samira."

I swallowed through the tightness in my throat. "I'm not."

We spoke a little more, and I gave him my address, then we said goodbye. I realized he hadn't said he would send me the flower, or if he even could. But I was certain he wouldn't let me down.

I leaned against the house and stared up into the star-filled night sky, remembering those words Detrand had said to me when we had last parted. "Be like the stars, Samira, and fight the darkness."

I held that thought as I slipped back inside. Luke and Briar were in the kitchen with Lynx all looking at me with hopeful eyes. None of them wanted to fall victim to such strong compulsion.

"It's on its way."

Lynx's shoulders dropped, and she smoothed her hair back. "Thank God."

"Who did you call?" Briar asked. She was shoving aside a bundle of sage so she could rest her arms on the table. Luke stood behind her chair, rubbing her shoulders. I'd known Luke for a long time and had never pictured him as the—how would Briar put it—pussy-whipped type.

"An old friend," I answered, "but that's not what's important. I learned something tonight. You might want to sit down."

Luke straightened, his hands lowering to his side. Briar and Lynx looked at each other then up at me.

My gaze focused on Briar, and I kept my voice gentle. "The fae witch lives. She never died. In fact, you made her stronger."

"Me? How?"

"They believe it's because you killed three alphas within a three-month cycle."

"That's a bad thing?" she asked incredulously.

Luke frowned. "Who's they?"

"Fae folk," I answered him.

At this, Lynx dropped into a seat next to Briar. The movement was so quick, had there not been a chair, she would've fallen to the floor. She stared at the floor and whispered, "The fae are involved?"

Briar threw up her hands. "How the hell would they know? You saw that bitch go poof just like I did!"

"It was a trick. She's in human form now, appearing as a male who calls himself the Phoenix."

"I'll find and kill him," Luke growled.

"I wish it were that easy." I walked to the refrigerator and grabbed my thermos of blood. It was halfway gone. I'd need to get more blood soon. I only had a few bags left in the deep freezer I kept in the basement.

"Let's just find her, then we can figure out how to kill her," Luke said.

I lowered the thermos from my mouth. "That brings up our next problem. She can shapeshift into anyone. She can *be* anyone. And no one knows how to find her."

I let my words sink in as they all looked at each other.

Briar was the first to speak, her voice low. "And I assume she, or the Phoenix, is still after the Abydos?"

I nodded.

"Is the blood safe?"

"It's in the safest place on earth. I am certain that she cannot get her hands on it."

Briar's shoulders relaxed a little, but she still held her serious expression. She'd kept the Abydos safe for so long that, even though I watched over it now, she still carried the burden in ensuring its safety.

Outside, a sudden gust of wind rattled the kitchen window. The cold chill snaking up my spine reminded me of something. "Have any of you seen an exceptionally tall, thin man with a bald head sniffing around here?"

Lynx shook her head.

"Do you have a stalker?" Briar asked.

Luke's eyes had gone to the window, his muscles tense. "When did you last see him?"

"A couple of hours ago. He followed me home, and I saw him at Sinsual the other night. Whoever he is, he's extremely powerful. I felt it."

"Could it be this Phoenix person?" Lynx asked.

"Maybe, or it could be fae."

"Fae?" Briar asked, wrinkling her nose. "Why would they be following you?"

I opened my mouth then closed it. She didn't know about Eddie, and I didn't feel it was my place to tell her. Or to tell her about Black Glen. "The bottom line is, now that Korin is back in town, I fear we may be in over our heads. We need more help. I've already reached out to the fae and they will help us anyway we need. But it's not enough."

"You have the Silver Claws at your disposal," Briar said.

"We need more. It's time we called upon the Witches of Rouen."

CHAPTER 12

*A*s I laid down for the day, burying myself into my coffin, I was reassured by the last several hours. Briar had talked to Roma and she had agreed to meet with us to discuss how the Witches of Rouen could help. They, too, had sensed a growing evil and were anxious to stop it. The problem was they lacked leadership. They had never been a real coven, just a group of misfit witches who, like other supernaturals, had found themselves drawn to Rouen and all its mystical qualities.

Briar wasn't the only one to get things moving. Lynx also stepped up and spoke to a few distant cousins in the area. She did not, however, speak to her immediate family, the Morgans. They belonged to the Order of the Crimson Night, an old coven of witches that had always aligned themselves with the Principes Noctis. They would not be helping us. In fact, we were going to do everything possible to keep them from knowing what we were doing, as they may attempt to stop us.

With Roma's help organizing the Witches of Rouen, the fae's help, and the muscles of the Silver Claws, we would be in a good position to not only try and rid Korin from our city, but also try to uncover the

Phoenix's true identity. Only then would we be able to stop her from raising Trianus again.

But deep down, even with all this help, I knew it wouldn't be enough. We needed one more group on our side. The vampires. And I was the only one who might be able to turn Korin's coven against him.

Whatever positive feelings I had moments ago turned cold and full of rage. Korin had to go. It couldn't be just about driving him from town. His hold over so many was too powerful. No, that hold had to be severed permanently.

I punched at the top of the coffin in frustration. For me to kill him, I might have to release all of the Kiss of Eternal Night. It had taken me years to come back from that last time I'd embraced the Kiss. I punched again. I couldn't go back to that again. There had to be another way.

Because I was so angry, the sun's light rising into the sky had very little effect on me, and I couldn't sleep. Only short bursts that were always interrupted by nightmares of Korin and all he had made me do to others. All the many heads severed by my hands ...

Night came at last, and I jumped from my casket, anxious to shed it and the trapped memories. I couldn't hear anyone upstairs. Briar was probably at Fire Ridge, and Lynx out with her second cousins. She wanted to tell them everything before we all met at midnight in our living room. It could get crowded. I wasn't sure who Roma was going to bring.

I dressed quickly, knowing I didn't have much time. I wanted to return to Winter's Cove to talk to Teddy to tell him about the cure Lynx was working on. Maybe he and Kristina could finally break free. Others too, if they wanted. But it wasn't just them I wanted to talk to. I had to know how much of a hold Korin had on Faithe. I had to get her out of there.

Upstairs, I found an assortment of cakes and cookies all recently baked and spread along the counter. The table was also covered, but with ingredients for the spell Lynx was working on. There wasn't an exposed flat space anywhere. Lynx must be nervous about tonight. I only hoped she hadn't inadvertently mixed any recipes.

After downing a microwaved blood bag, just barely heated, I headed out. A faint breeze blew through the warm air, carrying with it the scent of the ocean. It made me think of home, my human home near the Black Sea. Sometimes I thought about returning, but I never did. I wouldn't recognize it after so much time passing, and I wanted to remember my childhood place as it was.

I parked in front of Winter's Cove and headed up the stairs, my footfalls heavy against the stone steps. I hated this place and couldn't wait to be free of it. Maybe I'd get a chance to burn it down like I did the first one.

It had been cathartic before, and I would love to see it burn too.

A few vampires were huddled in the entry way when I walked in. They were wearing evening attire, tuxedoes and long, shiny black dresses, as if they were going out for the night. I didn't recognize them, which meant they were newer vampires. They cast me a long look, their gazes sliding up and down me with disdain. I hated the thought of what they might do in the city tonight. This coven was not a human-friendly one. They wouldn't kill them, as to not bring attention to our kind, but they wouldn't be gentle, either.

I walked past them into the living room. A young woman who looked more child than adult sat at a grand piano. Her long and slender fingers danced across the keys, playing a haunting melody. There were at least a dozen vampires spread throughout listening or talking amongst themselves. They, too, were dressed up. Maybe the other vampires weren't going out. Maybe this was the beginning of a dinner party.

I glanced down at my own clothing of black leather jeans and black tank top. I didn't fit in at all, but when had that ever stopped me? I approached the nearest vampire, a female who looked vaguely familiar. I think she had joined the coven shortly before I left. "Can you tell me where Teddy is?"

"Samira, right?" she asked, extending her limp hand to me. A diamond bracelet hung around her dainty wrist. "My name is Gwen."

I ignored her outstretched hand. "Nice to meet you, but I'm in a hurry." I didn't want Naburus to catch wind of me being here.

Gwen's expression soured. "He's back—"

"Samira!" a voice hissed from across the room.

My whole body stiffened at the sound. After I inhaled a deep breath, I turned around. "Hello, Michael."

Michael, my first lover when I joined the coven, strolled toward me. He was tall and muscular with blond hair to his chin. His stunning blue eyes, the color of the sky lit up by lightning, looked me over. My hand automatically curled into a fist and it took me a moment to loosen it. It was unfortunate he'd decided to approach me. For him.

He stopped in front of me, tugging at the sleeves of his tux. "I heard you were here the other night."

"You heard correctly."

"You didn't come see me."

I raised my eyebrow. "And?"

He leaned toward me, inhaling my scent. "I am head of security now. It would have been polite of you to do so."

"Congratulations on your new position. I remember how you coveted it."

Snorting, he leaned back. "Do you also remember how I coveted you?" His gaze fell to my lips. "And I'm accustomed to getting what I covet. Always."

I gave him a casual, unaffected stare. "You haven't changed one bit."

"Good evening, Michael," a deep, clipped voice said. A breath passed my lips and a shiver rolled down my back. *Mateo.* I tried not to light up, and failed, as I saw him stride towards us, his eyes focused on Michael. He also was dressed in a fancy suit. Apparently I was the only one who hadn't received an invitation.

Michael looked from me to Mateo, his expression darkening. I had left Michael for Mateo, who used to be head of security. Clearly time had not softened Michael's anger toward me. Or Mateo and Michael's anger towards each other.

Michael sneered. "Isn't this grand? Mateo and Samira, together again."

"We're not together."

Michael feigned surprise. "But I thought you two were soulmates, destined to be one since the beginning of time? Isn't that what you told me, Samira?"

"We are." Mateo's voice was firm, and he turned towards me, a half-smile on his face. "Isn't that right, *tesoro mio*."

My darling. It was sweet when Mateo meant the words, but now they were used as a weapon against Michael. It was petty and beneath Mateo, especially since we were no longer together. Mateo touched my hip possessively. "And you are *not* to touch her."

Michael sucked up to Mateo. "You do not have the authority to order me around in this house."

I placed a hand on Michael's chest and gently pushed him back. "I didn't come to start trouble. I just need to talk to Teddy, then I'll be on my way."

"Ah, another one of your boy toys. You sure leave a trail of them wherever you go. Such a thorough vampire slut."

Before I could do it myself, Mateo punched Michael in the face. Michael's head jerked back as his lip split and blood ran down his chin. He brought his thumb up to swipe it. He licked it, grinning. "Mmm, I always liked a spirited mate. Looks like you picked a good one, Samira. He's a lot like me."

Growling, I stepped in between the two, but Mateo reached around me to stab Michael's chest with his finger. "You will watch your mouth. You may have power over me in this house, but all I have to do is drag you outside where I rule Rouen."

Michael raised his eyebrows. "Ah yes, the new King of Rouen. But what happened to the true leadership of your coven?"

Mateo didn't respond but held his gaze firmly.

Michael hissed in his face. "You were only permitted to lead the coven because those above you couldn't fix the problems with the first batches of Scorpion's Breath. Korin killed them for their mistakes, leaving you in charge. You didn't earn the position. The blood of my lost friends gave it to you."

Mateo's body tensed, and I thought he might punch him but instead Mateo said, "Careful, Michael. Your jealousy is showing.

You've craved your own coven for centuries, but Korin will never allow it. Is it because he doesn't trust you?"

"It is because he needs me to protect this coven, since you no longer do."

"Are you certain?" Mateo edged closer to me, brushing his chest against my back. My mind zeroed in on that tiny spot of connection between us. And the way he was standing, the possessiveness of it. I wanted Mateo to go away, to let me fight my own battles. At the same time, I wanted him closer, to touch me as he had done before.

Michael snarled, his fangs descending. "Be careful, Mateo. As Korin gives, he may also take away. One word from me about your *trustworthiness*, and Korin could destroy your coven in seconds. And then you will never be allowed to leave his presence again."

"I would like to see you try," Mateo purred, then, gripping my stomach, pulled me to him tightly. My heart jumped at the movement. Smirking over my shoulder, Mateo ran his finger up my inner arm. Goosebumps prickled my skin, and I hitched a breath.

Michael's eyes raged as he followed Mateo's finger all the way up my arm, over my shoulder towards my neck. Warmth pooled in my stomach, my bones ached, my heart stuttered and my mind shattered. Need and desire controlled me. I couldn't stop from turning my face, baring my neck to Mateo.

It was instinctual, every pore in my body responded to his touch. I held my breath, waiting to see if he would bite me.

Did I actually want him to?

Mateo's hand slid down to my wrist, holding it loosely, allowing me to pull away if I desired. Then he leaned in, lightly scraping his fangs over my neck and a small moan escaped me. I shut my eyes, closing myself off to him as a soft red marked my cheeks, embarrassed at how I had betrayed my need for him. I wanted to push him away, to tell him to go to hell. To run and never return; facing the love of my life who had ruined me was too painful. I couldn't stand the temptation of his presence any longer.

But I knew I could not do so, because we were in a match of wills, and showing a united front to Michael was more important than my *feelings* right now. And so, I allowed his lips to brush over the sensitive part of my skin once more, placing small kisses at the base of my neck, licking the thin, sensitive skin right over my pulse, causing my nipples to stiffen in anticipation. He lifted his face to smirk at Michael again. "She is beautiful, isn't she?"

Michael clenched his fists, his face red with fury. Instead of addressing Mateo, he turned to me. "This is the second time you've come into our home without proving yourself."

Mateo tightened his hand, as if he might punch Michael again.

"Proving myself?" His words woke me out of my sensual dream. He had to be joking. "I used to be a part of this coven. Why would I need to prove myself?"

The side of his lips turned up. "Because it's been a long time, centuries, in fact. You may have gone soft. We can't have weak vampires in our home. You remember Korin's rule."

"Weak members, even weak visitors, bring shame upon our coven," I repeated, the words bitter on my tongue. Of course, it was Korin who decided what constituted as weak.

"You will need to go through a trial to prove your worth," Michael said.

Mateo looked from me to him. "And what exactly would this trial entail?"

He smiled, slow and cruel, and trained his eyes on me. "Something I've wanted for a long time. Fighting me to submission."

CHAPTER 13

"No—" Mateo began, but I interrupted him.

"Done." Maybe if I could beat him down, he'd finally leave me alone and let go of his vendetta toward me. Plus, if I could beat him, it might make other vampires in the coven respect me, and maybe even turn against Korin when the time came. And, if I was being honest with myself, that's what was most important.

He lowered his head in a small bow. "I'll set up the training room. It will be great entertainment for tonight's dinner."

"Let's do it now. I wasn't planning on staying."

"Ah, but you will. I command it." He eyed my clothes. "In fact, I have the perfect dress for you to wear. I'll have it brought to you." He turned and walked away, confidence in his step. I pushed away from Mateo, ready to flee his presence, but he tightened his hand on my wrist.

"Walk with me," Mateo said, releasing me as he turned the opposite direction.

I groaned inwardly and followed after him, ignoring the excited whispers of those around us. It had probably been decades since they'd watched a fight like the one they were about to see. The other vampires around us had come to their feet to watch our exchange and more had filed in from other parts of the house. So much for trying to keep a low profile. I caught Teddy's eye in the crowd, his eyes full of worry. I didn't see Kristina or Faithe.

Letting go of the casual attitude he'd shown earlier, Mateo clinched his hands in fists and walked briskly to the other side of the mansion, his anger radiating out in waves. He yanked open the library door, nearly tearing it off its hinges, and slammed it against the back wall.

When he turned towards me, his eyes were cold and hard. The honey-eyed man I once knew was gone, and before me stood a man filled with rage and bitterness. "Why do you insist on fighting him? If you do this, Korin will find a way to take advantage of the situation. He's got you on a hook; he'll slowly drag you back into his world. Is this what you want?"

"What happened to you? In just a few short days, you've changed. What is Korin planning?"

He groaned. "You know I cannot tell you that. Why do you insist on asking these questions? Right now, I am talking to you about Michael. He wants to take you from me again. I will not let him do that."

"Ahh, I see." I folded my arms across my chest and casually leaned against the door jamb. "This isn't about my involvement with Korin at all. But your desire for revenge against Michael."

He growled, bearing his fangs. "You did not see yourself when he was done with you the night you told him about us. There was not a spot on your whole body that did not have a wound. He carved you apart. You had to be infused with blood just to stay alive. It almost killed me to see you in such pain. I would've murdered him if Korin would've allowed it. Instead, I nursed you back to health, praying to whatever god may exist that you would live to see another night."

Fire raged in his eyes, spreading into my chest. I'd forgotten that night. Mostly because I was unconscious through most of it. But the reminder of it brought back my own feelings. I'd felt so helpless as he'd beat me in a fit of rage, just as my own human husband had beaten me. Korin had killed my husband for the very act, yet had allowed Michael to still exist, with no repercussions.

Rage from deep within me boiled to the surface. I was a lot stronger now, and it was time Michael learned his place. "This fight is mine."

"Time has strengthened you, Samira," he said, "but it's also strengthened him. Please, I beg you, don't do this. Assign me to do it in your place."

"This isn't about me. You *want* to fight him."

He hissed and closed the space between us. He laced his fingers through the back of my hair, pulling my head to the side. His lips traced up my neck, scraping my skin with his fangs. His breath came out in strained huffs as he pressed his lips to my ear, whispering. "Every time I think of him, I want to slice him into pieces. I will kill him one day for what he did to you."

I growled, pushing him away. "Stop, Mateo. Stop acting as if I belong to you. This is not your battle. I will fight him, and I will win. But this isn't just about revenge. I need to be in a position of respect because one day soon, I'm going to break Korin's ability to compel you, to compel all of you. And you forget," I hesitated in saying my next words, they were so painful, but I forced them out, "you choose Korin over me that night. Any claim you had on me is finished. Stop touching me, stop trying to stand up for me like some damn gentleman from the ancient days. We may be forced to fight as we had centuries ago, but we no longer live in those times. I am fully capable of defending my own honor." I waved my hand between us. "And we are no longer *anima gemellas.* Get that through your thick skull."

He snarled, the fire still in his eyes. "Never, my love. I let you go once, but I will never do that again. You may reject me now, but you *are* my soulmate and I will find a way to prove it to you."

I huffed, giving up on this ridiculous conversation and left the room. I hurried so that he wouldn't see the pain in my eyes. I never wanted him to know how badly he'd broken my heart when he had chosen to stay with Korin and the Buio Sangre. I'd pushed those feelings so far down inside me, I'd almost forgotten how painful they had been. But being around Korin and Michael was bringing everything to the surface. I needed to get out of here as fast as possible.

Just as I turned the corner, I ran into Teddy. He grabbed my arms to steady me. "What's wrong? You're shaking." He glanced over my shoulder. "Is Mateo bothering you?"

"I'm fine." I forced a few calm breaths into my lungs. "Is there somewhere we can talk? With Kristina?"

"Sure, but I'm supposed to tell you a dress is waiting for you in the Summer room upstairs. Michael insists you wear it to fight in too."

"Whatever he wants. He'll regret fighting me, though. I'm going to make a fool out of him in front of everyone."

Teddy grinned, exposing his dimple, and turned with me down the hall. "I bet you will."

"Have you seen Faithe?" I asked, glancing in rooms as we passed.

"She's in Korin's quarters. That's where she spends most of her time."

Dread ate at my stomach. "How can I get her alone?"

"It's difficult these days, but she'll be at the party."

"What is this celebration about?"

He eyed me sideways, his face reddening beneath the faint light in the hallway. He worked his jaw as if trying to find the words.

"You can't say, can you?"

He shook his head. "But I — I can tell you that his work is finished."

He gasped as if even saying that had taken great effort.

I froze and turned to him. "What do you mean by finished?"

"Ready to be rolled out," he said, choosing his words carefully.

I lowered my voice. "Listen, I have a friend working on something that will break Korin's compulsion. If I can get this to you, will you tell me everything you know?"

"You can do that?"

"I'm going to try."

His shoulders sagged with relief. "I'll tell you whatever you want to know. It's been terrible carrying this burden around."

Music playing in the distance found its way to us.

"Dinner will be soon," he said. "You better go change."

"Will you pass on what I told you to Kristina?"

He clasped my hands. "She will be just as glad as I am to hear it."

Before I left, I asked him one last question. "When did Korin become so powerful with his compulsion?"

"Recently. It took everyone by surprise."

"Any events leading up to it?" Maybe if I could figure out where the power came from, I could destroy it.

"He only said it was a gift. A gift from someone named the Phoenix."

There's the connection. Korin would've done anything for more power, including selling out his own kind. The Phoenix probably knew this, too. I wondered what Korin's own coven would think if they found out what he'd done. So far, they probably believed Korin wouldn't use the new drug on supernaturals, but I'd seen otherwise.

I hurried to the Summer room to change. It was a guest suite in the corner of the mansion, decorated in light gold and pale yellows. An ornate four-poster bed was pressed against the wall. Resting on a plush velvet comforter lay a familiar-looking dress. I gasped and almost stepped back, but shook my head and approached it. There's no way it could be the same dress I'd worn that night I'd ended it with Michael and yet, the similarities were uncanny. Long, form-fitting and strapless on one side. I ran my fingers down the silky black material. It even felt the same.

No doubt this was another way Michael was getting back at me, but what didn't make sense is how he knew to have it made. I held the material to my nose and inhaled. It smelled brand new. This development worried me. It was as if he knew I was coming.

When the music downstairs changed to something dark and melancholy, I stripped my clothes and pulled the dress down over my black bra and panties. The material was so soft and light, it felt like warm breath whispering against my skin every time I moved. I might've loved it had it not brought horrible memories with it.

I ground my teeth together. This is what Michael wanted. For me to feel like a victim once again. But I wouldn't let him have that power. Not again. If he wanted me to play a role, I'd play it.

In the bathroom, I combed my long hair, twisted it up into a French bun, and removed several strands of dark hair to frame my face just like I wore it that night. I also found some dark makeup and applied it around my eyes and reddened my lips. I stared at my reflection, looking so much like the woman I used to be, but I was anything but. Tonight, however, I would play his game. I'd pretend to be that woman again, right up until I slammed him on his ass in front of his whole coven. I couldn't wait to see the look on his face. The shock on Korin's face would only be a side benefit.

I reached the top of the staircase sweeping down to the grand lobby. Mateo appeared just then, as if he'd sensed me coming. His mouth parted at my appearance and eyebrows lifted. He looked impeccable in his dark suit and hair combed back. My gaze lowered to the white rose in his hand. They were my favorite.

As I descended the stairs, Mateo's expression changed to something dark and deadly. He stared intently at my dress, his gaze not leaving it as I moved down the stairs. I reached him and rested my hand on his arm.

"Michael had it made for me." He didn't respond, except to grind his teeth together, the sides of his jaw bulging. "I hate it as much as you do, but he wants to play head games. It's fine. It's just a stupid dress. I'm not going to let Michael's old resentment affect me." His eyes finally met mine, they were dark and angry. I gulped. "And neither should you."

His eyes only grew darker. "I want it off you."

"Too bad. You know I have no choice in this. And it would be wise for you to accept it, as I have. Otherwise they will win."

He lowered his gaze as if he couldn't stand to look at it anymore. Nodding, he held the rose out for me. "For the woman who owns my body and soul."

I rolled my eyes, an uncharacteristic motion for me. Briar must be rubbing off on me. "Thank you, but not necessary."

"Take it." He took hold of my hand and squeezed gently, his eyes hardening. "If only to counter Michael's mind games."

"There's the Mateo I know." I nodded and let him place it in my open palm. His fingers caressed the sensitive skin on the top of my wrist in a circular pattern. He trailed his fingers up my arm, leaving heat in their wake. "You truly are the most beautiful woman I've ever encountered. I don't know how I let you go."

My gaze turned hard. "Well, you did."

I brushed past him and walked into the living room where music filled the air. The space had become more crowded. There were at least three dozen vampires scattered throughout the room, each as handsome and beautiful as the next. Probably half lived here while the others preferred to live elsewhere, but those under Korin's command always came when called. There were also many of them that I recognized as belonging to the Sangre Nocturnas. They must be under command to return here as well, and why Mateo was so upset about it.

Vampires weren't the only ones in the room. There were eight humans wandering around in skimpy attire with glossy eyes and distant expressions. Both men and woman approached different vampires, showering them with attention and showing off the veins on their necks and arms. Someone had compelled them well. It made me sick.

Scanning the room, I searched for Korin and Faithe, but they weren't here yet. I spotted Kristina in the corner curled on a couch, despite her short cocktail dress. Her eyes were closed.

"You look divine," a voice said behind me.

I turned around to face Michael, forcing my lips into a seductive smile. "I love the dress."

His eyebrows lifted in surprise. "You do?"

Stepping toward him, I slid my palm up his hard chest and stared into his eyes. "Yes. It reminds me of the night I ended our sorry excuse of a relationship. It was one of the happiest nights of my life."

He snarled and gripped my arm, his nails digging into me, but I didn't flinch. "You're going to regret that. I'll make sure of it."

Mateo appeared next to me, but I ignored him, still focusing on Michael. "Not when I beat you tonight."

Michael's nostrils flared and for a moment I thought he might try to fight me now, but just then a powerful energy blanketed the room, making several people gasp. Everyone turned toward the door.

Korin. And he wasn't alone.

CHAPTER 14

*K*orin entered the room wearing a suit matched with a black cape and a thorned, metal crown. Faithe's arm was linked through his and she held her chin high. She wore a long, crimson gown with the front cut so low, the gap reached her belly button, exposing a good portion of her breasts. The girl I knew would never have worn a dress like this.

I remembered the first time my eyes had been opened to Korin's cruelty, thanks to Faithe's kind heart. Faithe had only been with us for a decade after we returned from Africa. For the most part, she'd managed to avoid Korin. Our coven was much bigger then with many divisions across Europe. It kept Korin busy.

But one night, I decided to take Faithe with me on one of my many errands for Korin. I believed it was time to start training Faithe on coven business in hopes she could work alongside me.

I had prepared her for what might take place. Our orders were to root out a group of shifters who had crossed over into our territory. Back then, that was a huge insult. I expected a few to resist and even told Faithe we might have to kill some. She wasn't happy about it, but understood.

However, when we arrived, we found something more than a

small group of shifter men. It was a large community with families. Many with children and women. All hungry and cold. They had recently fled their country because, in addition to being shifters, they were also Mongols who were no longer welcome in their country.

Faithe begged me to leave them be, but I had a job to do. Not once had I ever considered disobeying Korin. I attempted to chase them off the land, but the shifters were willing to stay and fight. They had nowhere else to go.

The small battle turned bloody, which only fueled the men under my command. Faithe begged me to stop, even shielding a shifter woman with her own body to prevent the woman from dying by my sword. This gave me pause, and I looked around at all the carnage.

"These people are me!" Faithe had cried. "I would be dead had a kind woman not spared me. *Be* that kind woman, Mother. Don't kill these people because they are different. They only want to live, and our coven has plenty to spare!"

Her words seared my heart, and I stopped the attack, but by then the damage had been done. Almost all had been killed.

When we returned to the coven, I was prepared to be punished for not fulfilling Korin's orders. But it wasn't me who was punished. It was Faithe.

Korin had stripped her in front of everyone and whipped her back until blood ran over her bare buttocks and down her legs. When he was finished, he locked her up for thirty days with no food or water. The ordeal nearly killed her.

That was when I decided to plan my escape from Korin and the coven, taking Faithe and Mateo with me.

Korin's dark gaze surveyed the room, taking in everything about it. He paused when our eyes met and nodded an approval, but when he saw Mateo by my side, something cold flickered in his eyes. Briefly, but I saw it. It made the hair on my arms lift.

"Welcome, friends," Korin began. "Tonight is a special night, and I'm grateful you could all be here to celebrate it with me. There have been some challenges along the way," his eyes flashed to mine, "but we came out victorious, and soon everything as you know it will change.

In a good way. We are so close! So enjoy your evening. Partake of these gifts I give you and satisfy all your cravings. I hear we even have some entertainment tonight, thanks to Samira. We are honored to have her back among us, where she belongs. Make her feel welcome."

The woman at the piano began to play again. I hated these vampire parties. They rarely deviated from tradition. Music playing, humans offering, vampires drinking. And Briar complained that *I* hadn't kept up with the times! These people still lived in the eighteenth century. I'd love for her to give these vampires one of her shows. The corners of my lips lifted at the thought.

The night wore on painfully slow. I looked for every opportunity to speak with Faithe, but she wouldn't leave Korin's side. I watched her from a distance, the way she hung on his every word, her adoring eyes trained always in his direction. He may have been the only person in the room. She might be compelled, but her eyes lacked the familiar glaze. Maybe it was something else. A spell, perhaps.

Mateo didn't speak to me again, but he stayed close by, his gaze flickering around the room, analyzing everything as if it were a threat. He may not be in charge of security anymore, but those protective habits never left him.

The smell of blood, given freely by the humans, perfumed the air, and my stomach clenched in hunger. It had been too long since I'd surrounded myself with such temptation. Everywhere I looked, humans writhed on laps as the vampires partook of their life-giving blood. The smell was so strong, the hunger a driving demand within me, instinctual and powerful, making my heart pound with need, that I had to stop by the wall, clinging to it, to catch my breath.

Mateo watched me struggle from across the room, his eyes moving over my body with his own desire.

But he would not come to me.

I had already rejected him once tonight; he would not give me the opportunity to do so again so soon. A human woman approached him, batting her eyes and trailing her finger down her neck towards her large breasts.

I waited, still clutching the wall behind me, watching closely. Mateo's eyes hesitantly left my gaze to eye her offered wrist hungrily.

I held my breath, feeling heat ignite in my abdomen as he took hold of her hand and guided that sensitive skin to his mouth. His gaze slowly lifted to mine again. With our eyes locked, he pierced her skin. A moan threatened to spill from my lips as desire coursed through me. Even from across the room, I could smell her blood calling to me, mixed with Mateo's heated gaze.

His long tongue twisted across her wrist in a slow, tantalizing stroke. Then he moved his tongue up her arm, his eyes still boring into mine as if to tell me, show me, that this is what he would be doing to me right now if I'd allowed it. His mouth stopped at the top of her corset, his teeth scraping at the swell of her breast. He paused, for the barest moment. And then, she gasped as his teeth sunk into her, lips latching onto skin so tantalizing and fair. A drop of blood slid down, and I licked my lips in anticipation. My heart raced as fire skirted over my flesh, flaming my own need.

Mateo knew exactly how to entice me.

The dark prince of temptation.

I stared openly at him, watching him drink from her.

It would be so easy to give in.

No one back home would even know, and one sip wouldn't cause me to career back into that lifestyle. I was stronger now, able to stop whenever I wished.

Mateo's eyes simmered with need. The side of his mouth lifted as if he knew I would come to him. His finger flicked forward, an invitation.

I sucked in a shaky breath, my eyes still locked on his and took a step towards him.

Then, a bell sounded, and all eyes turned toward open double doors at the back of the room. I caught my breath, forcing my feet to stop. A servant dressed in white announced, "Dinner is served."

I fell back, clasping onto the wall again, my hands trembling. Thank heavens for the bell. I looked back at Mateo. He had left the human and was staring into the dining room, his face pale. The smell of blood wafted into the air, the scent so strong it was dizzying.

From my viewpoint, I couldn't see what he was seeing. I walked toward him and peered into the long and richly decorated dining room. My heart stopped, and my legs weakened.

Hanging from the ceiling by many wires, four humans, face down, had been punctured at various points in their bodies. Their blood dripped into strategically placed wine glasses. When one was full, servants would swap it out for another. By how quickly the glasses were filling, the humans had been given blood thinners. If they weren't dead already, they would be soon.

"Mateo," I breathed, feeling myself grow faint. He was by me in an instant, his hand on the small of my back.

"Don't react," he whispered low enough for only my ears.

Others shared my same shock. The horrific scene before us might've been accepted in the fourteenth century, but we had evolved as a species and were no longer this barbaric.

"What is the meaning of this?" a shorter, older looking vampire demanded. It took me just a second to recall his name. Petre. He had been with Korin almost as long as I had.

Korin slowly turned to him. "I told you, things are changing. Soon, we will no longer have to hide in the shadows, and we can live as we were meant to be."

"As monsters?" Petre shouted motioning toward the humans. "This may have been acceptable centuries ago, but we've grown beyond this. It is abhorrent and no longer our way!"

Several nodded their heads in approval.

Korin glided toward the center of the room, noting their disapproval. "I have ruled this coven for over a millennium, and what is abhorrent is the way we've been forced to live. A new dawn is coming. You will either embrace it or move on."

Petre looked around. Seeing dread on the faces of others must've given him courage, because he said, "Then we move on."

He walked across the room, his head up, but before he could pass Korin, Korin lifted his hand, looked directly into my eyes and snapped his fingers. Petre burst into flames. He began to flail, screaming in anguish, and then, as if someone had poured concrete into his veins, he froze in horror. The flames intensified, cutting off his cries into tortured gurgles followed by bone-chilling silence as the crackling fire began to roar.

Korin stared at me as the flames consumed Petre, his skin melting like candle wax. I stepped forward, determined to stop him, but Mateo wrapped his arm around my waist, holding me still. His lips came to my ear, whispering so softly that no one could hear him.

"You may have once been Korin's favorite, but that was a long time ago. Things have changed, Samira. He will make an example of you if you try to stop him."

My eyes darted back to the dining room. Naburus was also there, staring hard at Petre, mentally holding Petre in place. Together, Korin and Naburus slowly killed Petre as we all watched on in horror. The smell of burning flesh made me nauseous, and I bent forward in agony. Mateo held me tighter, forcing me to stand straight. Korin could not see my weakness.

Just as I straightened, Korin's eyes flicked to me, showing me that he had taken note of it. He grinned, his eyes glazed over in amusement. Then Naburus's hold over Petre broke, and Petre writhed and screamed, a wretched noise like a dying animal. I would never forget that sound.

Korin's eyes drifted to Petre again, his mouth turned up in a smile, and Mateo stroked my hair, whispering in my ear again.

"This is a test, specifically set up for you, a way to tempt you to stand up to him. He will cut you down in a second if you try it." His voice lowered in a snarl. "And then he will kill us both because I will not stand by and let him touch you." His hand tightened on my side. "We will have our moment, Samira. I swear to you this night that Korin will receive payment for what he has done to us."

I turned to him, surprised at the sharpness in his voice, the steel in his golden eyes. Before I could respond, Petre dropped to the floor, a burned stump. Before the flames could spread, Korin swirled his fingers. The motion extinguished the flames.

Korin stared down at what was left of Petre and a look of sadness came over his face. "I truly am sorry that it came to this." He bent over, touching him lightly, making a shiver of disgust roll over me. "Move on well into the next world, old friend." He lifted his head and addressed the rest of us, his face hardening. "Anyone else want to move on?"

When no one answered, he reached back for Faithe. She hurried into his arms. "Let's eat then. I'm ravenous."

I remained where I was, rooted in my spot with raw terror, as the others filed into the dining room reluctantly. Mateo was whispering something in my ear, his hand pressing firmly on my back, but all I could see, hear, and smell were Petre's terrified cries as he burned alive, the humans hanging from the ceiling, Faithe as she clung to Korin's arm.

Korin radiated happiness; he loved to see people fear him.

His display of power worked. Fear coated my insides, burning brighter and hotter until it became a raging inferno. Korin would die for this. My vision focused.

Korin was standing in front of me. "I asked you a question."

"She's nervous is all," Mateo said, covering for me. "Of course she'll partake of the feast. She may not be a full member anymore, but she will honor our ways, as new as they may be."

My eyes slid to his. *Partake?* What was he saying?

"Mother." Faithe rested her hand on my arm.

The touch brought me fully to the present, and I stared into her eyes. There was something there, something I didn't expect to see. Fear. Regret. Horror. I blinked.

"Come join us," she said.

I recoiled inside. Had I really been tempted to drink from a human only moments ago? Now, I had no desire to ever touch a human again. I hadn't drunk from them in over two centuries.

"Please?" Faithe's voice held a hint of worry, big enough to draw my attention. If she was compelled, subtle hints would be the only way for her to convey her true feelings. Her large eyes stared into mine, as if begging me to stay.

Was she asking for my help?

The thought sparked me into action. Some part of Faithe was still in there. I had to help her get away from this monster. "Yes."

I moved to go into the dining room, but Korin stopped me and motioned Faithe and Mateo forward. Mateo looked from him to me, his muscles tightening, but I flickered my eyes to the dining room, telling him to go.

As soon as they were inside, Korin leaned toward me and whispered his sickening breath into my ear, "Don't even think about winning the fight against Michael. If you do, I'll help your precious Faithe move on just like I did Petre. If you defy me, she will die tonight. Do you hear me? Die."

CHAPTER 15

A painful lump filled my throat as I walked into the dining room, feeling Korin's cold gaze on my backside. Throw the fight with Michael? The idea made me ill, but the sensation disappeared when I accidentally glanced at the humans hanging from the ceiling. I had no idea how I was going to eat. This went against everything I believed in.

Michael rose from his seat across the dining room table near the head, where Korin was to sit. "I want you next to me, Samira. Before we fight, we should get to know each other again."

The rock in my throat became heavier, but I did as he ordered. This was not the time or the place to fight, not when I'd seen a glimmer of life in Faithe's eyes. *Play the part.*

Michael pulled back a chair, and I lowered next to him. Mateo sat across from me on the right side of Korin. His gaze shifted between Michael and me, his mouth turned down. Faithe sat next to Mateo, her eyes downcast. On the other end of the table, far from me, thank goodness, sat Naburus. Close to him, unfortunately, were Kristina and Teddy. I would've far preferred their company, but I was sure I had deliberately been placed away from them.

Servants hurried through double doors from the kitchen and set plates of warm food in front of us, starting with Korin. Goblets of blood from the humans above us, hanging like grotesque chandeliers, were also served. Most of us remained still, staring at the blood as if it were some foreign, disgusting food.

A man with blond, slicked back hair and sharp blue eyes took his goblet and drank it down quickly. A few others reached for theirs, as if now given permission to drink. They licked their lips and giggled, asking for more.

But the majority remained motionless, fear and hate in their eyes. Korin stared down those who did not drink and some shifted uncomfortably under his cold gaze. When it was obvious most had no desire to drink the blood, Korin slammed his fist onto the table, making silverware and plates jump. "Drink."

At this command, veiled with deadly threats, everyone grabbed their warm glasses and tentatively began to sip. I reached for the goblet, my fingers slowly curling around it. The pull of warm blood so close, the smell so tantalizing, I couldn't deny the want that swelled within me. It had been a long time since I'd had fresh human blood. Lately, I had to resort to animal blood as the blood bank I had been using lately was growing low. Probably because of the recent influx of vampires into Rouen.

Feeling eyes on me, I looked over. Korin held his own glass, swirling the crimson liquid in his hand. He watched me beneath hooded eyes, his gaze honed in on my cup. I lifted it, sweat dotting my brow and, swallowing the lump in my throat, bowed my head slightly and poured the thick blood into my mouth. I closed my eyes to keep from seeing the dead humans above me, but groaned inwardly at the rich, coppery taste as it coated my tongue and throat.

I had forgotten how good it could taste. So rich, so tantalizing. Like warm summer nights and cool breezes. I glanced at Mateo; it reminded me of him. Of long, passionate lovemaking, or even just talking through the night.

He had waited for me to drink before taking his own sip, but when he did, he didn't seem to struggle with it as much as I had. He was still accustomed to drinking from humans, something he didn't have a problem with. Humans had killed his entire human family when they found out Mateo had been turned into a vampire. Though Mateo may not be deliberately cruel to them, he held no love for them either.

I tore my eyes away from him, my fingers trembling in anticipation. I wanted more blood, and I hated myself for feeling that way.

Before I could enjoy it further and to prevent myself for asking for seconds, I turned my attention to the roasted vegetables and smoked lamb on my plate. The taste of it, pale in comparison, replaced the tangy flavor of the blood in my mouth.

Michael lowered his own cup and turned to me. "How long have you been in Rouen?"

"Years," is all I offered. I would not indulge him in pleasantries any more than I had to.

"How many, to be precise?"

"Why does it matter?"

"He searched for you," Faithe explained. "He sent several vampires all over the world to find you."

I looked from her to Michael, shocked. "Why would you do that?"

"Because Mateo wouldn't."

The realization stung more than I thought it would. After Mateo had rejected me, I thought when I disappeared he might try to find me after our history together, but apparently, it was my ex-lover who had taken the time. A part of me had hoped there was still a spark left between Mateo and me that he would've at least tried.

"It's none of your concern," Mateo growled at him.

I hated them all. "It doesn't matter how long I've been in Rouen." I gave Michael a cold stare. "I didn't want to be found."

He slid his cold and clammy hand over mine. "But your place is with this coven, even if others think it isn't. And despite our shaky past, I'm glad you are back."

My gaze flickered to Mateo. His expression tightened at the sight of Michael touching me.

"I'm just visiting," I clarified and removed my hand out from under Michael's.

Korin watched it all, a smile teasing the corners of his mouth as if he knew something the rest of us didn't.

"Why this city?" Korin asked, tilting his head.

Michael's hand moved to my shoulder where he played with the dress strap between his fingers. I tried to shrug him off casually, but he maintained the intimate contact.

"Rouen suits me," I said.

Korin set his glass down. "Is it because of your roommates?"

My blood chilled.

"I find them fascinating. A Morgan witch and an Alpha. Both very powerful. I sense it inside them both. However did you find them?"

I needed to change the subject and fast. I didn't want Korin anywhere near them. "There was an open room. That was all." I turned to the servant passing behind me. "Could I have more blood, please?"

He nodded and handed me a nearly full goblet from the middle of the table. The blood flowing from above had slowed.

"You enjoy human blood?" Korin asked.

I forced a smile. "It is in my nature, after all."

"And soon we will find out if you still have that fierceness I used to crave so much." Michael's fingers caressed my shoulder and down my arm beneath the table, then skirt up my upper thigh. My eyes widened at the closeness to an area I never wanted his hands near again.

Mateo must've sensed what had happened because he jumped to his feet, nearly spilling his plate. Before he could cause a further scene, I gripped Michael's fingers on my leg, raising my eyebrow.

"I'm certain there are other ways of showing you how fierce I can be." Then I snapped his fingers back until they popped from their sockets. Flinching, he jerked his hand away and bit the insides of his mouth so harshly, I could smell his blood. I gave him a smile. "But I'm happy to show you in the ring. When do we fight?"

Michael pulled his hand back, his pained expression turning into a seductive smile. "Soon, pet. And when we do, I'll remind you how much you enjoy my heavy hand."

"Stop," Korin ordered Mateo. "Let's enjoy our meal. It's not time for entertainment."

For the next hour, I forced myself to interact with the others, pretending it wasn't killing me inside to act like nothing was wrong, that I wasn't dining with a monster beneath humans who had suffered and bled for our benefit. The only good to come out of it at all was my conversation with Faithe.

She told me all about her life the last three hundred years. Much of it sounded sad to me, but she didn't bat an eye at her talk of wars or being by Korin's side. She had helped him do things that used to horrify her. There was a moment, however, where we shared laughter. When the old Faithe came out and pure joy radiated from her eyes. It was brief and as soon as Korin's eyes were on her, a fascinated look on his face, she stopped. However swift, it strengthened my resolve and gave me the courage I'd need to throw the fight with Michael.

With most of the plates empty, and the humans drained of all blood, Korin rose from the table. "And now, let us retire to the training room where we will have the pleasure of watching Michael and Samira fight once again. We all know the fireworks that fly when that happens."

Several vampires, the ones who knew our past, laughed. I cast them a dangerous look, anxious to get this over with. I pushed away from the table and followed everyone outside and across the lawn to a tall building. I deliberately avoided Mateo, who clearly wanted to get my attention. Probably to beg me not to fight again. Useless energy. All throughout dinner, his frown grew deeper so that by the end he was practically seething.

Good. Let him be angry. Give him a tiny taste of the anger I'd felt, so many years ago. Besides, I was in this position because of him, partly anyway. If he had left with me so long ago, we could've continued with our plans to destroy Korin once and for all.

Before I could walk into the large building behind the mansion, Faithe pulled me aside into the shadows. "Be careful against Michael. He doesn't just want to fight you. He wants to shame you in front of everyone, the same way he thinks you did to him."

I figured as much, but now that I had a moment alone with her, I didn't want to waste it talking about Michael. I glanced around to make sure no one was listening. Knowing I didn't have much time, I asked the most important question first. "Are you happy, Faithe? Here, in this place with Korin."

She stared past me toward the forest beyond. Moonlight cast an eerie glow upon her face. "It's all I know."

My heart ached at the pain I heard in her voice. "Why did you come back?"

Her gaze shifted to me. "I didn't have a choice. He found me."

"How?" I had been so careful to hide her thousands of miles away, with people I trusted.

Her eyes met mine. "He killed them all."

"Who?"

"The whole Madabbe Tribe. When Korin came for me, he killed every single person. My friends, and even those I considered family." Her eyes grew distant. "He tortured my lover for weeks."

I closed my eyes, understanding her now, feeling her heartbreak rip through me. Of course, she went with him. I opened my eyes and gripped her arm fiercely. "You can still go, get away from him. Please, Faithe. I will help you. Don't let him break you like this."

She smiled. "All those things don't matter anymore. It's too late for me. I am already broken, *Moeder*." *Mother*. She said this last word with the old tenderness I remembered. "But it is not too late for you. You should run now, while you can still escape him."

I shook my head, refusing to abandon her again.

She swallowed, then looked beyond me. "Then it is already too late. Be careful tonight." She brushed by me and disappeared inside.

I inhaled a sharp breath and followed after her, mentally preparing myself for what I had to do. I would not let her down again.

The training room was a large open space with thirty-foot ceilings. Mats had been laid across the floor and all sorts of weapons, ropes, and chains hung on the wall. I had a suspicion this building wasn't just used to train new vampires.

"Where do I change?" I asked Michael who was unbuttoning his shirt.

"Change? You're going to fight in what you're wearing."

"No."

"Since you're so unhappy with your attire, I'll be sure to try and remove it from you as we fight. Choose your weapon."

I groaned and walked to the wall holding the swords. I grabbed what was the most familiar: two long and thin straight blades. I used the tip of one to cut the slit on my dress up higher on my hip.

Near the front of the room, Korin had lowered into a tall-backed iron chair. Naburus sat next to him, the IV pole at his side. They shared a look, then Korin returned his attention to the arena. "Begin," he ordered.

I glanced once at Mateo before walking to the center of the room. His eyes were on me, following me everywhere I went, his arms crossed casually against his chest. But the tic of his eye gave him away.

Michael met me in the center, his shirt off, holding swords that matched my own. "I'm going to enjoy this."

CHAPTER 16

$\mathcal{W}$e bowed to each other and just as I straightened, Michael flicked his sword forward, strategically catching a pin in my hair. My long curls cascaded down past my breasts.

"Much better," he said.

If I was going to throw this fight, then I was at least going to do it after I sufficiently beat him down. I jabbed the sword in my right hand forward, but he blocked it. I swung again, stepping to the side around him. Just a few blows to test his skills. He met them blow for blow.

I picked up my pace, swinging low then high, twisting and turning, my feet following the fluid motions. He stumbled back, his footwork not as graceful as my own, but his skills had improved dramatically. I dodged his blade just as it came over me, but I realized a moment too late that it wasn't me he was after. It was my sword. He knocked it from my grip. He quickly maneuvered himself between me and it.

With his two swords against my one, the fight became more even. He swung the blades one after another in a windmill motion. I stumbled backwards, avoiding their sharp edges. I spun out of the way and somersaulted back toward my other blade. He appeared there just as I reached it and slammed his foot on top of it.

I looked up at him, narrowing my eyes. Super speed was not supposed to be used during these combat sessions. "Changing the rules?"

"A lot has changed since you've been here." He stabbed both blades forward at different speeds. I blocked the first one, but had to swing my shoulder out of the way of the second one. With my balance off, he dropped one of his swords and grabbed my arm. He jerked me to him, slamming my back into his hard chest while his other sword came to my throat, freezing my position. The sword in my hand dropped to the floor.

Michael turned me toward Korin and the others. I tried to squirm, but the sharp edge of the blade pierced my skin. "See how weak she is now? Even her body is softer."

His free hand slid around my stomach and up to my breast. He squeezed it hard. A surge of dark and ancient energy rushed through me at once. He would regret not banning super speed.

My arms shot up and knocked the blade from my throat. I spun and kicked him in the chest so hard he flew back. All of this in less than a second.

He scrambled to his feet, the sword still in his hand. His nostrils flared, and his eyes burned into mine. He yelled and rushed me, but I easily stepped out of the way and swung my fist backward, catching him on the back of the head. He dropped to the ground. While he recovered, I walked casually and picked up both my swords.

As I walked back to Michael, I stared at Korin, hoping he could feel my hatred of him burning through my eyes, but Korin only tossed me a casual smile. Even though he'd ordered me to throw the fight, he was happy I was degrading Michael so thoroughly.

I let Michael crawl to his feet and grab both his swords. His chest heaved up and down as we circled each other. Confidence had left him and only fear remained. And everyone could see it.

I smiled smugly. "Want to give up?"

"Never!"

He charged me again, but this time I lightened up, meeting him blow for blow and making it appear easy. He growled in frustration, sweat glistening on his chest and matting the hair on his forehead. I flickered my sword toward his cheek so fast he hadn't seen it coming. A cut appeared, blood filling the space. He gasped and swung wider than necessary. He was growing tired.

I continued to spar with him, adding a few more nicks to his bare chest, but when I spotted Korin whispering to Naburus, I took the hint.

Slowing up my movements, I let his blade catch my arm. I pretended the motion hurt and dropped my weapon. He elbowed me in the face, dropping me to the floor. It hurt, but nothing I couldn't recover from quickly. Instead, I remained where I was even when he jabbed the tip of his sword into my ribs.

"Yield," he said.

I slowly looked up at him and bowed my head. He stared at me long and hard before turning and tossing his blades across the room. His hands lifted into the air at his victory, but anyone with a brain knew I had thrown this fight. A polite pitter-patter of applause echoed off the high ceilings.

"Well done, Michael," Korin said, but his voice was anything but proud. "Samira, you have not proven yourself worthy to come to this place again, but maybe allowances can be made given your history with this coven. I will ponder it."

My nostrils flared. As if I was begging him to return. The emperor without any clothes, a play for those in the coven.

His eyes darkened, and a smile crept up his face. "I am certain there are other ways you could prove your worthiness. Perhaps you could join me in my room tonight."

Sure, if you would prefer your balls removed from their sac. I came to my feet, smoothing my dress down, and bowed, barely suppressing my rage. I knew he didn't really want me in his room tonight, he preferred a more submissive type. And blonde hair. But it was meant to debase me, as I had debased his head of security.

While Korin asked if anyone else wanted to fight for sport, I walked to the exit, adrenaline pumping through my veins. I caught the eye of Teddy and Kristina, both looking at me sadly. I didn't see Mateo, but I didn't look that hard. I hated that he'd seen me in such a vulnerable state.

As soon as I hit the lawn, I lifted my dress, kicked off my shoes, and ran to the main house. I hurried up to the Summer room, my heart thundering in my chest. I threw open the door, slammed it behind me, and rested my forehead against it. My hatred for Korin filled my blood with such rage that I wanted to rush back down there and kill him. It didn't matter that I might lose. The ancient power inside me wanted it, too. I could feel it humming just beneath my flesh, could feel it encroaching on my mind.

"Take it off."

I spun around and sucked in a breath. Mateo was in my room. The top of his shirt was unbuttoned and his hair was a mess, as if he had been tugging his fingers through it. He did that when he was upset.

"What are you doing in here?"

"Take it off now." He moved toward me, his chest heaving up and down. "I can't see it on you any longer."

I pressed back against the door, resisting the pull I felt whenever he was near. Because of adrenaline from the recent fight and the fresh blood coursing through my veins, the pull to Mateo was even stronger. I groaned, needing to stay clear-headed. "It's just a dress."

"It is more than that and you know it. I want it off."

"Then you take it off me," I snapped. "I no longer let those memories haunt me." A lie.

Mateo crushed the space between us, his fangs drawn. His eyes glowed with fury, his hand holding the top of my dress with clenched fists. I met his stare, daring him to tear it from me.

He held my gaze, our chests tight with unspent breath as both fury and desire coursed through our veins, our emotions all mixed up from our demented night. I could not look away, *did not want to* look away. I needed his touch, needed him to remind me who I once was. That I could live and breathe and *feel* once. That, long ago, I'd lived as the humans did, with emotions and longing and love.

My whole body trembled in anticipation, waiting for him to wrench those feelings from me.

Instead, he closed his eyes, clinging to his sanity, forcing his rage to simmer. He lowered his head to my neck and inhaled deeply. I held my breath, waiting for something. I didn't know what. My lips pressed together tightly as his hands clung to the top of the dress, pushing against my breasts. The tips pebbled. His fingers had been the last to touch me tenderly there, and they longed for his touch once again.

"Samira," he moaned. And then he ripped my dress down the front, his lips trailing down my skin as he sank to his knees like a prince kneeling before his lover, his kisses burning fire into my skin. "You were always my *anima gemella*, my one true love. Why can't we be together again, as we once were?"

"You know why, Mateo." My voice was soft, husky, uncertain, as if... as if I, myself, wasn't even sure anymore. As if I would not stop him if he stripped me bare and took me to the bed to make love to me the rest of the night. His long, nimble fingers traced up my body, tugging the dress to fall from my shoulders and pool at my feet.

He had seen me bare and writhing under him. He had heard all my heart's desires and dreams.

And then he had shattered them.

And so, every time I saw him, I wore my shields before him, my hate and anger pushing him away like swords. And now, my panties and bra, a slip of lace, was still my armor, protecting my broken heart. I kept them on, when in the past I would have ripped them from my body.

And yet, in this moment, I was never more naked and vulnerable before him. Because he was stripping me bare. Not only of my clothing but of my anger for him that had festered my heart into hardened stone. With every touch, with every trace of his fingers, he sent fire through my veins into my cold heart, warming it with tenderness, melting my ice with his love.

He paused, leaning his head on my stomach, his breath heaving. I silently begged him to take me, to release me from my anger. *Please,*

please, please, Mateo, the thought a whisper against the tip of my tongue.

His hands came to my side and squeezed gently, his fingers pressing just above my hip bone. I held back the moan that so desperately wanted to release, but I shook my head. Forcing myself out of this trance. I had to keep my wits about me. Korin or Michael could enter at any moment.

"Mateo, we must stop—"

He shook his head, keeping me from speaking as he raised his head, his eyes directly over my bellybutton, his lips so close to where I wanted him, his hot breath warming my core. I gave in to the emotions threatening to tear me into two, just like my dress, and moaned my agony. The need to have him inside me, the need to have his lips over my flesh, burning me with their touch. The agony that he had shredded my heart into pieces had taken me centuries of pain and spilling blood to get over.

"Samira," he breathed, making me still. His tongue flicked out, sending flaming desire to the center of my thighs, teasing me.

"Please," I begged, clinging to his shoulders, but I didn't know if it was a plea to stop or continue.

"I can't."

I hissed, anger and righteous indignation filling me. "Then why are you here, Mateo?" He looked up into my eyes. "Why do you strip me bare, until my bones ache, my skin flames, and my very essence longs for you again? Will you leave me again, rending me in half with your wicked eyes and simpering smile?"

He didn't answer, and I backed away, sliding away from his touch. "Just leave. Leave this room and never return to me."

His face snapped to me, fire in his eyes. "You have no idea what I had to go through for you."

"*You* have no idea the pain I went through because of you!" My voice was fire and rage. I wanted to storm the mansion, slice through every wicked vampire in this household, including the humans who'd given their bodies so freely to the evil that dwelled here. I caught my breath, counting down from ten, trying to control my rage. I couldn't let it get to me, couldn't let the darkness of the Kiss as it hissed its tempting snare take over my body. When I was done, I opened my eyes, steeling myself. My voice was soft. "Just leave. Please, Mateo." I almost begged him. He was breaking me apart.

He stood up, fire still in his gaze. "I suffered as you will never know to keep you safe. These last centuries have been torture for me." His eyes betrayed the truth of his pain and agony. "And despite what Michael said, I did go looking for you. Many times."

"I don't believe you."

"I did." He nodded. "And I found you every time."

"Liar." I scowled, biting my lower lip so harshly blood dripped from it. His eyes darted to the blood and his tongue snaked out, licking his own lips. But he did not taste me. Instead, he swallowed hard.

"I sent the Ames de la Terra after you. I knew they could help you. And when you were too much for them, I begged an old friend to take you in."

I sucked in a breath. "Detrand."

He nodded, his eyes still hardened. "Detrand took you in as a favor to me. And you do not wish to know what I had to do in return."

I laughed, the noise sounding strange to my own ears. "I can only imagine."

He scowled, looking away. Then he stepped closer and brought his finger up to my chest. He traced it in between my breasts and I sucked in a breath. He moved it over my neck to my mouth. He stared there as he spoke. "I would do anything to take that night back." His finger traced my lips, causing me to shiver, then it moved to my cheek to trace it lightly. "I love you, Samira. I always have and always will."

His hand clasped the back of my neck, digging his fingers into my skin as he clutched it, tugging at my hair. "I cannot take you tonight as I wish because my life is still tied to Korin. But I *will* find a way to break his compulsion." His eyes were fierce, his face hard and serious. "And when I do, neither the powers of heaven, earth, nor hell will keep me from you."

I opened my mouth, surprised, about to confess the potion that

Lynx was making when someone knocked on the door. I quickly stepped back just as the door opened. Mateo blinked to the other side of the room near the window. He leaned against the wall, appearing unnerved by who stepped through.

Korin and Naburus.

CHAPTER 17

orin's gaze flashed from me to Mateo, his expression
unreadable. I picked up my street clothes from off the
floor to get dressed. "Can I help you?"

Naburus raised his hand in a stopping gesture. "Don't cover up."

I felt his power tug on me, trying to still my muscles, but I fought
against it, angry that he would try to force me to stay undressed. But I
didn't show my anger, instead I gave him a cold and indifferent look.
"I will not."

"Obey him, Samira," Korin warned. He glanced at Mateo. "You
need to leave."

"I think I'll stay."

"Leave," I snapped, not wanting him to interfere with whatever
these two wanted from me. If Mateo stayed, it would only end badly
for him. Any leverage we had against surprising Korin would disappear. When Mateo didn't budge, I added, "I mean it. Get out of this
room and don't ever sneak into any room of mine again. This body is
no longer yours."

He stiffened and leaned away from the wall. "I had only come to
admire."

He walked toward me, his eyes shielding any feeling and Korin called after him, "Go straight to my quarters. I have business with you."

I inhaled a slow breath hoping Mateo wouldn't be punished for being in here.

Naburus shuffled toward me, dragging the IV pole behind him. "You are a strong, powerful woman, Samira."

"What do you want?"

"You did well tonight," Korin began as Naburus circled me, eyeing me up and down.

I lifted up my shirt to pull it over my head but Naburus yanked it from my hands and tossed it to the other side of the room.

"I lost," I growled, trying hard not to punch the skinny, aged vampire in front of me. He smelled like salt and iron.

"But you obeyed. First you drank human blood, then you lost against Michael." A smile tugged on the corner of Naburus' lips. "You're learning to obey."

"Because I don't have any other choice."

"There's always a choice. You just happened to choose to obey Korin's command."

I frowned. "That's not what that was."

Naburus looked back at Korin. "I want to taste the Kiss inside of her."

"No." I said the word with as much force as I could.

"Let him," Korin said.

I searched Korin's eyes. He was giving me another order to see if I would obey. "And if I don't?"

"Then Faithe is going to have to do all sorts of naughty things to me. Things I know she doesn't like."

A cold and painful chill worked its way up my bare back. I'd do whatever it took to protect my friends, and he knew it. I wasn't strong enough to fight him after I saw what he did to Petre. The chill of this thought seeped past my skin and into my bones, making them feel brittle and weak.

I was powerless, something I hadn't felt in a very long time.

I held my breath, counting to ten in my mind, giving myself five reasons why I should do this. If I could think of five, then it would be my choice and not his demand.

Everyone I loved would be affected. He would start with Kristina and Teddy. The fact that they were seated so far from me and next to Naburus was a statement he knew I cared for them. That was two reasons.

Briar and Lynx would be next, hunted for my disloyalty, compelled to harm themselves, and possibly commit suicide. That was four.

Then there was Mateo. Even though Mateo was strong, I had no doubt Korin would torture him the most and force me to watch. That was five.

And then there was Faithe. The woman I'd let down, because I chose to leave her behind.

She was reason enough to do it. I was responsible for her because I turned her, introduced her to Korin.

Six. There were at least six reasons why I had to do this, and that didn't include all the other innocents who would get caught up in his rage if I disobeyed. I steeled myself and met his eyes. He smiled, knowing he had won. I tilted my head, a reluctant offering.

"That's it, Samira." Korin's words slithered across my flesh, making my skin prickle.

Naburus inched closer, the wheels on the IV pole squeaking behind him. He leaned over and licked my neck with his slimy tongue.

"Yum, sweat," he said and opened his mouth wide to give room for his long incisors.

His fangs pierced my skin fast and hard. I grimaced at the sensation, knowing he wasn't trying to be gentle. A vampire's bite could either be incredibly sensual or terribly painful. He went for painful. Feeling blood leave my body was a funny sensation, almost like being turned inside out. It had been centuries since I had allowed someone to drink from me. I held myself still, even though I wanted to pull from his disgusting bite.

Naburus's mouth on my neck didn't last long; his bite was purely for research. He never cared about anything else.

He pulled out and leaned away, swishing my blood in his mouth as if it was fine wine. He swallowed and grinned, blood coating his teeth.

"The taste is surprisingly sweet." He ran his tongue over his incisors and drew his brows together. "But there's something else there. Heat and power similar to the difference between the sun and stars."

He lifted his hand and touched my forehead with his long and bony finger. "You are dangerous."

My gaze shifted to Korin, who had set his mouth in a firm line.

"I am nothing," I said to placate him.

"I know you mean to interfere with my plans," Korin began, taking Naburus' place in front of me, "Things are already in motion, and there is nothing you can do to stop them. I hope you believe me when I say that, because otherwise, it's going to cause you and everyone you love a lot of pain and heartache." He stepped closer, touching my cheek softly with his finger, and I suppressed my shutter. His eyes locked on mine. "I tell you this because I truly care about you. I thought of you as a daughter once."

"Is that why you haven't killed me yet?"

He smiled and patted my cheek. "No, child. You are much too valuable to destroy. For now. But if you attempt to stop me, your time will come much slower and with more agony than you can bare."

He glanced at Naburus who was running a long fingernail between the lines of his teeth. "Come. Mateo is waiting."

As soon as they left the room, I quickly dressed, dying to get out of here. I checked the time. Almost midnight. It felt like several nights had passed since I'd come to this place. How I had managed to live with Korin for over a century was beyond me.

Keeping to the shadows, I slipped away from Winter's Cove. Things were so much worse than I expected. Korin had too strong of a hold on the coven. Even if I managed to break his compulsion on them, he still had that ability to make others burst into flames. Fear was a powerful motivator, even against me, and he knew it.

I couldn't take him on, not directly. But what would hurt him the most was to get rid of the drug that made his precious Hydes. He had big plans for them, something beyond what I was seeing. As for the Hydes he'd already made, I didn't know how to help them. I doubted we could obtain enough holy water treatment like what we'd given Briar. I'd called in all favors with my contacts in the Vatican to get that for Briar. Besides, holy water wouldn't work on vampires. It only melted them from the inside out.

Reaching outside, I paused, my hand on the doorjamb and thought of Mateo, my body warming again. Had he meant all those words, or was he just overcome by our history in a moment of weakness?

Everything here was too familiar; it was almost as if we hadn't been apart all these years. But we had, and I needed to remember that.

As soon as I was safely hidden within my car, I rammed my fist into the steering wheel of my car, frustrated by the night's events. I hated Michael and how he had touched me. I hated Mateo for stripping me bare, and then refusing to go any further. I hated Korin for using my love for Faithe to control me. And I hated Naburus for his stupid science and just for existing. I hated that we probably couldn't save the supernaturals who had been forced into Hydes. There just wasn't enough time to find a cure, nor did we have the means to try and hold them.

I breathed in deeply, trying to keep calm over the choking sensation threatening to cut off my air. I needed to find a way to stop Korin, a way to rescue Faithe and the Hydes. And, I needed a way to keep Mateo from breaking my heart again.

CHAPTER 18

*P*unching through the darkness, I sped to Lynx's home. *My home.* I hadn't been to my hotel, Trevisan, for weeks. It just didn't have the same feel as the one I occupied now. In its own way, living with Briar and Lynx had become a new coven of sorts where I felt I belonged. They cared about others and we worked together to help this town.

I parked in the driveway and exited the vehicle, noting Roma's car and Luke's bike out front. I stood still, focusing my senses on the surrounding area. That tall man who had followed me so close to home still worried me. I didn't like unknown variables.

When I was certain there was no danger, I headed through the back door, following the sounds of many voices. Lynx was in the kitchen, her hair a mess and the room in even worse condition. All sorts of bottles, plants and flowers, and different shaped bowls lay scattered across the counters and table.

Her eyes lit up when she saw me. "Samira! Your friend is an angel! I received the Corpse Flower only a couple of hours ago. He sent me a whole dozen. I can make batches for several supernaturals." She shook her head, as if marveling over it. "I don't know how he got it here so fast."

I chuckled. Detrand was no angel. Nor did he pretend to be. If she looked closer, she might find the reason he was able to get it here so quickly was probably through nefarious means. "I'm glad. How close are you to finding a cure?"

"I'm almost done." She held up a plastic gallon baggie. "I'm freezing the rest of the flowers to use later." She took hold of my hand and tugged me toward the table. "Let me show you my potion."

I stared down in a large bowl of red smoking liquid bubbling around what looked like twigs and bones. "I don't know what I'm looking at."

She looked from me to the potion, then laughed uncomfortably. "Right. I guess not. I'm just so excited because this is a serious upper-level spell. I don't think my cousins could even pull it off."

"You have great talent." I smiled at her and nodded my head toward the living room. "Who's all here?"

"Go see for yourself. It's quite the group. The witches are nice, and I'm even related to one of them. Distantly."

Just as she said it, a girl who looked Lynx's same age walked into the kitchen. Her hair was red like Lynx's but a lighter shade. They also shared the same eye color.

"How's it coming—" She froze when she saw me.

Lynx quickly introduced us. "Denise, this is Samira. She's my roommate."

Denise's mouth remained open. My appearance could be startling at first, the predatory nature of my vampirism gave people with good instincts a warning to stay back.

"Nice to meet you," I said. I didn't extend my hand.

She blinked and cleared her throat. "You too." She shifted her gaze back to Lynx. "Do you need any help?"

While they talked, I walked out of the kitchen and into the living room which was buzzing with conversation. All that stopped when I entered the room. I remained rooted in my spot even though I felt like shrinking under their stares. In addition to Luke, Briar and Roma, I recognized Gerald, Fire Ridge's head of security, and Loxley, the shifter who'd taken up to following Briar around. Seated next to

Roma was an older, dark-skinned man with short black hair peppered with gray. Even though we'd planned this meeting, I still didn't like strangers in this house.

Briar untangled herself from Luke's lap and sat up. "Holy shit, Sammie! You look like the Disney Princess no one dared film."

"I just came from a dinner party at Winter's Cove. It required..." I waved a hand in front of my face and rolled my eyes, "this."

She turned back to Luke. "Sorry, but I'm switching teams. She's hotter than you."

He growled and pulled her back into his lap. "You're not going anywhere."

She laughed and wrapped her arms around him.

"Who are these people?" I asked, mostly referring to the guy next to Roma, although I was still unsure about Loxley since I didn't know much about her. Any one of them could be the Phoenix. We needed to be more careful who we let in.

Roma shifted her weight on the sofa and motioned to the man next to her. "This is Owen. He used to hold a leadership position when our witch coven still existed. He will take up the leadership role again as we're reorganizing."

"Then the witches will help us?"

"We will," Owen said in a deep voice that pleased my ears. "We've had a few witches disappear recently, and our seers tell us it's because of a growing evil in Rouen. They also have predicted that if we can't stop it, we will lose many more. We were grateful when Roma approached us. We can't fight this on our own."

I watched his movements, his small mannerisms, looking for anything suspicious. "What is your last name?"

He hesitated briefly before answering. "Williams."

I committed it to memory and looked at Roma. "And you're willing to come out of retirement to help organize the Witches of Rouen?"

"Hell yes! I've seen how you precious girls have suffered." She reached over and squeezed Briar's knee. "Besides, I always knew my

140

fighting days weren't over. I've been saving up for this battle. Something tells me it's going to be a doozy."

"I'm glad you're here. Thank you." I turned to the shifters. "Gerald, thank you also for coming. Who sits next to you?"

It was Loxley, of course, but we'd never been formally introduced. She barely looked eighteen and had dark, wavy black hair with red undertones and tan skin. She jumped to her feet, smiling nervously. "I'm Loxley. I'm a newer member of the Silver Claws."

"Last name?"

"Evans." Her wide, sky blue eyes looked from Briar to me.

There was something about her that set me on edge, a wisp of a dark shadow lurking in her eyes. "You're a shifter?"

She nodded quickly.

"Why are you here?"

Briar leaned away from Luke and toward me, scowling. "Why the third degree? I asked her to come."

I continued to stare at Loxley, trying to focus my sixth sense upon her. There was something about her, something I couldn't detect... I looked at Briar. "Why did you choose her to come?"

Loxley picked up her jacket from behind her and glanced at Briar. "I should probably go. She's freaking me out, and this isn't really my scene."

Briar hopped off Luke's lap to rest her hand on Loxley's arm. "Stay. I invited you because I've seen you fight, plus you're smart." She cut her gaze to me. "Can you chill out? Loxley's good."

I lowered my head and stepped away, but beneath my eyelashes I continued to watch her. Whatever she was, she was more than a shifter. She might not know it and may never. I'd seen it before. Supernaturals who aren't aware of their family tree. One species could've mated with another and those recessive genes lay in wait for perfect conditions before revealing themselves.

Or she was hiding something.

"What have you all been discussing?" I asked.

Briar relaxed her stance toward me but she remained by Loxley.

"So Roma said they're going to try to run some location spells to see if they can track down this shady Phoenix person."

I glanced at Roma. She was nodding her head.

"And the Silver Claws are all on standby until we know something more," Briar continued. "Really we're just waiting on new information and we can't get that unless—"

"It's done!" Lynx called from the kitchen. She hurried into the room with Denise behind her. Both were grinning wide.

Briar pointed at her and finished her sentence. "We have the cure."

"That's wonderful, Lynx!" Roma said. "I always said you were the strongest Morgan witch."

"Don't let Cassandra hear you say that," Owen added.

"When are they going to be here so I can test it?" Lynx asked Briar. She smoothed the stray hairs away from her face.

I glanced at Briar. "They?"

"Well, Angel. Mateo might come too. I texted him just before you came. So where were you exactly? A dinner party?"

I nodded, grinding my teeth.

"How was that?"

"Telling. It made me realize just how dire our situation is. Korin has been gifted great power and is more ruthless than ever."

Lynx walked over and stood next to me and Briar, her eyes full of concern. "Are you okay? Did something happen?"

I almost inhaled a hitched breath as all my feelings from the evening rushed back, but I blinked, walling them back up. It would do me no good to admit how Korin had forced me to do things I would never consider before, how seeing Faithe again like that tore at my heart, or how Mateo's behavior stripped me of my defenses.

It wouldn't do any good to admit how ... how *afraid* I was.

I blinked once more, one last check on my emotions before I spoke. "I won't describe the horror I witnessed. Whatever plans we put in place, we need to do them quickly. Korin's power over the others is only growing."

I didn't want to admit he also held power over me. With those impossible choices he gave me, what else was I supposed to do?

A familiar scent entered my nose and warmed my body. "They're here."

CHAPTER 19

*A*ll eyes traveled to the front door. A moment later, it opened. Angel walked through first, his gaze going straight to Briar. He didn't bother looking at anyone else. Briar seemed to notice too, and her cheeks reddened.

Mateo came in and walked past me without even as much as a glance. Very different from the man I had been with only a few hours earlier. This was a sharp reminder why I must stay away from him. He played too many games.

He stopped near the fireplace and turned to Lynx. "Is it done?"

She nodded quickly and swallowed. "I'll go get it."

With Mateo's tall height and intense gaze he could be quite intimidating. I remember being afraid of him too when I'd first met him. But that fear had turned to passion in a short amount of time. Maybe too short.

Lynx returned holding a glass partially filled with a brown liquid. Dark chunks of something swirled within. "I know it doesn't look the best, and its taste probably isn't much better, but it should work."

"And if it doesn't?" I asked.

She flinched. "Then it's going to make someone very ill, hopefully not worse."

"Could this kill them?" Briar asked, a hint of worry in her voice.

Mateo held out his hand. "Let's get this over with."

"I will go first," Angel said, stepping in front of him.

Briar came to his side. "Um, no. Let Mateo go first. He offered to drink the shit juice first."

He stared down at her, his gaze softening and a smile tugging at the corners of his mouth. "A little shit juice won't hurt me, I assure you. Besides, it's my duty."

"There is no need for those formalities here," Mateo said. "I don't want you harming yourself if—"

Angel's hand snapped forward and grabbed the glass. He swallowed half of it and handed it back to Lynx before anyone could stop him.

"Asshat." Briar stared at him with disgust.

"You should sit," I said and moved a chair beneath him. His face was beginning to pale.

Roma slid back on the sofa further away from him. "You don't look so good."

"Angel?" Mateo asked.

Angel's legs buckled, and he dropped to his knees, his face grimacing. Luke rose to his feet as did Gerald. Loxley stayed back by the door, looking like she wanted to bolt.

Briar knelt by Angel's side. "What's happening? Are you okay?"

His head snapped back, eyes open wide. He might've tried to answer her, but his jaw was clamped too hard, making the muscles on the side of his face bulge.

Mateo looked at Lynx, worry creasing his brow. "Is this supposed to happen?"

"I don't know!"

"Just give him a minute," Roma said. "Let the potion weed out the compulsion. It's powerful magic we're dealing with. It's not going to feel good."

Angel fell over, his back arching painfully high. His legs began to shake, followed by the rest of his body. Briar tried to hold him still but it was like trying to calm an earthquake.

"Do something!" Briar shouted at Lynx.

Luke rested a hand on her shoulder, but she shrugged it off.

Her burst of emotions toward caring for Angel surprised me. Clearly her feelings for him ran deep. I wonder if even Briar knew how deep they went. For the first time, Mateo and I locked eyes, an understanding passing between us.

Angel's body fell flush with the floor, and he sucked in a great breath.

"It's wearing off," Roma said. She was sitting on the edge of the couch leaning forward eagerly.

"Angel?" Briar asked. She stroked the hair away from his face.

Slowly, his eyes came into focus.

Mateo bent down next to him. "How do you feel, old friend?"

He groaned and touched his head. "Remember that time we were captured by the Season Witches?"

Mateo grimaced. "That bad, huh?"

I frowned and looked at Mateo. The Season Witches? I wondered when he had encountered them. It must've been after we were together. It wasn't that long ago that I fought alongside the witches with Aris Crow in Coast City to take down Bastian, a vampire on the Ministry who attempted to take over the city. The witches had been helpful, but I wouldn't want to get on their bad side.

When Briar had Angel sitting up, I asked, "What can you tell us about Korin?"

Angel glanced at Mateo, his face turning ashen. "It's not good, Mateo."

Mateo looked like he wanted to say something specific, but his mouth slammed shut. He nodded instead. "Tell them what you know, for I cannot."

"Korin took the Nocturnas to a large building a couple of weeks ago. It looked similar to the building where we fought against the Hydes in the swamps." He looked at Gerald. "You were there."

"Don't remind me," Gerald said, his chest tightening.

"The layout was similar," Angel continued, "which makes me think maybe he has many more buildings just like this. Though this one held many more supernaturals. Rows and rows of cages with long tubing connecting them all."

"What was in the tubes?" Lynx asked. She lowered onto the sofa's armrest, her face a mixture of elation and concern.

I patted her arm. "Well done."

She beamed at me.

"Korin said it was Scorpion's Breath with a kick," Angel answered her question.

I resisted the urge to scowl at Mateo. This all started because of him. If he valued human life even a little, all of this may have been avoided.

"Were witches also being held captive?" Owen asked, his attention solely focused on Angel. If Owen was uncomfortable with all of our presences, he didn't show it. This made me watch him closely. No one should feel comfortable around this much predatory power.

Angel nodded. "Several, in fact."

I straightened the glasses on the bridge of my nose. "How many did you say there were?"

Angel slowly came to his feet with Briar by his side. "Dozens, but I only saw a portion of the building. There could've been even more."

Briar finally noticed Luke's gaze on her and purposely turned from Angel. The dynamics between them was becoming complicated. I was surprised I hadn't noticed it sooner. "I've heard of a few people missing, but not that many. Where are they coming from?"

"Neighboring towns, maybe," Briar said. "I'll have the pack start asking around."

"What does he plan on doing with them?" I asked Angel. "And when?"

He shook his head. "I wasn't given that information."

Mateo removed his suit jacket and draped it over the back of the chair. He spun on Lynx, nearly making her fall from her perch on the arm rest. "Give it to me."

She held out the rest of the brown liquid. He stared at it briefly before tossing it back into his throat.

"He must have more information," Roma mumbled.

My body tensed as I watched the color drain from his face. He grabbed onto Angel for support, his eyes widening in pain.

"It will only last a minute," Angel offered.

Mateo dropped to the floor, his knuckles as white as an arctic snowcap. I felt his agony in my chest, then hardened myself against it; being around him was making me weaker. I almost went to him, but rooted my stance.

"I don't want to watch this," Loxley said. She was still hovering by the door.

Gerald backed up to her, his own face grimacing at what Mateo was enduring. "Let's go out on the porch."

Mateo's body had begun to tighten and shake. He fell to his side, his back arching painfully high. His muscles were flexed so tight that his form fitting dress shirt began to tear at the seam of his shoulders. His body flipped onto its stomach, and he growled as if trying to fight against the magic battering his body. More of his shirt tore.

That's when I saw it.

The faded, almost healed, distinguishable marks of a cat-o-nine-tails whip. I swallowed hard, my chest tightening. I'd seen the wounds many times before. One of Korin's favorite methods of punishment. Nine leathered tails, each tipped with a hard leather knot to provide the most pain. Sometimes Korin would weave nails through those tips. By the brief glimpse of Mateo's back, that's exactly the kind of beating he had received.

But why? Had Korin punished Mateo because of something I did? The thought made me ill.

I looked up, meeting Angel's gaze. By his expression, he had seen the marks too, but he didn't look shocked like I did. He looked angry, at me. As if I'd been the one to whip Mateo.

Mateo rolled onto his back and sucked in a great breath. His body still twitched, but the worst of it was over. Angel bent down. "How did it feel?"

"As you de- described," he stuttered. "Although I might prefer the Season Witches means of torture."

Chuckling, Angel helped him sit up. "It will continue to burn, but it will be manageable."

Briar looked at him, surprised. "It still hurts?"

He didn't answer.

On an exhale, Mateo said, "Korin plans on attacking the heart of the city soon, maybe in a matter of weeks."

"Attacking?" Lynx gasped, a hand on her stomach. Denise moved closer to her, looking just as horrified.

"For what purpose?" I asked.

"It's a dry run for something bigger."

"How much bigger?" Luke asked, his voice deep and gravely.

Mateo rose to his feet with Angel's help. He slipped his jacket back over his torn shirt and looked at each of us. "Rouen is to be the birthing place of Trianus." He looked at the witches. "As you know, the earth holds great power. There are a few tears across its surface, one of them being directly below Rouen. They plan to tap into that power and use it to raise Trianus. Korin's job is to prepare the city to greet him, which means humans must come under his control."

I sucked in a breath. "It's Coast City all over again."

Everyone in the room looked at me, but I didn't bother wasting time explaining further. Instead, I said, "We have to stop it. Whatever it takes. I've seen firsthand how humans and even supernaturals suffer when one of our kind gets too much power. No good will come from this."

Briar slammed her fist down. "I second Sammie. We must stop it, no matter the cost."

"I third it," Lynx added.

Angel assisted Mateo into the chair. Color still hadn't returned to Mateo's complexion when he said, "I think all of us are in agreement that Korin must be stopped. And now that we are no longer compelled, we can give the," he glanced at Briar, "shit juice to our people, which will give us more numbers."

"As long as you don't get compelled again," I said.

Lynx stood and paced the room. "Maybe there's something to protect them from that happening again."

149

"As far as I know, there isn't. Not for vampires. It would be a wonderful gift if there was." I turned to Mateo. "You must act as if you are still compelled, until the time is right. Even if it means you must do something you don't wish to do."

"Samira's right," Roma confirmed. "Vampires can't be protected from compulsion, but others can. Humans and witches, for example."

"I didn't know this," I said, immediately interested. Roma nodded. "This could help us greatly."

"Shifters?" Briar asked.

Owen shifted his position on the chair, leaning forward. "It depends upon how much human DNA is in them. For some, it may work. Roma and I, along with the Witches of Rouen—" He turned to Lynx. "Of course, you are welcome too."

Lynx's face lit up as he continued.

"—will create a special thread for people to wear. It's worked in the past and should work again."

"Good." I noted Mateo, staring at the floor with a distant look in his eyes. Something was bothering him. "What is it, Mateo?"

"There's more." His eyes slowly rose to meet mine. "Korin is working with someone, a man named the Phoenix."

"We've heard of him, but what you may not know is he is the same smoke beast we fought at Fire Ridge."

Angel frowned. "I thought Briar destroyed it."

"Me too," Briar said, rolling her eyes, "but apparently all I did was give that fae witch bitch more power when I killed Vincent, the third alpha in a short amount of time. Now she's running around as some bald, tall dude that's uber powerful."

Roma cleared her throat. "How do we find this person?"

"Maybe there's a spell," Owen offered.

Lynx opened her mouth. "I can look—"

Roma touched her arm. "Let us do it. You're going to have your hands full creating more shit juice. Brilliant work, by the way."

Lynx smiled shyly. "Thank you."

I drew my attention back to Mateo. The way his finger slowly tapped against the chair as if in sync to a metronome. And the way his lips tightened and relaxed. I knew all his movements. Knew what they all meant. "That's not what's bothering you. What else?"

He hesitated, his Adam's apple bobbing on his throat. "He said when the time is right, he plans on taking your blood."

"I was told they already had my blood." I didn't admit the fae had told me this, or that they, also, had my blood.

"They do, for testing purposes, but they want more."

I thought of earlier at Winter's Cove. "He tasted my blood earlier tonight."

Mateo sat up straighter, his eyes sharpening into points. "When? Who?"

"Naburus insisted he have a taste."

Mateo's golden eyes burned the dark, orange color of the sun's rays at sunset. I could practically feel the heat from them against my skin. "He should not be touching you."

Briar glanced at me with a twinkle in her eye and lifted her hand to her mouth, forming the letter O with her lips. How she managed not to say something was beyond me.

I shifted my gaze back to Mateo. "You say that as if I had a choice."

An uncomfortable silence blanketed the room; I hadn't explained to anyone what had happened there.

Mateo just shook his head. "You don't understand." He exhaled a weighted breath. "The Phoenix and Korin don't just want a little bit. They want every last drop."

CHAPTER 20

The room exploded in an array of voices. Through it all I stared at Mateo, and his pained gaze bled into mine. I'd seen that look before. The last time we were together, and he made a vow to meet me on the Teragony Bridge at midnight. We were going to run away together. Leave Korin once and for all.

He never showed up.

Had I known what that look meant, I might never have gone to that bridge. And now, seeing it again, I knew he was helpless to prevent what was about to come. Compelled or not, Mateo would not or could not intervene.

"Enough." My power-infused voice silenced the room. "Korin will not have my blood. We have the upper hand. He doesn't know how we will free the vampires from his control, and we will use that to our advantage. As for the Phoenix, the witches will find the person, and we will destroy him."

I eyed everyone in the room, focusing on the ones I didn't know very well. Owen remained calm, his face a mask of mystery and power. Denise still stood behind Lynx, a wall of grace, but her eyes held a hint of worry. Gerald and Loxley had come back into the room in the middle of the conversation. Loxley looked everywhere but at us. Something about this conversation made her extremely uncomfortable.

"What's the plan?" Briar asked.

If someone in the room was the Phoenix, we would have to be very careful about making plans. "We will decide later. For now, some of us should scout out security at White Pine where Korin is storing the Hydes. We need to know what we're up against."

"I'll go," Angel said. "I know how to find it."

"We'll join you." Luke grabbed Briar's hand, and she nodded.

"Me too." Gerald looked back at Loxley. "Would you like to come?"

She chewed on her lip. "I'm actually going to head back to Fire Ridge. This is out of my league."

Briar walked over to her with Luke. "Actually, I need you to do something for me. When you get there, ask everyone to reach out to shifter packs in neighboring cities. Have anyone call us if they're missing shifters. If they do, write down the names and which pack they're from."

Loxley nodded. "Yes, Alpha."

Angel opened the door, and they all left. Briar cast me an encouraging look over her shoulder before she disappeared outside.

Roma stood, along with Owen. She glanced at Lynx and Denise. "Let's go, too. I'll reach out to the others to meet at the Apex in one hour."

"It's late," Owen warned.

"They'll come. We can't waste any more time."

"Thank you, Roma." I bowed my head slightly. I was glad to have someone like Roma take charge of the witches. They needed someone who had already proven themselves as a leader in the past, someone with a good reputation. Otherwise, like it often did, there could be a play for power among the younger ones. It's how the witches fell the last time, all those years ago.

"I can stay if you'd like," Lynx said to me, her voice low.

"Why would you do that?"

She shifted her weight onto the back of her feet and flicked her gaze to Mateo. "Emotional support."

I chuckled a little. The action felt uncomfortable, and yet, it releases some much needed tension. "I'll be fine."

From the front door, Roma asked, "Are you coming, Lynx?"

She nodded and said goodbye to me, leaving Mateo and I alone. I approached him slowly, noting his occasional grimace. "How are you feeling?"

"It still burns, but I've had much worse."

My eyes flickered to the top of his collar, where I could barely see the sign of the whip marks. "Why were you punished?"

He averted his gaze and adjusted his jacket around him tighter. "It doesn't matter."

"Was it because Korin caught us in my room? Are you supposed to stay away from me because I'm a traitor?"

He didn't say anything.

I crept closer and lowered into a chair opposite him. "Tell me."

"I should go."

Not this again. "Because Korin orders it, or because that's what you want?"

His shoulders lowered, and his eyes mirrored the movement. "Does it matter?"

I waited a few seconds before I responded. "It should. You either believe in me, or you don't. But you cannot pretend to care for me and yet ask me to walk away from this. If you truly knew me, you would know that is impossible. I will not stand by as he tortures those people and attempts to take over this city."

"It is that reason I know you so well that I ask you to leave. You will push him until he does something you cannot take away, and it may be your very life." His eyes grew serious. "I mean it, Samira. He will not stop until you are dead, and he has exactly what he wants."

I jumped out of the chair, indignant. "You forget, Mateo. I am fire, and I am might. It was me who lead the northern realm against the fae invasion of the fourteen-hundreds, and slit the dragon Ravana's throats while he slept, all ten of them, also killing all his royal guard in the process."

"Yes, I remember," he interrupted, standing up, his face red with anger. "I also remember that you were the breaker of my heart, which is much more difficult to overcome than all those things."

I blinked, surprised at his audacity to say that *I* broke *his* heart. Ignoring it, I moved on. "I was Korin's executioner for a reason, and he has yet to see the new me. The stronger me. *He* should be afraid of *me*. And if you cannot support me, then leave." My voice was venomous as I spat my words.

"Samira, you do not know Korin anymore. He has changed, and his powers have grown. I don't even know all he's capable of. I'm not certain he does, either." He stood up slowly, unwilling to look away from me as he came to his feet. "And I will not stand by and let him take you and use you, as he has so many others."

"Mateo," I growled. "I am not leaving Faithe."

"It is already too late for her."

"It is not. I will find a way to protect her."

"I heard her tell you this herself, and I agree with her." He swallowed hard and I knew it cost him to admit to this. "I love Faithe as I loved my own sister, as a daughter, perhaps. But she has chosen her path in life. Your love for her blinds you."

"Just as your feelings for me blind you."

He scowled, as he took a step back. "We will have to agree to disagree on this point. Despite what you think about me, do not doubt I will protect you as much as I am able." He nodded his head slightly. "I bid you good night."

As soon as he was gone, I sucked in a breath and slammed my hand across the back of his chair. It sent both the chair and the table flying, and they crashed against the wall, then clattered to the floor in a great mess of jagged wood. I took in another breath, calming myself by counting down. When I was done, I picked up the broken pieces, studying them. They were easily fixable.

At least I had something to do for the rest of the night. I couldn't let anyone see how my conversation with Mateo had affected me. I'd fix the chair and table, and then I would find a way to resolve the problem with Korin.

And then, the Phoenix.

* * *

I HAD NEVER BEEN MORE glad to be so busy than I had been the last few days. It helped to keep my mind off Mateo. I did regret some of the words I'd said to him, especially since he was right. Korin had new powers, and even before he had them I wasn't certain I could beat him in a battle. I shouldn't fight with Mateo; I needed his help. But it infuriated me that he tried to get me to leave, to stand in for me and not allow me to fight my own battles. I shoved those thoughts away when they crept in.

He was a distraction I didn't need right now. Not when there was so much going on.

Briar and the Silver Claws, with Angel's help, had learned everything they could about security at White Pine, where Korin held supernaturals captive. We also discovered Korin was manufacturing Scorpion's Breath 2.0 there. Briar said the cloud coming out of the building's smokestack reeked worse than Angel's breath after drinking SJ, the name she'd given to Lynx's anti-compulsion potion, short for what she'd originally called it: shit juice. Somehow, and much to my dismay, the name stuck.

Security at White Pine was worse than we feared. Not only were there dozens of Hydes acting as guards surrounding the building, but there were also half a dozen vehicles patrolling a ten-mile loop around the property. From what Briar could gather, these cars had been outfitted with all kinds of weapons. Plus, Briar had discovered magic on the property as well; spells meant to be security. Angel couldn't get close enough to know what kind was being used or what it might do to intruders, just that it was there.

We needed more help, and I knew just who to call upon.

Briar walked in the door at exactly the same moment I walked upstairs from the basement, having just woken up at sunset. Really I hadn't slept. Only laid there in thick blackness on comfortable padding. I'd picked out the nicest coffin I could find when I first came to Rouen. I hated hard bedded coffins, which most were. The dead had no need of comfort, the salesman at the funeral home had told me, laughing even. I assured him, with my strongest predatory glare, they did. I left that funeral home with the nicest coffin the man owned, made special with extra padding added to the inside.

"You received my message." I walked past Briar to the refrigerator and grabbed my thermos of blood. Someone had covered my label with another one that read: "Yummy tomato juice." And beneath it, in smaller letters: "P.S. I promise." I recognized Briar's handwriting.

I didn't give her the satisfaction of acknowledging her new label as I drank down what was left of it. It was salty and cold and left me still hungry. I didn't like that sensation deep in my stomach. The constant ache as sure as the ticking of a clock. Though I was tempted to find a way to ease the ache, I kept it there, never fully satisfying myself. For in that way, I was able to keep the Kiss's darkness from fully rooting itself inside me.

The Kiss of Eternal Night's powers became stronger when it fed on rage, grief, and even gluttony. And the more I indulged those emotions, the more I gave up control to the Kiss, which smothered my humanity.

Detrand had helped me bring it back through much pain and suffering. Now, that constant pain in my stomach served as a reminder. Briar always gave me a hard time for not showing emotions, but one day I might explain to her why I had to keep them to myself. One day she might understand why I refrained from feeling anything the Kiss might take advantage of.

Sometimes, during the day when I lay in my coffin and the house was extra quiet, I could hear the Kiss whispering encouraging words. It wanted me to drink and drink and drink until my stomach could no longer hold all the warm blood. It wanted me to seek revenge toward Mateo for abandoning me. It even wanted me to experience joy like I used to, wild and free.

But I knew the Kiss's tricks. The moment I indulged, it would take over.

"Why did you want me here so early?" Briar asked, eyeing the label on my thermos hard as if to draw my attention to it. I ignored her. I'd been looking for an opportunity to teach her patience. This was the perfect moment.

"We need to go see Eddie."

"My boss? Why would we do that?"

"He might be able to help." I grabbed the keys to my car hanging on a hook near the door.

"Hell, no. We are not involving humans."

I said nothing and walked out the door. Briar continued to complain, even as we drove away from the house. In the beginning, her sarcasm and opinions on everything had grated on all my senses, but lately I welcomed the distraction. I turned on my cell phone, illuminating the notification that Lynx had called, and set it on the center console next to a business card. It was Owen's and bore the Apex symbol.

"Are you even listening, dead-face?" Briar snapped.

I'd learned the more I ignored her, the worst her insults became. I continued to ignore her and turned down Main Street.

"We cannot involve Eddie. Do you understand? Besides, he's not going to be there this early. We're wasting our time."

I passed by the road leading to Sinsual.

She whipped around, watching it pass. "Where the hell are we going?"

I continued to drive, enjoying her growing discomfort.

She slapped the dashboard. "Hey, anemic poser! I asked you a question."

Pulling into a parking lot, I turned off the car. "We're here."

She swiveled in her seat and peered out. "A Chinese restaurant?"

I opened the door and headed inside. It had been a while since I'd been here. Small red paper lanterns hung in rows across the ceiling. Their faint light illuminated a couple dozen tables resting upon cheap linoleum floors. There were a handful of customers in the restaurant. I moved away from them, knowing it was safer.

Briar grabbed my arm and spun me around, her face pinched. "What the hell are we doing here?"

"I'm hungry." I dropped into the nearest chair and looked around, specifically focusing on the rear of the restaurant. I checked the time.

Briar pulled out a chair across from me and sat down. "Are you doing this on purpose?"

"What?" I asked, but I couldn't stop the twitch at the corner of my mouth. I hoped she wouldn't notice but she was too perceptive.

She leaned forward and hissed, "You little shit."

"Just relax and get something to eat. I'll explain everything soon." I tilted my head, curious. "Don't you know where we are?"

She glanced around. "Why would I?"

"You're an Alpha in Rouen. I'd think you'd know all the important places."

She opened her mouth, but closed it when a waitress approached our table. The waitress's brown eyes lit up when she recognized me. "Sweet Samira! You're back. I wondered when I'd see you again."

"Hello, Kuriko. How's Da Chun?"

Briar looked from me to Kuriko, her eyebrows raised.

"Growing like a weed! I can't keep up with her. You want your usual?" She swiped stray hairs away from her face.

"Yes, please, and give Da Chun a hug for me."

Briar's mouth fell open. She managed to collect herself long enough to place her order. As soon as the waitress left, she swung her head back to me. "Who the hell are you? And since when did you give hugs?"

"Children need hugs. I would not deny them something so easy to give, would you?"

She leaned back in her seat and folded her arms. "I don't know you at all."

"No, you don't. And that is a good thing." Part of me spoke the truth. She couldn't know the dark parts of me, how close I constantly hovered to a powerful darkness that could destroy not only me, but everyone around me. And yet, I wished she could know the person I used to be. I mourned that person often, especially since meeting Briar and Lynx. I could see in their eyes what they thought of me. Boring, stuffy, uncaring, unfeeling. All of which wasn't true.

"Tell me about this place," Briar ordered.

I nodded my head back toward a door at the rear of the restaurant. "This is the entrance to the Apex."

"Where the witches meet?"

"Lynx called me earlier saying they have the first batch of SJ ready. She wanted me to come get it and to finally meet the Witches of Rouen. I detected a hint of fear in her voice, so I brought you, just in case. I have a tendency to rub people the wrong way."

She laughed. "And I don't?"

I blinked. "I see what you mean."

"Why the ruse? And why say we were going to see Eddie?"

"Because, Briar, you need to learn patience. And maybe we still are."

"This was a lesson?"

"You are pack Alpha and a Komira. These are powerful positions that require strength, fortitude, and courage, all qualities you have. But they also need patience, gentleness, and the ability to know when to shut up. Sometimes, when you are still, you will discover things you might not have otherwise."

"What truth would I have discovered in this lesson of yours?"

I sighed and told her about my cell phone and the business card. "Little clues, insights into people, are always around you. Be patient and alert and give truth a chance to reveal itself."

"This was a stupid lesson."

Kuriko returned to deliver our food. She set a warm, steaming cup of thick crimson liquid in front of me. This was the closest I'd ever allow myself to come to drinking straight from the vein.

"It smells wonderful," I said. "Thank you, Kuriko."

"Anything for you." She set Briar's plate of rice and chicken in front of Briar. "It's nice to see you with someone, Samira. The heart needs friends."

I bowed my head. "Wise counsel."

After she left, Briar leaned forward. "She knows you're a plasmatarian? How?"

"Have you forgotten my lesson so soon? Look around." I brought the spoon to my mouth and savored the warm blood as it coated my tongue.

She paused, her gaze circling the room. If she was paying attention, she'd spot the small pentagram in the corner of the window. The yellow canary in a cage near the register. The symbol of earth on the door as we walked in. The customers who smelled of jasmine and iron. The cook with a strange, bluish birthmark on his neck in the shape of a snake. Briar might've also noticed the tattoo of a triangle on Kuriko's palm. The signs were everywhere had she been looking.

Her gaze returned to mine, eyes wide. "This place is full of witches."

CHAPTER 21

I didn't give her the satisfaction of showing my pleasure at her answer. "Enjoy your food, Briar. And think about my lesson."

This time, she didn't say anything, and we enjoyed our meal in silence. I hoped she did actually take my words to heart. I feared with what was coming in our future, it would be important for Briar to catch the little details. It was the only way to read people like Korin.

I checked the time on my phone.

She pointed it. "Ha! That's the second time you've checked the time. See? I can pay attention."

"Lynx should be here." I frowned and looked up at the old wooden door at the back. The symbol of fire was etched into its center. It opened just then, and Lynx slipped into the dining room. Her red hair had been straightened and pulled tightly into a pony tail. It made her look different somehow, with long bangs sweeping over the side of her face. The light freckles across the bridge of her nose stood out more than usual, and her green eyes appeared more alive. She even had a little pink patch of a blush on her cheeks, subtle enough that only a vampire would notice. She'd been using magic.

Lynx spotted Briar. Her brows drew together. "Hey, Briar. How come you're here?"

"I wanted her to come," I said. "I hope that's okay."

She forced a smile. "Sure. Come on back, but please, let me do the talking. They are a ... spirited group right now. Not everyone agrees with working with vampires and shifters."

And that's exactly why I brought Briar. As long as she tempered herself, and listened to them, they will see her as a great resource and valuable ally. But there was the secondary reason for Briar's presence. Witches could be dangerous. I needed someone with me who would back me up should there be trouble.

We walked through the opening. As soon as the door closed behind us, the temperature dropped considerably. Behind the door lay the beginning of a metal, spiral staircase.

Briar shivered. "Why is it so cold?"

Lynx glanced over her shoulder as she led the way down. "Magic works better in cooler temperatures."

I'd only been here two other times, nearly forty years ago. The long dark stairway leading two stories below ground smelled the same. Rosewood mingled with animal blood. The last time I'd come here, it had been by force. A group of witches had attempted to recreate the power of the Red Tree Witches, a powerful coven who had existed centuries earlier, and had tried to take over the city. I had been captured while trying to stop them. For two weeks, I remained imprisoned while being forced to endure various means of torture. They wanted the names of those I worked with, but I gave them nothing. However, I had learned valuable information about their coven. Once I had the information I came for, I escaped and told the Ames de la Terra. Within a day, their group was destroyed.

"What are these witches like?" Briar asked. "Are they cool or total bitches?"

I eyed her sideways. "This is one of those times where you shouldn't talk. Take in what you can."

"What Samira said," Lynx added, nodding her head.

Briar groaned, but remained silent the rest of the way. At the bottom of the stairs, we turned down a long hallway. Old lights flickered above us, creating shadows at our feet. A strange tingling began to lift the hair on my arms. We were getting close to the Apex.

At the end of the hall, Lynx turned left and stopped in front of a metal door with a keypad on the side. This was new. She didn't bother shielding herself as she pressed a five digit code into the pad. I memorized the numbers and glanced at Briar to see if she was doing the same. She rolled her eyes at me, mouthing, "Duh."

Beyond the door, a great room opened up with twenty-foot ceilings painted black with witch symbols painted in white strategically placed throughout the room, just as I remembered. In the center of the ceiling, clear glass partially glowed with moonlight. Above the glass, a long tube traveled through the earth and the building above it into a great smokestack, but it never held smoke. Only captured moonlight via a mirror as the moon tracked across the sky.

Scattered across the stone floor, two dozen witches stopped talking at our arrival and faced us. Much to my dismay, I didn't see Roma. I was hoping she'd be here to facilitate a conversation between us. Owen, however was. He stepped apart from the group.

"Welcome to the Apex," he said. He wore a long dark robe, a hood at his back.

The rest of the witches, consisting of both men and women, wore normal street clothes. Several of them eyed us dangerously. I took in what I could about them in case one of them could be the Phoenix. A few of them held the faint outline of guns hidden within their jacket pockets. A few others openly held wooden stakes, which was telling about how much they trusted me. As if they'd get close enough to me to be effective.

Lynx introduced us. "This is Briar, Alpha of the Silver Claws, and this is Samira."

Briar snickered and mumbled to me. "You don't get a title. I'll be happy to inform them that you're a Breaker of Men."

I ignored her. "Thank you for inviting us here to your sacred place. We appreciate your willingness to work with us to stop those who wish to harm this city."

"Who said we wanted to work with you?" a woman said with long black hair. She openly twirled a stake in her hand.

"That must be the bitch," Briar mumbled again.

Lynx shot Briar a dirty look, then looked back at the group. "Like we've already discussed, Amanda, we need to work with shifters, vampires, and whoever else we can to fight Korin and the Phoenix. It's the only way we can prevent what's happening."

Amanda shook her head and looked at the others. "I still can't believe this. How can we even consider working with a Morgan witch? Has everyone forgotten what her ancestors did to ours?"

"That was a different time," Owen said, his voice hard.

"We don't want to cause problems," I offered. "We came for the SJ. It is important to free vampires from Korin's control so they might aid us."

Amanda snorted. "We don't know that they will help."

"Amanda," Owen warned, "enough. This has already been decided. Go grab the SJ."

Amanda tossed her wooden dagger hard across the room. It bounced off the wall and clattered to the floor as she stormed away.

"I thought they wanted to work with us, Lynx," Briar said.

"Most of them do. There's just a lot of bad blood."

Amanda returned, holding a briefcase. She handed it to Owen, then spun on her foot toward us, her hands outstretched. A blast of invisible energy hit all three of us, knocking us to the floor. "I won't let you ruin us again!"

Air exploded from my lungs. I remained down, resisting the urge to jump to my feet and remove her head. Briar began to do just that. I grabbed her arm, keeping her down. "Wait."

Her arm shook under my grip, and I could tell it was taking every ounce of strength not to fight back. Lynx rose to her feet, her eyes alive and pulsing with raw energy. She snapped her hand forward in Amanda's direction. Amanda yelped as her body rose several feet into the air. The other witches in the room gasped and stepped back. Even Owen, for the first time, looked concerned.

Lynx twisted her hand rotating Amanda's body until she was

hanging upside down. Lynx strolled over to her, keeping her right hand in the air.

"Put me down, you crazy bitch!" Amanda shouted. She frantically waved her arms around, probably trying to use her own magic, but she was no match for Lynx.

Lynx brushed her fingers over Amanda's face and across her lips. Amanda's mouth closed tight with magic. "What happened in the past will stay in the past. We have no desire to control witches or harm them in anyway. We only want to find and destroy the Phoenix and men who might be helping him, like Korin. Samira and her vampire friends, Briar and the Silver Claws, are not your enemies. We can help each other. That's all we want. Then, when this is all over, you can go back to living your miserable life wishing you were as powerful as me."

Briar opened her mouth probably to follow up Lynx's words with something sarcastic, but I flashed a look to silence her. This was Lynx's moment and she had to establish herself as a dominant figure among her kind. Someone to be respected. Someone to be feared.

"We want that, too," Owen said.

Lynx stepped to the side of Amanda's dangling body to survey the rest of the group. "Will the rest of you support us or do you want to end up like Amanda?"

Lynx kept her hand up in the air, mentally suspending Amanda in the air. She hid her other hand behind her back. It was shaking.

"We will join you." A woman stepped forward. Several more added their approvals until every one of them was nodding.

"Good," Lynx said. Her gaze shifted back to Amanda. "That leaves just you. Will you be good or do you need to leave town for a while?"

Amanda's mouth became slack. "Fine," she growled.

Lynx snapped her fingers. Amanda fell to the ground with a grunt.

I came to my feet, taking Briar with me. Owen walked over and handed me the briefcase. "There are three dozen ampules inside. They can either be injected or ingested. The user will need a good thirty minutes to recover, so be sure to inform them."

"Thank you. We really appreciate it and will return the favor any way we can."

"Just help us find our missing brothers and sisters. Another one of us came up missing this morning. A girl barely eighteen."

"I knew her," Lynx said, her eyes tearing.

Briar rubbed Lynx's arm. "We'll find her. My pack included. We really do want to help."

Amanda came to her feet and brushed herself off. "One chance. That's all I'm giving you three."

"That's all we need," Lynx answered.

"What can we do to help?" Owen asked.

"We're making plans soon. Lynx will let you know. And thank you for helping. We can't do this without you." I looked from him to the witches. "Without all of you."

Lynx said goodbye to them and led us outside.

"Where was Roma?" Briar asked.

"Trying to convince the rest of the witches to join us." Lynx opened the door leading out of the restaurant. "These were the ones who were interested in what you had to say."

"You mean that wasn't all of them?" She rubbed at her head. "That's a lot of power if we can get them all to agree to help."

"We will," Lynx answered confidently.

I hoped she was right, but I wasn't going to hold my breath. There was too much history between witches and other supernatural species. Too much pain. It would be the perfect group for the Phoenix to blend into and cause strife among us all. I'd have to be more diligent than usual around them.

"You were pretty amazing back there," Briar told Lynx.

"About killed me. My head is pounding."

"Go home and rest." I opened my car door and set the briefcase inside. "You did well tonight, Lynx. And even you, Briar."

She turned to me, her eyes wide. "I did?"

I nodded. "Yes. You managed to keep your mouth shut."

"Oh." She frowned, while Lynx tried not to laugh. "Yeah, yeah, I'm starting to get it."

"Are you two heading home?" Lynx asked, still smiling.

"We have one more stop."

Briar groaned. "I was hoping to have fun tonight with Luke and a bottle of chocolate syrup. Maybe a sausage or two."

Lynx grimaced.

"We have to go see Eddie," I said.

"You were serious about that?" Briar gaped at me. "I told you, we can't involve humans. Tell her, Lynx!"

Lynx laughed, a tired sound. "I'm staying out of it. I'll see you soon."

She walked back toward the restaurant, her head down. Not even a shadow of the person she'd been inside the Apex. A leadership role would be taxing on her, but in time, I didn't doubt she'd rise to the occasion. Once she figured out where all that power inside her came from. Not even I knew the answer to that.

"Get in," I told Briar.

She mumbled a string of curse words, but did as I asked.

I pulled away from the curb. "When we get to Sinsual, I want you to pay attention. Notice the small details. Use all your senses."

"It's a smelly club. I'd rather not."

I said nothing else as we drove back to Sinsual. As her questions went unanswered, she fell into a tense stillness instead of arguing. She was learning.

Adjusting my grip on the steering wheel, I eyed the briefcase at Briar's feet and thought of Faithe. A dark and familiar pain stung my heart. I tried not to entertain it for fear of letting the Kiss spread its poison past my heart and into my mind. Instead, I pushed back against the rage and kept my thoughts to a minimum. If Faithe was being compelled into staying with Korin, then this SJ could change all of that. She could run away far from him, just like she had when I also disappeared all those centuries ago. But would she be safe? He'd found her once before. I doubted Korin would give up. Which left me with only one option.

Kill Korin.

CHAPTER 22

Sinsual was just beginning to get crowded, which I was grateful for, but that was all due to the time. It was barely nine o'clock. Within a couple of hours, this place would be packed with bodies, all ignoring the allotted human capacity sign at the front. Clear negligence on Eddie's part, but I had bigger things to worry about.

Briar and I walked past the bar. A human man called out, "Hey Briar! Give us a show!"

She looked back at me with a hopeful gleam in her eye. I shook my head.

"Maybe later!" she called back to him. To me, she said, "I miss it, you know. The opportunity to just let go and not have anything to worry about, no decisions to make."

"You're Alpha now. That is part of your sacrifice as a leader." I said the words because they were the truth, but I knew how she felt. I couldn't remember what it felt like to let go anymore. Every action I made, and even my thoughts, had to be tempered and well thought-out.

"I'd only admit it to you," she said as we walked up the stairs to Eddie's office, "but sometimes I regret it. Becoming Alpha."

"It can be a heavy burden," I agreed. "That feeling only verifies that it was the right decision. The best leaders do not crave power, but lead because they must."

Briar stopped me before going into the office. "I still don't know what we're doing here. I don't want Eddie to get hurt."

I searched her eyes and knocked on the door. "Do you trust me, Briar? Because that is the real issue here."

She nodded.

"I cannot give you the information you seek because it is not my truth to tell. But pay attention and you may discover something."

Her eyes narrowed just as Eddie's voice said to come in. We entered the room, and I closed the door behind us.

Eddie sat behind his desk, a pen in his hand. He pushed aside a stack of papers. It only took me a few seconds to spot the faint glimmer of light around him, nearly translucent. Eddie wasn't really here. This was a projection of himself. I glanced at Briar, but she didn't see it. Not yet.

Eddie looked from Briar to me. His gaze lingered on mine. "What are you two doing here?"

"Um … " Briar looked at me, waiting for me to answer.

"Did you want to work tonight?" he asked hopefully, looking at her.

"Sorry, but I think my bar dancing days are pretty much over."

He leaned forward, resting his elbows on the desk. "I'm sorry to hear that, but I guess you have more important things to do."

She frowned and looked at me.

"Eddie," I began, "we need your help."

Briar's frown deepened. "Are you about to ask him for a loan? Because I am swimming in my money now."

"Quiet." I looked back at Eddie. "It's time. We found a highly guarded warehouse and need help getting inside."

His mouth tightened, and he leaned back with a thoughtful expression. "We'll need more details."

"We?" Briar glanced from me to him. She narrowed her eyes. "What are you?"

"You haven't told her?" Eddie asked me.

"It's your secret to tell."

Briar shifted her weight. "Told me what?"

He sighed. "I'm fae."

She stared at him and blinked. "Well, butter my ass and call me a biscuit. Why didn't you tell me?"

"Just like you told me you were a shifter?"

She snorted and waved her hand at him, dismissing his indignation. "Good point, fae boss."

He turned to me. "Can you meet me at Black Glen in twenty minutes? I'll meet you out front and escort you in. I want to hear this in person. Folas will want to know as well."

"What the hell is Black Glen? And what do you mean *hear it in person*? You're right here!"

"I'm not. I'm using astral projection."

Briar looked at me, mouth open. "Is he serious?"

"Very. And Black Glen is where fae folk live," I answered. "Let's go."

I turned to leave, but she stopped me.

"Hold up." She walked around the desk and stared at Eddie. "I can see it now. This weird shimmer around you. I've seen it before, but thought it was some kind of spiritual aura thing."

She reached out with a pointed finger and touched his chest. Her finger went right through him.

"Don't do that." Eddie rubbed at his chest. "It feels weird."

"But it doesn't hurt you?"

"No."

"This is the coolest thing ever." She cocked her fist back and punched it through his face. "That's for lying to me."

His face evaporated but then returned to its form. "Briar! You're giving me a headache."

"How long have you known I was a shifter?"

"Since the first day I met you. It was hard not to feel your shifter powers pulsing from you."

"Then you know about the Silver Claws?"

"Of course. I know everything about you. And would like to say that I'm quite happy you quit taking protection money from all the locals."

She grinned and flicked at his head. "You're welcome."

He groaned and rubbed at the back of his neck.

"Are you finished, Briar?" I asked, checking the time. I wanted to make sure I'd have enough time to meet up with Mateo to give him half of the SJ. "We need to go."

She narrowed her eyes at Eddie. "I'll be seeing you real soon."

"I'd love to have a chat about your Komira status sometime." His eyes glowed with mischievousness.

She sighed loudly, brushing her hand through his astral projection as she waved him away.

We left Sinsual, Briar complaining the whole way that Eddie didn't tell her he was fae. I listened for a while, even inside the car, but finally I'd had enough. "This is on you. You should've noticed he was different."

She flopped her head back into the headrest. "It's barely noticeable!"

"But it is noticeable. These are the small details I need you to pick up on. It could save your life someday, maybe even other's lives."

She dropped her head to the side, looking at me. "This is that important to you?"

"Of course! Have you not thought about the Phoenix being able to change forms? He could be anyone around us. We need to look at everyone with an eye of scrutiny. Notice every little detail, something that might give away his identity."

"I guess I never considered that." Her voice was quiet, and she remained silent, deep in thought, all the way to the park.

After I parked, I exited the car with Briar at my side and walked to the front entrance. Moonlight just barely illuminated the tops of the trees. If it weren't for nearby lampposts, we'd have been bathed in darkness.

I squinted my eyes, just barely detecting a faint shimmering in the air. "What do you see?"

Briar stared into the park. This time, instead of questioning me, she focused her gaze, and I felt a burst of power pulse outward from her. "Something is different here. I feel power, lots of it. And the air ... it's almost like I can see the hum of electricity within in it. But that can't be possible, right?"

I smiled, proud of her. I knew she was strong enough to notice the details; she just needed to allow herself those quiet moments to spot them.

In a low voice, I breathed the same words, in Eddie's native tongue, he had spoken last time we were here.

Briar stared at me with wonder on her face. "What language was that, and what did you just say?"

"It's the language of the ancient fae. 'By the moon's light upon the floor, reveal the secret, open the door.'"

"Door?"

I motioned my head toward the park. Briar slowly turned and jumped when she saw rows and rows of houses and shops appear before her. "Is this Black Glen?"

I nodded and walked toward it. "Come on."

It took her a moment to follow after me. She didn't say anything for a long time as we weaved our way through the numerous houses and shops, bustling with different fae folk who all seemed to have a destination, despite the late hour. This had to be the first time in her life Briar was speechless.

I checked the time. Twenty minutes was nearly up. I circled back to the entrance to meet Eddie. I wanted to give Briar time to take in what she could about the fae, and I also wanted Eddie to know I could get in here without him, something he would surely report to Folas. I didn't want them to underestimate me. *Ever.*

We stood just inside the entrance staring outward at the street. A man on a bicycle peddled past completely unaware of the great city bustling just to the side of him. Eddie was there, looking up and down the street wearing a tight t-shirt and jeans. I noted the top of a pitch-fork tattoo peeking out the top of his shirt. It looked similar to the one Folas had on his arm.

"Eddie!" Briar called.

He turned around and frowned when he saw us. He searched beyond us and hurried over. "How did you get in?"

"Easy," I answered.

Briar punched him in the shoulder.

He flinched and rubbed at his arm. "What was that for?"

"Just want to make sure it's really you."

"Where's Folas?" I asked him. I wanted to get this over with. I was anxious to return to Winter's Cove.

"Up at Warwick. We'll go there now."

While we traveled to the center of Black Glen, Briar asked Eddie all sorts of questions about the place. I listened in. Most of the information was useless, but I did learn the fae "moved" Black Glen to Rouen nearly two hundred years ago. This surprised me. That meant they had been here for the witch's wars. It made me wonder how involved they had been. Secrets had been revealed about the Ames de la Terra's movements in taking out the witches, and I had never uncovered how they had been revealed. The information had made us almost lose the war.

"This is Warwick Castle," Eddie said at the gates to the grand estate. "Our King and Queen live here. They've been ruling for the last five hundred years."

He walked inside and circled around the back like before.

Briar reached out and touched a purple rose petal in passing. It shimmered beneath the moonlight. "This place is amazing. Can I show Luke sometime?"

"No," both Eddie and I said at the same time.

He whirled around, his expression dark. "It will put his life at risk, do you understand?"

Her eyebrows lifted. "What about my life?"

He glanced back over his shoulder and looked high up at a tower, almost as if he was afraid someone was watching us, but I saw no one. "You are an Alpha and a Komira. That gives you certain clout among my kind, but if you were ever to reveal our secret without our permission, there would be severe consequences. And Briar," he leaned toward her conspiratorially, "we have eyes and ears everywhere in Rouen."

"What about dicks?" She grinned but when he didn't respond, she swallowed. "Fine. Message received. And what about Sammie? This isn't the first time she's been here."

He snorted. "She's been gifted with the Kiss of Eternal Night. She can pretty much do whatever the hell she wants."

Briar gaped at me. In an uncharacteristic move, I winked at her and began walking after Eddie.

"Hey!" she called after me. "Don't do normal things! It freaks me out."

If only she knew. In another life, Briar and I could've raised hell together.

We had just reached the stone archway when Eddie stopped. A tall and lean figure walked toward us, his head down. As he drew closer, Folas looked up, moonlight illuminating every dark shadow of his angular face. His eyes, dark before, now glowed an eerie blood red.

Eddie's body grew tense. "Is something wrong?"

"The King and Queen want to meet our guests."

"I don't think that's necessary," I protested. Meeting the King and Queen of the fae could prove more risky than helpful. They were known for being self-serving with big tempers.

His sharp eye moved towards me. "Unfortunately, I am unable to help you unless the King and Queen give their approval. I'm sorry."

I looked away, frowning, but not surprised. I'd garnered their attention. It probably had something to do with my blood. Folas' gaze roamed to Briar. "Who are you?"

"This is Briar," Eddie said quickly, as if that was all the explanation he needed.

Folas's chin lifted, and he leaned forward a little to inhale her. "I've been wanting to meet you."

"I can't say the same."

He studied her for a moment and opened his mouth like he wanted to say something, but Eddie interrupted him. "Shall we go through the front entrance then?"

Eddie didn't wait for a response. He turned and the rest of us followed. I eyed Folas as we walked, noting how he studied Briar. He had already taken a sample of my blood. Would he want one of hers as well? Somehow, I needed to gain the upper hand against him. I had a feeling he would surprise me with his true motives at an inopportune time.

Eddie walked up the steps until he reached tall silver doors etched with all kinds of fae symbols. I recognized many of them, but not all. I'd only lived with fae folk for a short time in the fourteenth century, just long enough to learn their language and culture. It had been invaluable knowledge when we fought against their invasion. Knowledge is everything in war.

Leaning forward, Eddie exhaled a deep breath onto the vertical crack between the two doors. The doors slowly swung open, revealing a grand entryway filled with white light. The bright color was everywhere. White marble floor, white walls, a chandelier filled with white candles that burned, not yellow and orange, but with white flames. The color reflected through the many glass statues throughout the room. Several were as tall as Folas. Sculptures of men and women, frozen in time. The only other colors in the room were found in the garden paintings hanging on the walls.

"Should I take off my shoes?" Briar whispered.

Neither Eddie or Folas responded. They just stood silently, so we did the same. A few seconds later, a maid with long white hair and wearing a short white dress appeared, her frame thin and waif-like. "How may I help you?"

"We're here to see the Queen and King," Folas said. "On their orders."

She lowered her head. "They're waiting for you. Right this way."

She glided across the shiny floor, her feet barely skimming the surface. It wasn't until we started walking that I realized Briar's footsteps made no sounds. Neither did mine. It was as if the room absorbed all noise. It was an odd sensation, like dreaming while being awake. I glanced over at Briar, meeting her gaze. She seemed to be feeling the same thing.

The woman with white hair floated down a wide hall straight ahead. Her hair lifted into the air like spider's silk to a breeze I couldn't feel. On each side of us, vibrant paintings depicted beautiful creatures I'd never seen before, all happy and dancing in ornate gardens. The colors of the flowers and plants were some of the most vivid I'd seen, and yet, in each one, a storm brewed in the distant landscapes, angry and dark. Veiled threats seemed to be everywhere in this bright place.

At the end of the hall, the slight wisp of a woman turned right and stopped. She motioned us toward a glowing light at the end of the hall.

"It's warm in here," Briar whispered. She removed her jacket.

Eddie stopped. "This is as far as I can go. Folas will see you the rest of the way. Pay attention, ladies."

Briar and I shared a wary glance. What had we gotten ourselves into?

CHAPTER 23

olas nodded farewell to Eddie and continued onward. Briar and I followed reluctantly behind. I knew very little about the King and Queen of Black Glen, other than what I'd overheard in whispered corners over the years. They'd won their titles in a great battle fought in Europe. Their victory had united several fae communities, a feat none had seen for over two thousand years. It made me wonder what kind of people they were to illicit such a following. They either led by fear or love, but not both.

As we walked, the light grew stronger and stronger until I had to shield my eyes. Briar did the same. But a few steps later, the light appeared at our backs. It was like we had walked through a wall of light separating the other part of the castle from this—I looked around—great throne room. This area was just as bright but had more color, more blues and greens, yellows and oranges all painted into the walls and ceiling in great swirls that appeared to be moving in gentle circles. The pattern shifted all at once and the lines sharpened and reversed, pointing in our direction as if they were watching us.

"Come," Folas said.

"What the hell?" Briar breathed, looking around in awe.

"Stay alert," I warned, focusing in on those lines that moved with us. Some of them crowded together, briefly forming what looked like little animals with beady eyes, but just as quickly the lines would untangle and move along the walls toward the front of the room.

I followed their direction, my heart racing, something it didn't do often. I slowed my breathing and made myself become detached from the situation, almost clinical.

Rows of people stood on the side of the room, silently staring at us as we passed. Two figures sitting on thrones in the front of the room came into focus almost as if the light above them had been shielding them until just the right moment.

The man on the left perched on a black-and-gold throne etched in thorns and red roses. It was padded with extra thick and billowy cushions, magical and seamlessly sewn into the throne, complete with an attached leg rest, giving it a modern, La-Z-Boy recliner feel. He filled it, and then some, with his blubberous body.

His dark blue shirt barely fit him; buttons stretched to the max. A white cape wrapped around him and spilled to the floor. Dark and full hair looked like it had been dropped on top of his head with no regard as to where it should lay. Parts of it covered his forehead, but the other half looked like it had been swept back too many times by chubby fingers. His thick legs were spread wide and squished beneath a black skirt. I'd seen a few other men in Black Glen wearing similar skirts. It must be an old custom some of the men clung to.

To the right of the King, sat a woman just as distended, lazily reclining in a similar throne. Her stomach was so far bloated that it jiggled in protest like Jell-O at a kid's birthday party as she struggled to sit up. Her dress, made of green and purple velvet with puffy sleeves and a long train, stretched over her body. A walrus could've worn the gown better.

Folas bowed low in front of them. From the corner of my eye, I spotted Briar looking at me as if to see if I would bow, too. I remained upright. They were not my King and Queen, nor would they ever be. Briar followed my example and straightened taller.

"Your majesties," Folas began, "May I introduce to you, Samira,

179

bearer of the Kiss of Eternal Night, and Briar, Komira and Alpha of the Silver Claws pack."

The King reached for a tray near his throne and scooped up a large green grape from off its top. He bit into it. Juice ran down his chin. He rotated his fat head toward his wife and sighed. "What do you say, dear? Should we kill them just to see if we can?"

Briar lowered into a defensive position, her hand nearing the blade in her boot. I also adjusted my stance, wishing I would've brought my swords.

Folas cleared his throat. "They've come to help solve our problem with Korin."

The Queen eyed us greedily, picking at her teeth with a sharp bone. "They don't look all that interesting to me." She turned back to the king. "I say we put them in the ring, Haemen. Let them fight each other to the death. The one who comes out the winner gets to leave with her head intact."

I took a step in front of Briar, a protective move, even though Briar had no need of it. "We come in peace and are only looking for help to stop Trianus from rising."

Haemen's throne shook as he struggled to sit up. After two attempts, and failing, he growled. His leg rest moved in a slow motion, magically folding back into his chair as the back of it came forward, pushing the king upwards.

Folas kept his posture submissive, but his eyes darted to the crowd a few times. I followed his gaze, searching through the throes of people to where his eyes landed. Then I saw her.

She was the most beautiful woman I'd ever encountered. A thin but muscular frame and long golden hair lay in loose curls all around her shoulders. She was dressed differently than the others, more modern but also very regal for a woman of lower status. She wore a long, form-fitting white gown with sleeves that reached her wrists into the shape of a point. Just above the swell of her breasts rested a giant diamond pendant, reflecting all the white light in the room into an array of colors, some I didn't recognize.

And her eyes were staring right at me.

I blinked, twisting my head back to Haemen. After what felt like several awkward moments, his chair finally positioned itself upright. Instead of standing, he leaned forward, leering at us.

I wondered if his legs would even hold him, but I maintained a polite, but alert, posture. Fae glamour was meant to deceive, and he could probably be at me instantly, a dagger in my stomach, if he so desired. Haemen's eyes wandered over us for a moment, then slid over to Folas where his gaze lingered, his cheeks flushing briefly. He blinked and licked his lips before he drew his attention back to us. "Let them kill each other."

At the wave of his hand, our clothes transformed into white fighting leathers. We both held a long, sharp knife in our hands. I could strike out at Briar in an instant, before she even knew what to expect, but I wouldn't. I wasn't fooled by their charade.

"No. I refuse to fight her." I threw my knife to the ground.

His lips twisted up in a sneer. "Then you have just forfeit your life."

"I don't think so." I held out my hand to Briar, who placed her own knife in it. In the blink of an eye, I stood behind Folas, my knife at his throat. "Tell me, how much is the life of your lieutenant worth?"

"Calm yourself, vampire," a gentle voice said. The woman from the crowd stepped forward, her hands clasped together at her waist. She was tall, having several inches on me. Her ice blue eyes held a calculated, intelligent look as she strode towards us. Both Briar and I moved at the same time, ensuring that the king, the queen, and the new fae woman was in our line of sight.

Her eyes never strayed from the blade at Folas' throat as she came near me. "You say you want to work with us. We've had outsiders come to us in the past with similar motives, but in the end, each species serves their own kind. Why should we think you are any different?"

"I can't speak about the past," I began, my hand still tight on the knife and Briar close to my back, protecting it, "but we all want the same thing. To stop Korin and the Phoenix from bringing Trianus back from the dead."

Haemen snorted, his eyes tight and ever shifting to Folas. "Our kind can take care of those beasts just fine, when the time is right. You are a fool for indulging them, Oona."

"Perhaps." Oona stopped in front of us. "But they intrigue me. Why go after Folas instead of taking the opportunity to fight their way out or killing each other?" She said the last part without any emotion, as if it would mean nothing for me to kill Briar.

"Because he seems to be the most valuable fae in the room," I answered. "Wanted not only by the King, but—" I loosened my hold over Folas and took a step back, bending slightly in a polite bow and lowering my hand, my palm out, offering her the knife. "also by the Queen."

Briar gasped, her face snapping towards the woman, her eyes wide. The woman on the throne disappeared in a puff of smoke and Folas glared at me hatefully. But the woman, the real Queen of the Fae, only held my gaze with an amused expression.

"You are swift and observant." Her nose wrinkled. "But I have yet to determine if your motives are altruistic or not." She turned to Briar, eyeing her up and down. "As for you, I don't like what you're wearing. It's too rough for such a beautiful face."

Briar narrowed her eyes. "I don't know whether to say thank you or punch you in the face."

"You'll do neither. It's beneath your status." She snapped her fingers. Briar's body glimmered, and in the next second, her fighting leathers transformed into a long black gown, cut so low in the front, her breasts nearly burst from the thin material.

Haemen grunted then chuckled, relaxing now that Folas was safe. His eyes roved over Briar's body. He reached for several more grapes, shrugging. "Eh."

"Whoa," Briar gasped, staring down at her dress. "Nice rags, but not really my thing."

Oona, the Fae Queen, ignored her and approached me. "I can feel your power, different from the wolf. Yours is darker. More dangerous than hers. By the shadows in your eyes, you know how deadly you are, correct?" She narrowed her eyes. "Your glasses are an interesting touch. You have no need of them. Why do you wear them?"

"I'd like to discuss our plans," I said, trying to avoid Briar's questioning eyes. She didn't need to see or know the dark side of me.

Oona's slender finger brushed my cheek, leaving an icy coolness in its wake. "Such control you have! I wonder, what would happen if you unleashed the Kiss's sweet poison?"

I leaned forward to stare into her eyes, summoning just a hint of it to the surface. "You don't want to know."

She visibly shivered.

"Have you heard enough, my Queen?" Haemen asked, looking bored. He adjusted his weight, trying to lean forward, but in doing so, he had to spread his legs wider, exposing himself fully to us.

"Holy purple cocktapus," Briar breathed, her face paling.

Oona spun around toward Haemen. "I have not had enough. Not even close."

Haemen groaned and wiped his face with the back of his hand. "Send them away or kill them. We don't need their kind in our palace. They are stinking up the place."

"Your majesty, please," Folas began, but the King interrupted him.

"Can you or can you not do your job?" he roared. "Must you rely on help from a blood sucker and a mutt?"

Both Briar and I bristled. While Folas explained to him our importance, Oona returned her attention to us. She ran a finger up Briar's arm and hooked it into the top strap. She pulled it down slowly, seductively, nearly pulling it off, but stopped just short of it.

"I like your body," she said to her. "You're soft in all the right places."

"That's what I hear," Briar answered.

Oona turned to me. "And you. Your body is hard, but I feel heat burning through your veins."

"Enough!" Haemen yelled at Oona. "Leave. All of you."

"I want them," Oona said, eyeing Briar and me. "For the evening."

"I can't stay," I blurted, flustered by the sudden turn of events. I had things to do, not be some fae Queen's plaything.

Haemen chuckled. "My Queen gets what she wants. Go with her and if she's satisfied by sunrise, you may just leave with your life."

"I will not—"

Briar grabbed my arm hard, silencing me. "We'll go. It could be fun, the three of us."

Folas glanced from me to her, his mouth turned down. By the hesitant look in his eye, he hadn't expected this either.

"Then it's settled. Follow me." Oona gracefully turned and guided us toward the wall to the side of us. I thought it was a dead end, but as she approached, a section of the wall slid back, revealing another hallway. I glanced back at Folas and Haemen. The King burped and shoved more food into his mouth, leering at Folas, who just stared after us.

My heart was heavy as I continued onward. What were we doing? I couldn't have some tryst with my roommate and a fae Queen. What was Briar thinking? What was I thinking following after them?

I needed to get out of here and quickly.

CHAPTER 24

I glanced to the sides, searching for an exit, but we only passed closed doors. I didn't dare escape through one in case it was a dead end.

Briar glanced back at me, smiling, a twinkle in her eye. I found nothing humorous about our situation.

Almost at the end of the hall, Oona opened a door and motioned us into a large, richly decorated room with silvers and blues, set onto a backdrop of flat black. Glass sculptures of gnarled and twisted trees grew in the corners of the room. It reminded me of a frozen forest trapped beneath a starry night.

Briar closed the door and walked seductively toward Oona. "Where do you want me? On my knees or on the vampire?"

I choked on the growing saliva in my mouth.

Oona and Briar stared at each other and both their lips curled up into smiles. Then they glanced at me and both burst into laughter.

"You should see your face!" Briar cried, holding her stomach and pointing at me.

I looked back and forth at each one of them, truly stunned. "I don't understand."

Briar wiped at a tear at her eye and, in a mock voice that I gathered was supposed to sound like me, said, "Stop talking, Briar. You must be observant and pay attention to the little details."

"That's not how I sound."

Oona's face relaxed into a comfortable smile, watching us carefully. "I take it the student has become the teacher?"

"Hell, yeah, I did." Briar strutted across the room to me and slapped me on the back. "You totally thought we were going to have a threesome, didn't you?"

"I, well, I," I stuttered, blood heating my face. "Didn't you?"

"Nah. I've had enough people want me that I know what desire looks like. Her body," she glanced over at Oona, "which is amazing, by the way, was doing all the right things, but the look in her eye was saying 'get-me-the-hell-away-from-this-disgusting-free-baller'. Am I right?"

"You pretty much ... how do you say it? Nailed it?" Oona walked over to a white leathered chair and gracefully sat down. "Join me, please. We have so much to discuss."

Briar hurried over and jumped on a sofa, stretching her legs long. Her black dress bunched at her hips and barely covered her thighs. "Could I get my street clothes back? This is super uncomfortable."

"Just an illusion." Oona snapped her fingers, and Briar's jeans and tank top returned.

I inhaled a breath and slowly exhaled as I joined them, sitting in an identical chair as Oona. Unlike Briar, I actually liked the leathers. They easily adjusted to my movements and were more comfortable than the ones I usually wore. Except ... I looked at Oona. "I actually prefer black."

"No problem." In an instant, they were black. I took a moment to admire them, while recomposing myself. Very rarely was I taken off guard like that, but clearly I was lacking in the sexual desire arena. It made me wonder how much of Mateo I had misread.

"I apologize for the ruse," Oona said, swiping long curls away from her shoulder. "But the King only understands two things: food and sex. I have to use both quite frequently to get what I want."

"And what is it you want?" I asked.

"I heard what you said about Trianus, and Folas has told me the same. I was there when Trianus came the first time. It nearly destroyed our species. We cannot let him rise again."

Briar sat up. "The King doesn't feel the same way?"

"He thinks we are stronger now, and we are, but this time is different. I can feel it. Korin's involvement is making it worse. I've seen the creatures he's created out of supernaturals. He cannot be allowed to continue. It could create something worse than Trianus."

"I don't know about that," Briar said. "They're terrible, but killable."

Oona raised her eyebrow. "How do you think Trianus was created in the first place? Creatures evolve, become more than the original intent of the maker." When Briar didn't answer her, she continued. "Folas will be instructed to help you in whatever ways you need. Just ask."

Her eagerness to help us worried me. We'd only just met. "Thank you for the offer, but wouldn't you like to be involved?"

"The safety of my people is my most pressing concern. It won't be too long before we are effected, no matter what the King thinks. And yet, I am bound to his command." She shrugged, as if there was nothing else she could do about it.

"Have you tried talking to him about it?"

"I am highly skilled in reading people. I know when to press him, and when to wait." She paused, giving me an assessing stare. "The moment I met you two, I felt, not only your power, but I sensed your hearts. You chose not to fight, but to analyze the room for our weakness instead. A wise choice. You are both strong and want good, but you also battle darkness."

"Isn't that bad?" Briar asked.

"Not when the desire to shun the power is there." She gave Briar a small smile, holding her hand to her chest, over where her heart pounded. "All of us have darkness inside of us. You'd be surprised how many entertain those dark, rhythmic heartbeats when they think no one is watching. And yet, I don't feel that with you two. You abhor it, but also accept it." She paused, tilting her head to the side and dropping her hand. "Although, I must admit, there's something missing. A piece to the two of you. Is there another?"

Briar and I looked at each other.

I turned back to Oona, thinking of the prophecy. "Lynx, a witch."

Oona's eyebrows lifted and she smiled. "She is the sun to your moon and stars."

Briar nodded. "That about sums her up."

"I heard of a prophecy once," Oona began, her eyes lifting to the silver ceiling, "that spoke of three powerful sisters who would be involved with Trianus somehow. I can't recall it, but I wonder if it was about you three."

"A prophecy?" Briar exclaimed. "About me? That's so badass."

I stood up, not wanting to discuss the prophecy right now. It was one that, in my mind, would never come to fruition. I'd give my life to make sure that happened. "Do you trust Folas?"

She nodded. "The fae will always be concerned with our own interests firsts, we do not hide this fact. But he is trustworthy. He will not steer you wrong."

I nodded, tucking this little bit of information away. I was still uncertain if we could trust her, but for now, I would. "When can we meet with him? I'd like to discuss plans with him right away. We recently discovered where Korin keeps his monsters and must act quickly to stop him."

"Of course." She rose with me and led us to the corner. As she approached, a small section of the wall sunk back. "Follow this to the end. It leads to Folas's study. You'll find him there."

Briar flashed her a knowing look. "You and Folas having a sordid affair?"

"Not this week." She winked at Briar.

Briar laughed. "I like you. We should hang out more. I bet you have lots of cool shit in this palace."

She laughed a beautiful, sweet sound. "I do. When this is all over, I'd love to show you all of my amazing 'shit.'"

She turned to me, her expression tightening, and placed her hand over my heart. "Your darkness is raw and growing. I believe you will overcome it, but I'm not sure you believe you can. Your fear may have severe consequences."

I lightly grabbed her wrist and lowered it. "I've been managing just fine for centuries."

She tilted her head, analyzing me again with those cool eyes. "But something's changed."

"Her ex is in town," Briar said as she unwrapped gum from its silver package and popped it into her mouth. "But don't worry. I'll make sure he doesn't break her heart again. If he tries, I'll break him."

She said this with such passion that it surprised and touched me. "Thank you Briar—I really mean that—but I can handle myself." I sighed. "Let's go. I have other things to do tonight." I shifted my gaze to Oona, but only let our eyes meet briefly. Her insight into my soul was unnerving, reminding of Sersi. "Thank you for your assistance."

She bowed her head in acknowledgment. While Briar said her goodbyes, I jogged down the steps, anxious to see Folas. If I didn't go over to Winter Cove early enough, I'd get stuck there for the day, something I didn't want to do.

Briar caught up to me, popping a gum bubble in her mouth. "I really dig that Oona chick."

"She needs to mind her own business."

"I rather liked her insights into your heart. And if what she says is true, you need to be careful. Or at least talk to me or Lynx about it. Don't bottle that shit up. I know first-hand how quickly things can spiral."

"I appreciate your concern, but I'm fine." I stopped in front of a wooden door and knocked quickly. Too many personal conversations in a short amount of time had me on edge. I took a quick moment to calm my pulse and clear my head. By the time Folas opened the door, I was a mask of control.

"Oona said you'd help us." I walked past him into a small room decorated in rich reds and dark mahoganies, the complete opposite of the rooms we'd just left. Briar joined me.

189

"I will, but we must keep our movements as secret as possible. The King cannot find out. I hoped he would see reason, but too many years of peace have made him soft."

"And fat," Briar mumbled.

Folas gave her a sharp eye, but said, "What do you need from us?"

And here came the tricky part. I searched his eyes hoping to spot any kind of deceit.

"We found where Korin is creating his supernatural army," Briar blurted, clearly not concerned about Folas being the Phoenix. "But it's heavily guarded."

"We cannot fight," he said quickly. "The King will find out."

"That's not what we need," I clarified.

Briar frowned. "Isn't it?"

"What we need are your powers of illusion. If you can provide this, then the shifters and vampires, maybe even some witches—"

Briar snorted as if that was entirely out of the realm. I still held out hope they would come together.

"—will infiltrate Korin's building and rescue who we can. We have received word that there are many supernaturals being held there who haven't been changed yet."

He nodded his head, a thoughtful look in his eye. "We can do illusions. I'll choose my best men."

"If I may," I said, "we need to keep this operation to as few people as possible. As you know, the Phoenix could be anyone. We must be careful."

"I understand. I'll choose wisely. When will you need us ready?"

"When can you be ready?" Briar asked.

He thought about this. "I'd like to see the place ahead of time to know what we're up against and to choose the right kind of illusion. The wrong one and Korin will see right through it."

"I can take you there," Briar said. "Tonight?"

His eyes looked toward the ceiling as if he could see through to the King. "I can do that, but let me get word to the Queen in case the King asks for me."

While he circled to his desk and scribbled on paper, I turned to Briar, keeping my voice low. "I need to take the SJ to Winter's Cove." Ideally, I should take it to the Sangre Nocturnas, but I was being selfish. I wanted to try and get it to Faithe, Teddy and Kristina. They needed it more than the Nocturnas. They were under his control much stronger than the Nocs, plus they would probably have more information we could use.

"Will you have time to get some to the Nocs?"

"Possibly," I nodded, thinking. It was a hard choice, to decide who to give the SJ to first. "Or if Mateo is there, I can give it to him to pass along."

She grabbed my arm. "Be careful around him. I can tell he has strong feelings about you, but something's holding him back. Whatever it is, I fear it will end up hurting you more than him."

"I'll be careful, but so must you." I lowered my voice. "Things aren't always what they seem in this place, including the people."

Folas straightened, holding the paper in his hand. He crumbled it, mumbled a few words, then tossed it upward. What looked like a mouth on the ceiling opened up and swallowed the note. "Let's go."

Outside of Warwick, we met up with Eddie again. Briar would ride with him and Folas to Fire Ridge, where they would pick up Gerald and Luke, who knew the most about White Pine. With nothing left for me to do, I parted ways and drove to Winter's Cove, my hand on the briefcase, and my mind on Faithe. Briar assumed the restless darkness inside me stemmed from Mateo, and maybe some of it did, but most was because of Faithe. Even beyond Mateo, she was the only thing that mattered to me in this life. There was nothing I wouldn't do for her, including giving my own life. I prayed I could convince her to take the SJ and flee Korin once and for all. And while she was away, I would devote the rest of my life to hunting and killing Korin.

It was nearly one in the morning by the time I reached Winter's Cove. I emptied half the ampoules into the car and took the rest. Moonlight reflected off the silver trim of the great mansion. Pressure squeezed my chest as I walked up the stairs.

Gripping the briefcase in my hand, I pushed open the door and tensed just as I sensed someone standing behind it.

A hard fist crashed into my jaw, followed by two people flanking each side of me. They gripped my arms tightly.

Michael stepped away from me with a smug smile. "Just the bitch I've been waiting for."

CHAPTER 25

I sucked in a breath and fought against them haphazardly while I dropped the case and subtly kicked it to the side. My vision slowly began to clear.

"Take her to the dungeon," Michael ordered and let us pass. "And take her phone."

I glanced sideways at those holding me. I didn't know the name of the vampire on my right, but I'd seen him before. It was the silver-eyed one who had been at Sinsual with Silas. Teddy held my left arm, his eyes downcast.

"Teddy?"

"Sorry, Sam. I don't have a choice." He reached into my pocket and removed my cell phone. So Teddy was compelled, of course.

"Don't speak to her!" Michael called after us.

Just before they dragged me through the door to the basement, I glanced near the front door. The briefcase was partially concealed beneath a small table. I hoped no one noticed it.

The dungeon must be the oldest part of the mansion. The air held a tangy, moldy smell that only centuries worth of blood-soaked floors and walls could give. Korin loved the scent and had always refused to have any of his dungeon's cleaned. He said it added to one's suffering to see rusted bars, dirt floors, old torture devices.

"Why are you doing this?" I jerked back a little, but not anywhere near my full strength. That would be saved for later. Korin obviously suspected me of something. I had to know what and if my friends might be in danger, too.

"You'll find out soon enough," the silver-eyed vampire said to me.

Teddy held my arm gently. "Korin will visit you soon."

"And what's your name?" I said to the dark-haired vampire.

"That's Zane," Teddy offered quickly. "He joined us a decade back."

"Shut your mouth," Zane snapped.

I studied Zane from the corner of my eye. The way his gaze stay focused up ahead, the surety of his steps, his flexed jaw. This was a vampire who was sure about his place in the coven, strange for someone so new. Also odd I'd seen him with Silas. Could he be the Phoenix? Maybe plans between Korin and the Phoenix had been in place longer than I thought. I always assumed it was a recent merge, but that, I realized, was a foolish thought. Korin had never made moves without calculating for years, decades often. He didn't make decisions lightly.

We reached the bottom of the stairs, three levels beneath the mansion, to a small area that barely held three cells. Two lightbulbs hanging from the ceiling attempted to fill the space with light, but their efforts were in vain. Too many shadows, too many unseen ghosts, overwhelmed the small room.

When Zane briefly let me go to open the cell door, I whispered in Teddy's ear no louder than a breath, "Get the briefcase. Hide it, then drink it when it's safe and share with those on our side. It will break the compulsion."

He nodded once.

Zane turned around. "Get in."

I did as he said, reminding myself not to breathe. They left me alone, Teddy casting me a sorrowful look as the door closed behind them.

I approached the metal bars, my mind racing. Korin must've found something out about me. Maybe he'd seen witches at my house, or any of the others, for that matter. He never liked mingling with other species. He said it made us weak. But he knew he didn't own me anymore. Maybe he wanted information.

Sniffing the bars, I detected holy water, recently applied. I ground my jaw together and gripped the bars tight. I pushed outward, my palms smoking. The pain was sharp and immediate, but I continued to push until I felt the old metal began to break. I let go, gasping. This cell couldn't hold me.

The thought comforted me as I lowered onto a turned-over bucket. I'd stay here as long as necessary to find out what Korin wanted. I hoped this also gave Teddy enough time to take the SJ and also give it to Kristina and anyone else who wanted it.

The door leading to the dungeon creaked open. I came to my feet, expecting to see Korin, but instead, Faithe glided in. The shadows in the room seemed to attach themselves to her as she descended the steps. My heart picked up, then slowed to a near stop when I caught her pained expression as her eyes studied the walls and she smelled the terrible scents. That's when I remembered. Faithe had been imprisoned in a place similar for weeks before her captors had killed her adopted human mother. I wished I could take the pain from her. I'd tried once. And I would keep trying until I succeeded.

Her long black dress reached the floor, its silky edges dragging through the dirt as she walked towards me. She looked up at me, her pink eyes meeting my gaze. Her long white hair had been twisted up into a loose bun. "I didn't know he was going to do this."

I approached the bars, my chest aching. "I didn't think you would."

Her hands rubbed at her arms. "I hate this place."

"I know. You should go." I didn't like seeing her here, the dungeon of all places.

Her eyes met mine, pain radiating from them. "I've done terrible things, *Moeder*."

"We all have." I reached through the bars for her, trying to comfort her, but my hand met with empty air.

"Can you ever forgive me?" her words came out an appeal, the desperate plea of someone who had no hope, but wanted it.

"Always." Emotions crowded my chest, widening a shallow crack in my heart. Darkness bled out. I breathed in slowly, willing it back, willing the tears stinging my eyes to remain in their dark holes.

Her eyes closed as if she couldn't stand to keep them open any longer. "I don't like being here, but I have nowhere else to go. I'm an outcast. A monster in a world of beautiful creatures, but Korin accepts me for who I am."

I stepped forward, anger bordering on rage filling my entirety. "Korin is using you. And you are not a monster! You never have been."

"Then why do I feel this," she clawed at her chest, her eyes opening, "this ugliness inside me? It's eating me from the inside out, and I fear there will be nothing left soon."

"That's what he does! He wants you to feel worthless so he can control you." I gripped the bars, but recoiled when I felt the holy water's sting again. "You have to leave this place, Faithe."

"I can't."

"Because he's compelled you to stay?" I gauged her reaction, any small detail to give away what I already believed to be true.

She wrinkled her nose at the suggestion. "Why would he have to compel me? This is where I belong."

My legs weakened when I saw and felt the truth to her words. The others may have been compelled, but she hadn't. Her pupils hadn't fluctuated, her lips hadn't tightened. She was here, with Korin, of her own free will.

"Faithe, please. You have to get away from him. He's poisoning your soul."

She chuckled, as sound that snaked its way into my heart, furthering the crack across its surface. "What soul, Mother?"

"What if I found a way where we could both go? No separating. Just you and me. We will disappear."

"Together?"

"What I did before, it was a mistake leaving you. I see that now. I never thought Korin would go looking for you."

"Where would we go?" A glimmer of hope clung to her eyes. It was small, nearly drowning in dark shadows, but it was there.

"I know of a place, a beautiful place filled with light and peace. Many go there to find themselves again."

"Did you go there?"

"I did. After I left our coven, I wasn't in a good place. You were gone. Mateo and I —" I swallowed through my dry throat "—I was alone and didn't know how to exist without you, without him."

"So you sought after the Kiss of Eternal Night."

I flinched. "You know about that?"

She approached the bars, her dress swaying around her legs. "Of course. Korin kept a watchful eye on you, all those years. He told me everything you did." Her expression hardened. "You preferred to shut off your humanity rather than come find me."

"It wasn't like that. I believed you were safer without me around."

She wasn't listening. "After you battled and obtained the coveted Kiss, what did you do?"

I didn't like how she was baiting me. She probably expected me to cower, to hide in shame at what I'd done. But I wouldn't give her the satisfaction. She needed strength, and I'd show her what that looked like. Show her that despite how challenging life may get, how hopeless, one can still find their way back. The moon's shadow can only last so long before the sun rises.

"Let me tell you what I did, child." I summoned a fraction of my dark gift and expelled it through my gaze. "The Kiss burned through me, eating at every emotion I had until there was nothing left. And still it hungered. It nearly drove me mad until I realized the only way to calm the beast was to kill. Not just take lives, but rage right through people. The violence, the blood, was the only way to silence the Kiss's voice in my mind. Rage is its favorite snack, and I indulged it for a very long time."

My sudden candor and fury startled her, and she stepped back, paling. "What made you stop?"

As much as I wanted to, I didn't turn away from her. "A child not much younger than you when I found you. She had long blonde hair, eyes the color of fallen acorns, skin as pure and white as the first snowfall. She stood in the rain, alone on the street corner in the middle of the night. She was the only one left in her village that I had not killed."

I hesitated, afraid to say what happened next. But maybe it wasn't just Faithe who needed to hear it. Maybe I needed the reminder too, especially with the way I felt the darkness inside me swelling, growing into something deadly and all too familiar.

"What happened?" Faithe stared at me wide-eyed, but not with a look of horror like I would've expected but more of an understanding. It was in that moment, I realized Faithe truly had done some horrible things.

My voice lowered. "Just before I killed her, that young girl said something to me you had once said. 'Let me die, dark angel.'"

"I remember," she whispered.

"I saved you that day, but I wasn't strong enough to save that little girl, not in the way she should've been saved. Instead, I snapped her neck, a mercy killing compared to what I had done to the others. But by doing so, when she reminded me so much of you, it had opened a part of me that had been buried for a long time. A sliver of myself before the Kiss took over. It was just enough that I fled and hid in a cave, chained to its wall so I couldn't hurt anyone else. That's when they found me."

She looked up at me. "Who?"

"People who can also help you, if you'd let them." I didn't want to say anything else. I'm sure she had heard of the Ames de la Terra, but not in a good light. Korin would love to see that group destroyed.

"It's too late for me." A slight deflection in her voice told me otherwise.

"Listen to me, Faithe. There are plans in mo—"

"He's coming." She quickly backed up against the wall, as far away from me as she could reach.

I had been so focused on Faithe that I had missed the distinct sounds of approaching footsteps, followed by the clinking of a metal pole as it occasionally hit the top of a stone step.

The door opened and Faithe's expression melted into a mask of boredom as Korin and Naburus entered.

Korin's eyes flickered from her to me. He descended the steps, holding his hand out to Faithe. She smiled and accepted it, letting him pull her to him. "What have you two been talking about?"

"Nothing important. Sharing pointless memories." She ran her hand up his chest, making him growl deep in his throat.

"Why am I here, Korin?" I asked.

Naburus set his IV pole on the floor and pulled it along behind him, dirt gathering at its legs. He stopped just in front of the bars and sniffed. "You touched them. I can smell your burnt flesh."

I ignored him. "Korin?"

"Show me," Naburus demanded, a hunger in his eyes.

I raised my hands, facing my palms toward him. There was nothing to show. I had completely healed.

"No, no. Grab the bars again."

I ground my teeth together. "Is this really necessary?"

"Give my boy what he wants," Korin said. His heated gaze lowered to Faithe's. He tilted her chin upward and kissed her hard, while his hand lowered to her breast.

I grabbed the bars, every muscle in my body tight. I could snap the metal in two. Kill Naburus and attack Korin. The bars began to groan under the pressure.

Naburus giggled as he stared at the smoke rising from my hands. I barely felt the sting.

Korin jerked away from Faithe and sucked in a great breath. Blood dribbled down his chin. He must've bitten her tongue. Faithe wouldn't look at me.

"Why am I here, Korin?" I asked again, my voice loud and full of power. I let go of the bars. Naburus tracked my hands.

Korin's cold gaze focused on me. "I learned you were recently in Black Glen. I want to know why, and I want to know how you got in."

This startled me. Of all his questions, I hadn't expected this one. It worried me he even knew about its existence, a city that was supposed to be secret.

"I was invited there."

"Why?"

"The fae King wanted to know about several missing people in the city. He thinks vampires are involved." I kept my lie as close to the truth as possible to avoid suspicion.

Naburus reached through the bars, his fingers aiming for my hand. I jerked it back to his severe disappointment. He frowned and slowly withdrew it.

I glanced away from him to Korin. "I came here tonight to find out if there was any truth to it."

"And if there was?" Korin asked.

"Then I'm here to warn you. The fae King and Queen are not happy. For that matter, neither are the Witches of Rouen. If our coven does have anything to do with missing people in the city, I suggest it stop. We are making lots of enemies."

He scoffed. "The Witches of Rouen are unorganized amateurs, and the fae? They are cowards, hiding in their secret city. They've grown fat and lazy in their complacency."

"You could've asked me your questions without these bars in my face. Why did you lock me up?"

He approached the cell, eyeing me up and down. "How do you feel being imprisoned?"

A cold and violent chill raced up my spine. "What kind of question is that?"

Naburus looked over at him. "May I, father?"

"My son wants more of your blood. He said it made him feel better."

"No." I backed away from the bars. As long as I was behind here, I was safe.

"But you must."

"I don't have to do anything." My gaze flickered to Faithe. Color drained from her face, making me frown. What did she know that I didn't?

"You're right," Korin said. "You don't."

"Father!" Naburus pouted. An odd spectacle for someone who looked so old.

"You don't have to feed my boy, just like I don't have to do this." His hand struck forward like that of a viper and snatched Faithe. He spun her around to face me and placed her body between him and the bars. "This will only hurt for a moment, pet."

Snatching a fistful of her hair, he yanked her neck to the side and plunged his fangs into her neck. At the same time, he stepped forward, ramming her body into the holy water infused bars. The bare flesh on her face began to smoke, and she screamed, a terrible sound that wrenched my heart and cut off my breath.

He might just make me watch her die.

CHAPTER 26

"No!" I cried and rushed the bars. I tried to push her back, but Korin held her firm. Faithe's skin began to blister, and she cried out in agony.

"I'll do it! Just let her go."

Still fangs deep in Faithe's neck, Korin's gaze slowly met mine while her face melted.

"Please," I begged, his eyes glazing over in pleasure as he drank from her neck. He moaned, as the smell of her burning flesh stifled my nostrils.

"Please!" I begged again, falling to my knees. He watched me beg him, his lips twisting up in a crazed smile. My eyes darkened and let a flash of the Kiss flash in them. "Korin."

His grin grew wider. "Yes," he hissed, "that's it, Samira." But he stepped back, unlatching from Faithe and taking her with him. She sucked in several choppy breaths and sunk to her knees.

"Faithe?" I wished there weren't bars between us.

"Get up," Korin ordered me.

I did as he said, worry and anger storming inside me. A clashing of emotions I could barely contain. Once again, he'd given me an impossible choice, reminding me how much control he had over me.

I had to set Faithe free, had to find a way to release his control over me.

"Stick out your arm."

I slid my arm between two bars without question. Any slight movement to the left or the right would cause me to burn.

Naburus scooted over to me, the metal pole dragging behind him. Dirt had gathered so much at the bottom it pulled the tubing from his arm taught and jerked him back. He hissed and brought the pole next to him, nearly knocking it over.

His scowl disappeared when his eyes found the veins on my wrist. My pulse beat erratically just beneath the flesh.

I lowered my gaze to Faithe as Naburus punctured my skin and began to drink. Faithe, ever so slowly, began to heal, one cell at a time. She stayed on her knees, her hands lay limp in her lap, a defeated gesture. She stared into the distance, her consciousness anywhere but here.

Inhaling an angry hitched breath, I turned away as Naburus began to rub his crotch, moaning as he drank.

"Good boy," Korin said, his voice deep and throaty.

I could feel Korin's gaze watching me closely. Something about this felt wrong and not just because I had a psychopath drinking from me while he pleasured himself. This felt staged.

My rage grew. I slowly looked up at Korin, the Kiss's dark power seeping from my heart. A smile tugged at the corners of Korin's thin lips. Could he feel my rage? See it? I hoped so. I wanted him to fear it.

Just before Naburus let go, he pushed my arm to the side, singeing it against the poisoned metal. I didn't even flinch. I wouldn't give him anymore satisfaction.

Naburus unlatched and licked his lips. His eyes rolled into the back of his head as he experienced some sort of euphoric sensation.

"How long are you holding me?" I asked Korin.

"For a time. My boy might get hungry again." He looked down at Faithe. "Get up, pet. You look ill." He made a tsking noise. "I'll take you to your room."

Naburus exited first, his eyes still glazed. Faithe said nothing as she followed after him. She didn't even look back at me. Had she been part of this ruse? Or was she as innocent as I was?

Korin stopped, his hand on the door jamb. "I want you to think about what just happened. Picture my son in your mind drinking from you while he touches himself." He paused. "And I'll give you one more image to think about. Tonight, I'm going to have Faithe in every way possible. She's going to have to beg me to stop." He winked. "Sweet dreams."

The lights turned off and the door slammed shut.

Searing hot rage slammed through me, so powerful I stumbled back. I would kill him. Jerk his spine right out of his ass. I punched at the wall, my fist crashing through the wooden walls only to meet dirt on the other side.

The foreign presence inside me, the Kiss of Eternal Night, took hold of my emotions and surged forward. I gasped and fell to my knees as the beast inside me kissed itself awake.

I clutched at my head and gritted my teeth. I couldn't unleash it, not after all I'd done to hold it back. And yet, if I let it loose, I could very well kill Korin. And right now, that's what I wanted more than anything. He had to know I would want this. Did he want to die?

My blood turned to ice, and I snapped my eyes open in the darkness. This is what he wanted. This is why he put me in this cell, tortured Faithe in front of me and let his foul son feed on me again. He wanted me to get angry and lose control! The realization doused my emotions like a wet blanket.

I sucked in a breath and pulled myself into a meditation pose, hands resting on my crossed legs, and focused on relaxing and clearing my mind. Korin wanted me to embrace the Kiss, but why? And why wasn't he afraid of that happening? This concerned me the most. Based on what Faithe had said, he knew what I'd done when I'd given in to the Kiss before. Why would he want that, especially when, according to Mateo, he wanted every last drop of my blood? Why not try to take my blood while I was imprisoned? Maybe he still would. I sighed and continued to concentrate.

Time passed slowly. My bones felt the sun rise and with it came a nagging sensation across my flesh that made me itch. Only a tight space like my coffin would relieve it.

I huddled into the corner trying to make myself feel as tight as possible. My eyelids grew heavy, and I let a heavy sleep pull me under. If I slept, I couldn't think about Korin and the terrible things he'd done.

Nightmares invaded my mind. The kind I hadn't had in a very long time. They were full of violence, blood, tortured screams. All of it by my hand. I was death's reaper, riding on a bloody stallion straight to hell, taking everyone in my path with me. The trail of bodies behind me stretched long.

"Samira."

My eyelids flew open. My mind and body were numb. Just as it should be.

Lights had turned on. By the way my body was feeling it was nearing sunset. Teddy stood in front of the bars, glancing back toward the door as if someone else might be coming in.

"Are you okay?" he asked me.

"I'm fine. Did you find the briefcase?"

"I did."

"And?"

He glanced at the door again. "I drank the liquid, and I got to tell you, it felt like I was being burned alive by fire from the inside out."

"I've heard that, but did it work?"

"Ask me anything."

"Why did Korin imprison me here?"

"He said he wanted to scare and anger you. That's all. I thought it was strange, so did the others."

"What of Kristina? Did she take it?"

He nodded. "She cried afterwards. A lot. When she realized she was free."

"Is she going to escape here?"

"She wanted to say goodbye to you first. Korin's letting you out soon, but he's going to have you followed, so be careful."

"How's Faithe?"

"I haven't seen her, but that's not unusual. She doesn't typically leave Korin's room until later in the evening. Usually after he's left."

I frowned. "Where does he go?"

He shrugged and swiped the long hair from his eyes. "I wish I knew. He hasn't been telling us much lately." He hesitated before saying, "What comes next?"

"That depends on you. I plan on destroying every dirty thing Korin's working on this city, then I will kill him."

"I want to be a part of it." His words were backed by strength, his gaze just as fierce.

"It will be dangerous, living a double life. If he finds out you're not compelled anymore, he could kill you like he did Petre. Burn you alive. And you may have to do things you don't want to do."

"It will be worth it if we can take him down. I'm tired of seeing this coven suffer under his reign."

I smiled, the numbness in my chest lightening. It was good to know some of my old coven would back me.

"I programmed my number into this." He handed me my phone back. "I should go. Please keep me in the loop."

"Thank you. I will." I slipped the phone into my pocket.

He turned to leave, then stopped. "I hope you don't mind, but I let Mateo know you were here."

I hitched a breath. The thought of Mateo, the one person I used to always feel safe with, cracked through my apathy. I couldn't add more emotions to the ones I was currently trying to bury. "I wish you wouldn't have done that."

"Mateo's always been a good friend to me. He told me to watch out for you, and I swore to him I would. I'm sure he'll be here soon."

"I need to get out of here."

"You will. Soon." He said goodbye and left me alone again, leaving the lights on.

I settled back into my cell, thinking I'd be here awhile, but shortly after, Zane, the silver-eyed vampire, showed up. His black hair had been combed back, and he wore a long brown suit jacket. The planes of his face were all hard lines and angles. The cold look in his eyes wasn't any softer. Everything about him was a sharp edge, one I didn't want to get close to.

"How long have you worked for Korin?" I asked.

He unlocked my cell. "I don't."

"Did you used to work for Silas? Dominic?" Although odd for a vampire, it wasn't unheard of. I had seen him talking with the shifters, after all.

"Wrong again."

"Then who do you work for?"

His hand froze on the handle of the cell door. "He likes you, you know."

"Who?"

"The one who will usher in a new dawn."

"The Phoenix? What do you know about him, or should I say *her?*"

He filled the doorway with his tall and muscular body. A glazed look came over his eyes, and he licked his lips. "You are special. One day you may even be worshiped. May I touch you? Kiss you even?"

"No."

He blinked rapidly as if he'd never heard the word. "One kiss. Before it all ends."

"Am I free to go?" My pulse began to race. I didn't like being cornered. It made me think of that night with Michael when things went very very wrong.

"Give me what I want."

I stared at him, wondering what would happen if I killed him. Was he important to Korin? If so, Korin might punish Faithe for my actions. It wasn't worth the risk. But that didn't mean I'd give him what he wanted.

"Come here," I said, straightening and batting my eyes.

His mouth curled upward, splitting those hard, cruel lines on his face. He moved into the cell with me and lifted his arm as if to pull my head toward him. Before he could reach me, I knocked his hand away and rammed my knee between his legs. He coughed a high-pitched sound and doubled over.

"The next time you try to touch me, I'll remove your heart with my teeth. Tell the Phoenix the same goes for him."

I shoved him aside and left my cell, walking with confidence, but as soon as I hit the stairway, my calm mask shattered. Too many emotions. Too much anger, sadness, and fear. I continued on, the storm raging fiercely within me. I wanted to smash the whole house down. If I released the Kiss, I could do it in mere minutes.

I sucked in a breath, counting down from ten. When I was done, I started over again, unable to let go of my rage. I would kill Korin, take out Naburus with a flick of my wrist. And while I was at it, take out Michael, too.

I had to get out of this place before I burst!

Reaching the entryway, I wished I had enough strength to go find Faithe or say goodbye to Kristina, but I couldn't stay here another second. Not until I patched the holes in my mind and heart where the Kiss's darkness was tunneling through.

I flung open the front door and slammed into a hard chest.

"Samira?" Mateo asked. He gripped my shoulders, his brows drawn together with concern.

"Get me out of here." The words barely escaped my lips before he spun me around and carried me away.

CHAPTER 27

*L*eaving my vehicle behind, he opened the passenger door of his car and set me inside, then hurried to the other side. Grabbing the keys from the center console, he brought the engine to life and slammed the clutch into drive. I focused on the movements of his hands as they gripped the steering wheel, the tips of his knuckles as white as bone. My breathing hitched. *Concentrate.* Think of anything other than Winter's Cove. I studied the cuff of his black dress shirt around his wrist. The second button was undone.

"Tell me what happened," he said, glancing back and forth from the road to me.

My gaze wondered up his arm and to his chest. More buttons were undone, exposing the top of his chest. I used to run my hands over those hard muscles.

My breathing began to slow. I glanced out the side mirror. Winter's Cove was nowhere to be seen. "I hate that place."

He was quiet. Then, "Me too."

"We should leave and never look back. Take Faithe. Take our friends."

He didn't say anything. Not like I expected him to. I settled into my seat and leaned my forehead against the cool glass of the window. "Where are we going?"

"Somewhere safe and away from prying eyes."

I didn't ask him to clarify. Right now I didn't care. I should, though. I should be heading to Fire Ridge. Plotting. Planning. Figuring out a way to destroy Korin.

But I was too fragile right now. I could feel it. The mental patchwork in my mind was barely holding together. Rage, hate, anger, sadness, agony, the need to kill, to *destroy* all boiled beneath the surface, threatening to burst out in volcanic proportions. I had to hold it all inside, had to push it down so far that it would never come to the surface. Because if I gave into all those emotions, the Kiss would take over. And if that happened … I shivered.

If that happened, then God protect them all, because the Kiss turned all feelings into death and destruction. It would take over my life, my heart, my soul and use it to rage against the world.

I would kill Mateo, Faithe, my roommates, the innocent—the very people I tried to protect—all without guilt.

No. I had to keep it locked inside. I schooled my face into a mask of cold indifference, not blinking, not even thinking, except to contain the raging, boiling emotions inside.

As if Mateo knew how I was feeling, he didn't press me for details. He sped through the darkened streets of Rouen, all beginning to bustle with night life. I didn't focus on anything, just let it all whirl by, a mesh of color and sounds. My phone vibrated several times in my pocket, but I ignored it all. Occasionally, Mateo would glance at me but he remained silent.

We reached the border of the city and he continued driving. Past fields and through a forest. It was all a blur.

When the car finally stopped, I focused my eyes. We were parked on the shoulder near the tree line. He exited the car and came around to my side to help me out. I let him guide me.

"Not much further," he said as if I'd asked. I didn't care where we were going, as long as I didn't have to think or feel. Just a small break. That's all I needed.

Mateo guided me down a small ravine and up the other side, stepping over fallen limbs and rounding bushes. Ten minutes passed. The moon was just beginning to rise above the tree line. Its full light invigorated my skin. In the distance, the sounds of a waterfall tickled my ears. My shoulders sagged; water had always soothed me.

We walked up a steep incline and stopped at the top. We stood upon the edge of a cliff overlooking a raging river. Not much further way, the great river poured from the cliff's edge, billowing sprays of moisture in all directions. I could barely hear anything else but the thunderous downfall as it hit the rocks below.

It was like me—an endless flow of emotions pounding against the wall I built up to trap them, before they burst through and destroyed everything in their path. But the rocks below, strong and steady and unmovable, was exactly how I needed to be. I took in a deep, slow breath, attempting to contain them, the rage and anger burning inside.

I took another deep breath, and then another. I could be like the solid stone below, steadfast and immoveable.

Warm arms wrapped around my stomach and I closed my eyes, allowing Mateo to comfort me. A sliver of my anger slipped away. He smelled like the earth, like home, like warm beaches and the sun's rays I hadn't touched for hundreds of years. I yearned for the feel of it on my skin, soft and warm and comforting. But instead, Mateo was my sun. Or he had been in the past. I relished in it now, giving in to the temptation to just let him and me *be*. No thinking, no anger or heartache, just being together again, for a moment in time, like a ripple in the pond.

"Sometimes," Mateo whispered in my ear, "I come here when I need to think." He paused, and the silence of the forest stretched before us. His grip around me suddenly tightened, almost as if he was afraid I might fall from the cliff. "I've been coming here a lot lately."

I turned to him, still barely grasping ahold of my emotions. "I appreciate your taking me here. It's what I needed, but after this, you need to let me go."

He raised his eyebrow, amused. "I could never let you go. You are my *anima gemella*, my soulmate. *Sei la mia vita,* you are my life. The part of me I am always looking for but can never find, not when you are far from me. Or even an arm's length away. It is only in these small moments when you allow me to touch you that I feel whole again." He did not know, or comprehend, the danger right before him. He trusted me, but it was a lie.

I was a lion in wait, in a cage as thin as thread. In my state right now I could easily swipe the locks away and kill him.

I swallowed hard, forcing down the emotions enough to let me speak as the chipping at my heart began again. "No. I mean, you have to let me fight my own battles. I am stronger now. I deserve this, to fight for myself."

"I meant it when I said that without you, my life has no meaning. If you die, then I go shortly after. I cannot live *sin ti.*" *Without you.*

"Then let me take that chance. Take a chance on your *anima gemella.* Trust me to not only protect myself, but to protect you as well."

He sighed, running his lips on the top of my head, and I felt the pounding of his heart in his chest. "You do not understand why I must protect you, Samira. I have seen him slowly seduce so many people into his grasp, only to break them in half the minute they are the most vulnerable."

I turned in his arms and he pulled me closer, clasping me tight to him. His arms, so strong and steady, to the Kiss they were only brittle bone and easily sliced flesh. We were so close our faces almost touched. I swallowed hard. "Tell me, Mateo. How did *I* break your heart? How did you suffer so, when you were the one who chose *him,* and not me that fateful night so long ago."

He closed his eyes, shutting himself off to me, but still clasped me tighter, to him. His breathing came in and out in short bursts and his eyes fluttered under his lids. And then, when he opened them, they were cold, as hard as steel.

"He knew we were to leave that night."

I held my breath, waiting for the explanation I'd wanted for so long.

"He came to me, two minutes before I was to leave to meet you. He knew exactly what we had planned and had guards, hidden within the area, ready to take you." He blinked, looking away, no longer allowing me to see the pain in his eyes. "Michael was there too, waiting for the order. And if I did not submit to Korin fully, to allow him to compel me, then he would let Michael imprison you, rape and beat you. *For months.* But that wasn't all. Korin said he would bring you to the brink of death by torture, over and over, and then allow you to heal, only to begin it again. He called you a traitor, and that his punishment for traitors was just."

He blinked, and a tear tracked down his face. When he looked at me again, I could see, feel, almost *touch* the agony inside him. "And I was not strong enough. I tried to fight him, tried to kill him, but he was stronger."

My heart pounded, and my rage resurfaced. My insides ached until my very bones felt as brittle as twigs at the thought of them fighting. How easily Mateo could've died. And my armor, the very last of it surrounding my heart, melted into nothingness.

"And so I gave in," he said. "I begged him on my hands and knees, kissing the ground below him, to allow you to go. To stay his hand at taking you."

His tone turned vicious. "And he *swore* to me, swore it, that he would not kill you. That he would let you go." He swallowed hard. "But in return, I had to serve him. I had to do whatever he asked, even if it killed me inside to do it. If I didn't, he would threaten your life."

Just like Faithe, Korin knew our weaknesses, and did whatever necessary, no matter how horrible, to control those who resisted.

Shame rushed over me like a tsunami. All this time, I had doubted Mateo's love for me. Not only doubted him, but raged against him. I choked out my next words, not wanting the answer but needing to have it. "How long?" I paused and when he didn't answer, I asked again. "How long did you serve under Korin this way?"

"Centuries. Centuries of suffering. Of killing and torturing others. And I did it because of my love for you, to keep you safe."

My heart pounded, my stomach rolled at the thought that he had suffered for me. I took a step back, shaking my head, trying to protect him from myself. I stepped until I was at the edge of the cliff. "It can't be."

"Please, Samira." He held out his hand, pleading to me. "I had no other choice, *mio amore*. He always knew where you were, always. That is why Michael looked for you, because Korin commanded him to do it. And he would give me reports, showing me with his knowledge how vulnerable you were. And I knew I had to continue to obey. I could not rebel, or he would do worse things than kill you."

"Why didn't you tell me? Find some way to communicate with me?" My lips trembled, my gut squeezed at the horror.

"Why didn't *you* come to *me*?" He caught my hand, squeezing it tight. "How could you doubt me so? Doubt my love for you? I waited for you to return, to save me from my misery, to rescue me from my fate."

I closed my eyes, unable to face his beseeching, but I still heard it in his voice, his agony that I never came for him.

"You are my soulmate, and yet, you betrayed me when you left and did not look back." He tapped my chest. "You broke me, my love. The only person who could do it."

I clutched him, falling to my knees, unable to stop the torment inside. He was right. When he did not come for me that night, I only thought he had chosen Korin over me. I did not stop to think of any other option.

And yet, Korin had orchestrated it all.

Just as he had orchestrated Faithe to fall into his hands to force me to return to him. For what, I did not know. Except that in the end, I would only be a shell of myself.

I clasped at the earth, heaving, smelling the iron and minerals that laced the soil. The pounding water below became a drum, thudding and pounding, just like my heart, at the rage still simmering inside me. I squeezed my eyes, trying to force it down.

No, no, no. Please stop.

But it raged, like a beast with long, sharp teeth and claws just as deadly, pacing back and forth inside its boney cage inside my ribs. I screamed out in short bursts, attempting to release it bit by bit, but the Kiss only hissed and coiled, wrapping its temptation around my heart, slowly squeezing it tight, tighter.

Korin deserves to die. He killed all those people who were only protecting Faithe. He tortures her. He manipulates you. He hates you. He wants to drain every drop of your blood until your empty eyes stare at a cold, cloudless sky.

"No." I shook my head, trying to shake the Kiss' words inside me, tempting me.

Mateo touched my shoulder; he was kneeling at my side. "Sam. I… I'm sorry. I didn't mean it."

He turned Faithe against you. He forced Mateo to do things, horrible things, unspeakable things.

"NO." I grit my teeth together, ignoring Mateo's gentle hand on my cheek.

He made Mateo, the love of your life, your other half, suffer! He deserves to die. You should kill him now. He doesn't deserve to live one more second.

I pressed my head to the ground, pulling my hair between my fingers, tears streaming down my face. In hundreds of years, I had not let the Kiss get to me like this. Mateo pulled me onto his lap, surrounded me with his strong arms. I couldn't understand what he was saying, but his voice was soothing, his hands gentle. He ran them through my hair, tugging it tenderly, his words a soft caress. I leaned my head on his shoulder, allowing him to touch me in ways I had not permitted in so long.

The hiss of the Kiss still whispered in my mind but it slowly, ever so slowly began to subside and Mateo's words began to grow clearer. He was singing a song, the song my mother used to sing to me. I blinked my eyes at the realization of his words. I had only sung it to him once, revealed it in a moment of stillness centuries ago. And yet, he remembered it, or had learned it on his own.

The words were tender, and spoke of a timeless love.

I remembered my mother, my human mother; she had loved me. A wave of warmth washed over me, tears streamed down my face as I thought of a time, so much simpler than now, when all it took was the love of my mother to calm me.

I let him sing to me, his voice low and tactile, almost sensual in my ears. And now the words sung were of his love for me, that was everlasting, never ending. And it was the truth.

After all these years, after my betrayal, *he still loved me*. Even though I was wretched and soulless, filled with a power so violent, so strong, that I could wipe the Earth of every living creature with it. And yet, he knew this, and he still loved me. He still risked his life, just to calm me.

I did not deserve him.

I did not deserve his love.

I jerked out of his arms, stumbling forward. "Take me home, Mateo."

He blinked once, then twice.

"Please," I begged him now. "Take me home. You can't be near me. I'm … I'm too dangerous."

He stood up, his face angry now. "I told you once before, and I am telling you now." He gripped my shoulders, and the mere touch of him simultaneously kept me together and broke me apart. "I will never let you go. I did it once, and it was wrong. Even if I did it to protect you, I should've found a way for us to be together, and I will not give up on that now. I will smash through your walls until you come home to me. I know you're afraid. I know you think you're protecting me by keeping me away, but shoving everything you're feeling so far down where no one can touch you will only hurt you in the end. You are my soulmate. We were meant to be together. And I know that only love and passion can contain the Kiss. Only the unconditional love of your soulmate can help you."

I shook my head, hearing the hissing in my mind again, knowing that releasing my feelings over to him would only kill him in the end. "Let me go, Mateo."

His fingers dug into my skin, clinging to me, but I had to make him let me go. I wasn't strong enough to do it on my own. I looked him in the eyes, making certain to put as much feeling into my words as I could. "Let me go, Mateo. I do not love you anymore."

He gasped and took a step back, releasing me. Realizing what he'd done, he lunged for me again, but it was too late.

"I'm sorry." My desperate words were swallowed by the night as I leapt from the cliff into the darkness. Far enough to land in the murky, deep water, and I let it flow over me. The frigid blast of the water was a jolt to my system, a shock to my senses, and everything within me froze, including my feelings.

I stayed in the water only long enough to let my emotions calm enough that I could contain them, then I swam to the land and ran from Mateo, his voice calling my name an echo in my ears.

I ran from the only man I ever loved.

And from the only man brave and stupid enough to love me back.

CHAPTER 28

I raced through the woods, using as much energy as possible to burn through the rage churning through my mind. By the time I arrived at Fire Ridge, my body was exhausted, my mind too tired to do anything but exist in the moment.

Mateo's revelation had been an explosion in my mind. My betrayal settled deep into my bones and into the heaving pieces of my heart. I made a silent vow to him, to myself, that I would find a way to make it up to him. That I would save him from Korin, even if it killed me in the process.

But for now, I had to learn how to be around him and not lose myself in him. Mateo, Angel, and the Nocturnas were essential to getting rid of Korin. And so, I had to push back the feelings, the need to have him near me, to kiss his aches and pains away, to make up to him for my betrayal in body and soul. To keep it from surfacing and taking over my body. *Just for now.* Until Korin was dead and Faithe was free. Until the Kiss was settled again, deep in my bones, in my gut, silent and cold as before.

I stood in the woods of Fire Ridge for some time until a cool indifference filled my body.

Just as it should be.

It was nearing eleven o'clock at night. By the number of motorcycles and cars out front, half the pack was here. Since Briar became Alpha, it seemed more and more of the pack liked to hang out at their mansion. Dominic used to call people in, but the shifters seemed to want to be here now.

I opened the front door, taking in one last breath to ensure I was calm, and inhaled the smell of fresh meat and potatoes. I was ravenous. A few heads turned my direction at my arrival. They quickly glanced away. My presence may be tolerated now, but I wasn't accepted, which was fine by me.

Weaving my way through the living room and the few groups of people not outside, I searched for Briar. I came up behind her in the kitchen, sitting on the counter. Young Loxley sat next to her while Marge and Samantha, both wearing aprons, argued about which barbecue sauce to put on the ribs.

"You want spicy," Samantha was saying. "What kind of sick bitch puts sugar on their meat?"

Marge removed a rack of ribs from the oven. "If you don't watch that strawberry mouth of yours, I'm going to have to put my foot right through it. A real shame."

"The only hole you'll be breaking through is your daddy's."

Marge's nostrils flared. She lifted the spatula in her hand as if it were an ax. "Take that back! My daddy is the sweetest—"

"I smell vampire," Briar interrupted. She spun around and jumped to her feet when she saw me. "Dammit Samira! I've been calling and texting you all day and night!"

Forcing a casualness over my posture that was the opposite to how I felt, I pulled the phone out of my pocket, grateful I'd recently upgraded to a waterproof one. My clothes and my hair were already dry from the speedy run over.

There were a dozen messages on my phone from Briar. Using her own words, I said, "Sure as shit."

"Hey! Don't use my line! It only pisses me off more." She paused. "And yet, hearing you curse, it makes me feel warm inside."

"Do you want some ribs?" Marge asked me. "I've got some bloody ones I haven't cooked yet."

"Sure. And add some of that brown sugar sauce to it."

"Ha!" Marge said in Samantha's face. "Even a vampire likes sugar on ribs."

Briar laughed. "Come on, Sammie. Let's go talk in my office."

My gaze flickered to Loxley. She quickly lowered her gaze. Once again, I got the distinct impression of how different she was from the others.

I followed Briar back through the living room. Through the glass on the patio, I locked eyes with Luke. He saluted me and returned to his conversation with Gerald.

"Where have you been?" Briar asked over her shoulder. She turned down the hallway leading to a room she'd turned into her office. She'd torn down Dominic and Vincent's old office and made it into a place for any hurt or sick supernaturals that needed a place to stay for a while. I thought it was a fitting way to retrofit the space.

"Korin locked me up in the dungeon of Winter's Cove."

She jerked to a stop and whirled around. "The fuck? Are you okay? Why didn't you escape or call at least?"

"It was a dungeon."

"Don't deadpan me! And don't bullshit me either. You could've escaped if you wanted to."

"Then I didn't want to." I walked past her into the office.

She followed and closed the door behind her. Her office was painted a light gray with white trim. Posters of old eighties bands and TV shows hung on the wall. I recognized maybe half of them. A simple square table took up the back space of the room with a stack of cards scattered across its top.

I wrinkled my nose. "This looks like a room at the back of a bar where people conduct shady business."

She dropped onto a worn love seat and propped her feet up on a folding chair. "Thank you. It took a lot of time to get it to look like this. Now tell me more about this dungeon and why Korin threw you in it."

I briefly recounted what happened, leaving out many of the parts that might reopen the rawest wounds.

Briar lowered her legs and sat up. "So he wants you to go all beast mode? Why?"

"That's what I don't know."

"Then you better lock that shit up tight, because if Korin wants it, it can't be good."

"I am. How did it go with Folas?"

She sighed and leaned back. "He has some good ideas, some of them risky, but I'm glad we're working with them. Still can't believe that Eddie is fae."

"Mateo and the other vampires can't help. Not for a while."

"Angel alluded as much."

I tilted my head. "I've been meaning to ask you. Is something going on with you and Angel?"

She lifted her feet again and rested them on the chair. "The million dollar question. I love Luke, more than anything."

"That's not what I asked."

"But Angel. There's a connection I can't explain. A strong one."

"Those connections are hard to ignore." I looked away, not wanting her to see the expression in my eyes. "Especially for vampires. Whatever you're feeling, he's feeling it a hundred times more."

She was silent, thinking about this, then her eyes moved to mine, catching the pain in them. I'd let my guard slip for a moment.

She raised her eyebrow. "Like the one between you and Mateo?"

I nodded, blinking away the pain.

"So what do we do?" she asked, her voice sincere. I could tell she had thought about this a lot.

"We place one foot in front of the other and hope that one day that connection pulls us together." I took in a calming breath, aware of the Kiss that was just under the surface, careful to keep it down where it belonged. "Whether your connection is friendship or love, I do not know."

"And yours?" She leaned forward, eager to hear my answer.

I looked into her eyes, dredging up the courage I needed to say the words. "I need him."

A simple confession but one that shook me to the core. And, the truth.

Her eyes didn't leave mine. "And I need Angel."

We both stared at each other, the confessions between us binding us closer. I finally blinked and she looked away. I followed her gaze to the wall opposite. A man on a poster with stringy long hair, a guitar hanging from his waist, stared back at me while licking a microphone. "I hate your office."

"Of course you do." She patted my thigh and the mood lightened. "Let's go talk to Lynx and see if she has the witches on board yet. We're going to need their help. I'll grab Loxley and Luke, maybe a few of the others."

I stopped her. "What is it with Loxley? Why her?"

She thought about it. "There's something about her I like. A kinship maybe. She's an orphan like me. Plus, she's super strong and fast. It comes naturally, and that's real talent."

"What do you know about her?"

"She found our pack the moment she moved to Rouen after graduating high school up in Wildemoor. Her mother died in childbirth and her father died a few years later, not sure how. Her aunt raised her." She shrugged. "She has an asshole ex, but Luke put him in his place and now he doesn't bother her much."

"Was she raised by her aunt as a wolf?"

"I'm not sure. What's your interest?"

"I sense something different about her. I don't think she's a full shifter."

Her eyebrows lifted. "Do you think she could be the Phoenix?"

"I don't think so, but she is hiding something. Keep an eye on her."

Briar stared toward the door, nodding. "I will."

* * *

AFTER BORROWING one of the vehicles at Fire Ridge, I drove Briar and

Luke over to our house. At the last minute, Briar decided against bringing Loxley or any of the others. Perhaps she was just starting to realize how dangerous it was to discuss plans with so many people.

Three blocks away, I turned the corner, listening to Luke and Briar discuss Folas's plans when I spotted a familiar face standing beneath a lamp post, light reflecting off his shiny bald head. I slammed on the breaks.

"It's him." I jumped from the car, barely shifting it in park before I was out the door.

"Who?" Briar called as she also exited the vehicle with Luke right behind her.

"The Phoenix. I think." I didn't know for sure, but I felt it deep within my bones.

Luke and Briar followed my gaze. The tall man stared after us and didn't move as we slowly approached him.

When we were five car lengths apart, Luke asked, "Who are you?"

His all black eyes stared through me, and yet, I could feel them prying into my conscious. "Protect your mind," I said quickly.

The man's mouth opened, revealing an endless black pit. A sound seeped out, dark and raspy. "Mind your own business or there will be consequences."

The harshness of his voice made my bones ache and my flesh freeze. Pure evil stood before me. I'd only felt it a couple of other times. I held a hand out to Briar and Luke. "Back up."

"Hell no," Briar snapped. "This bastard thinks he can stand beneath a streetlight all creepy-like in the middle of the night and warn *us*? He should be on a registry, and I'm not talking about the wedding kind."

Briar leapt through the air, claws extended. The man smiled and stretched out his hand. A blast of powerful energy slammed into all three of us and tossed us back at least thirty feet. Luke slammed into the windshield of a parked car. Briar and I landed on our backs on pavement. Pain racked my body, and I moaned. Briar lay next to me, trying to inhale tiny sips of air.

"I'm broken," she grunted. "He's so dead."

I lifted my head toward the lamp post. "He's gone."

"Motherfucker." She rolled to her stomach and looked up, wincing at the motion. "Where's Luke?"

"He flew that way." I pointed to the left. My back felt like it had been hit by a sledgehammer.

"Oh shit." Briar grimaced and scrambled to her feet. "Luke!"

She ran-limped over to him. I pulled myself into a sitting position. Luke lay sprawled across the front of the car, unconscious, his chest torn and bleeding. I sucked in a sharp breath and ran to him. Every bone in my body ached. Whatever the Phoenix had hit us with, it wasn't just the force of the blow that had harmed us.

"Luke!" Briar removed her t-shirt and pressed it to his chest. She stared at me with pleading eyes. "He's not dead, right?"

I was already checking his pulse. "He's alive, but just barely. Let's get him to the car."

"Angel can help." Briar picked him up. I darted around my vehicle, opening the door for her. She said Angel's name over and over, her voice full of anguish. Their connection must be really strong if he could sense her call.

She carefully set Luke in the car and slid next to him, keeping pressure on the wound but blood still flowed freely. "Come on, baby. Hold on."

I could feel the anguish in her words; she really did love Luke, which made me move even faster. By the looks of that wound, he didn't have much longer to live.

CHAPTER 29

I raced home and jumped from the car, reaching the front door in seconds. If Angel couldn't help Luke, Lynx probably could.

As if she had sensed what had happened, Lynx came running out of the house. "What happened?"

"It's Luke," I said and hurried to the other side to help Briar. I helped Briar pick him up. His skin had paled a deathly white.

"Shit, shit, shit," Briar said as we carried him in the back door.

Lynx held open the door. "I knew something happened! It was the strangest thing. It was like a blast of pure evil raced through the house. It knocked me to the ground!"

Briar and I looked at each other. The Phoenix hadn't just hurt us, but he'd managed to harm Lynx, too.

"What the hell was it?" Lynx cried, as we carried Luke into the living room and laid him on the couch.

"The Phoenix." I glanced up at her. "Get bandages and whatever magic you think could help this."

"But what is it? I need to know exactly what hurt him before I can help."

A chilly silence settled over us. Briar carefully lifted Luke's shredded, blood-soaked shirt from his chest and pulled back the material. Deep and violent claw marks marred his chest.

Lynx sucked in a breath.

Briar growled. "What the actual fuck?"

"Any of you know what exactly did this?" Lynx whispered. "I don't know how to help without knowing."

The door flew open. Angel filled the doorway, his hair windswept, eyes alive. "What's happened?"

Briar stood, her bloody hands at her side. Tears stinging her eyes. "Help him. Please. I'm sorry I keep asking for your help. I just don't know what—"

He appeared in front of her and gripped her arms. "Shhh. You only have to ask."

Angel dropped to his knees by Luke and inspected the wound. "What did this?"

"The Phoenix," I said.

Angel licked his finger and ran it along the deepest claw mark first. "In what form?"

The question caught me off guard. Could the Phoenix have shifted into animal form so fast we hadn't noticed?

Briar answered first. "He was human when we saw him, and he hit us with this insane amount of energy. It even reached Lynx in the house over three blocks away. It knocked us to the ground, but it was more than wind. It's like it went right through me. My bones still hurt."

Angel's head snapped to her. "You're injured?"

She groaned and motioned to Luke. "Just heal the guy who's about to find out if Death is a man or a woman. I want to be surprised."

Angel returned to the task. "Why did the Phoenix attack you?"

"He warned us to stay out of his business," I said.

"Then he's afraid of you."

"I don't know why," Briar said. "He kicked our asses in less than a second."

I silently agreed with Briar, thinking of the prophecy. The Phoenix couldn't be afraid of us. If the prophecy was true, then we were supposed to help him raise Trianus. Or, really, her, now that I think about it. It was the mother of Trianus that started this all, the witch buried beneath the house. She'd taken on a male form. "Trianus's mother and the Phoenix are one and the same. We need to remember that."

"I haven't forgotten," Lynx whispered.

Angel licked his finger again. The deepest mark in Luke's chest had healed. Briar continued to apply pressure wherever Angel wasn't working, and she kept glancing at Angel, deep appreciation in her eyes.

"How do we stop the bitch?" Briar snarled.

"We can't stop what we can't find." I paced the room, thinking. "Eddie said they'd try to find the Phoenix. I can check in with him."

"I'll check in with the witches, too," Lynx said.

I glanced at her, noting her messy hair, the dirt under her fingernails. "Whatever it takes. How are the witches? United yet?"

"Mostly. I was with them earlier making more SJ. Another witch came up missing. They want to know when we can hit White Pine. They think maybe the missing people could be there."

"It's most likely," Angel said. "I saw many supernaturals there."

"We'll go tomorrow night, assuming Luke is better." My gaze dropped to him. The bleeding had stopped, but the wound still looked terrible. I asked Angel, "Will you be able to heal him all the way?"

He shook his head. "This was done with magic, but I will heal him as much as I am able and, hopefully, his body will do the rest."

"Thank you, Angel," Briar sucked in a breath. "I know I keep asking for your help and I'm afraid it will all be too much one day, but—"

He nudged her. "Shut up."

Her lips clamped together, and she gave him an incredulous look.

"What about vampire blood?" I asked, interrupting whatever this was between them. "We'll need his help tomorrow."

"Does vampire blood heal?" Lynx asked.

I walked over to Luke. Angel slid back. "Not exactly, but it will make him stronger. Briar, do you mind?"

"Juice him up." She parted his lips for me.

I bit into my wrist and held it near his mouth. Blood dripped inside. "The hope is my blood will jump start his own already heightened immune system and make the healing process much quicker."

When my wrist healed, I stepped back to let Angel resume his work. Already, color had returned to Luke's face. This was a good sign.

Briar began to speak soothing words to Luke, holding his hand tightly. Turning to Lynx, I asked quietly, "How's Roma?"

"Amazing. She's been working with younger witches, showing them all sorts of magic. It's good to have someone older around to show us some of the lost arts."

"Will she be with us tomorrow?"

"She said she wouldn't miss it. I just have to tell her what time. We have about five others who volunteered to go in with us. Others will go during the day and get as close as they can to set magical wards on the property."

"How does that work?" I'd always been fascinated by witches and their ability to manipulate the elements around them. As a young vampire, I'd dabbled in magic, but the magic that allowed a vampire's existence was extremely hard to access and took a lot of self-control, something I didn't have at the time.

Lynx pulled me to the corner of the room where she could talk louder. "It's actually pretty neat. We managed to get our hands on a Hyde's blood—"

I opened my mouth to speak, but Lynx raised a hand.

"Don't ask how. Anyway, we created some spells and cast it over the property to be activated as soon as a shifter, previously unknown to the property, crosses a boundary we created. But if a Hyde hits this pocket of magic," she made her fingers simulate an explosion, "poof!"

"Truly fascinating. Maybe one day you can teach me a little magic."

Her eyes lit up. "I'd love it!"

I smiled at her excitement. Of all three of us, me, Briar, and Lynx, I believed Lynx to have the most power, but hers, so far, was untouched. And that made her extremely dangerous and powerful. I never told her what I'd suspected the moment I met her—she was more than a Morgan witch. I'd met plenty of Morgans living in Rouen over the last century, and she was something more.

"Is your mother still pressuring you to train with the Ministry?" I asked.

Briar must've heard me because she tilted her head our direction.

Lynx's expression fell. "I've managed to hold her back, but it's just a matter of time."

I could tell by her expression she was afraid of leaving. I placed my hand on her arm in a comforting gesture, something I wasn't used to doing. "We'll find a way to prevent it. I know certain things that can sway Cassandra should we need it."

She lowered her surprised gaze to where I was touching her. "You have dirt on my mother?"

I leaned and whispered conspiratorially, "I have dirt on everyone."

She giggled a nervous laugh and averted her gaze, a motion that surprised me. Her heart was pounding. I was about to ask her about it, when Luke moaned. We hurried over and gathered around him.

"Luke?" Briar asked. She gripped his hand tightly.

His eyes fluttered open. He took a few seconds to take in his surroundings. His gaze settled on Angel kneeling next to him. He frowned as he glanced between his exposed chest and Angel, realizing what Angel had done.

He shoved Angel away and attempted to sit up. "What the hell happened?"

Angel rose to his feet. "You had your ass kicked."

Briar shot him a dirty look, then returned her attention to Luke, stroking his matted hair off his forehead. "That bald bastard zapped us with some powerful juju. You got it the worst because you—" She swallowed hard. "Because you jumped in front of me. Don't ever do that again, you asshole."

He chuckled lightly, staring into her face like the sun rose from it. "Don't need to be protected so much, and I won't have to keep doing it."

Angel walked over to Lynx and me. "Do you need anything else?"

I caught a flicker of resentment in his green eyes. If there really was a strong connection between him and Briar, it must be hard for him to watch Briar and Luke together. "I think we're good now. Thank you very much."

"Let me know how I can help tomorrow night. I know the vampires' roles must be limited, but we'll help where we can." He glanced over at Briar, whose attention was solely on Luke. "I have to go."

At this, Briar jumped up and walked Angel to the door. "I owe you big time."

He stared at her with intense eyes. "And one day, I may come to collect."

Luke sighed, running his hand through his hair. Then he slowly eased off the couch, clearly still in pain. His face was pale, and he was sweating. He slowly walked over to where Angel stood, whose eyes were only on Briar. Luke held out his hand. "Yeah, thanks man. I'm the one who owes you."

Angel looked down at it, hesitated, then shook it briefly. His gaze landed on Briar for a long moment, then he disappeared.

Briar stared after the empty space for a long breath, then turned to Luke. She pecked him on the lips. "I'm so glad you're okay."

He pulled her in for an even deeper kiss.

Lynx and I looked at each other.

"Coffee or whatever?" she asked me.

I nodded quickly and followed after her into the kitchen, leaving Luke and Briar alone. A few seconds later, Briar squealed out, and I swiveled around to see Luke throwing her over his shoulder. His eyes twinkled as he ran up the stairs, still in pain but clearly not enough to keep him from growling as he got to her bedroom door, then closing it firmly behind them.

I checked the time; it was well after midnight. I had hoped to head over to White Pine and scout out the area myself, but it had been a terribly long night already. Trying to control the explosion of emotions I'd endured earlier had left me drained.

Lynx handed me my thermos of blood. The label that had been on there earlier had been replaced with a crude drawing of a penis. Then a scribbled arrow and the word 'Mateo' next to it. I gave a tired laugh, and it felt good to ease the tension.

A door upstairs jerked open and Briar's voice called down. "Did Sammie just laugh? Lynx, take a picture."

"You do it!" Lynx called up, her green eyes twinkling with amusement.

"I can't. I'm only halfway dressed." Briar sighed and heavy footsteps came down the stairs. "Screw it, you guys know what boobies look like. I wanna see what Samira looks like when she laughs!"

"Don't!" Both Lynx and I yelled at the same time, and the footsteps stopped. Grumbling loudly, Briar turned back upwards and yelled out before slamming her door shut. "Fine! But only because I'm really horny!"

I sighed, a smile still teasing my lips. "We need something stronger to endure the next hour."

Lynx laughed and reached for the vodka above the fridge.

It didn't take us long to get tipsy, but the effects would be short-lived, especially for me. I could hear Briar's lovemaking and this made me drink more, faster, and harder. Lynx, too, seemed to be acutely aware how loveless our lives were at the moment and drank more than usual until the bottle was empty.

As the buzzing sensation in me abated, a sense of dread filled my gut. Lynx sensed my trepidation. "It's going to be bad, isn't it?"

"I don't know if that's the right word." After the way the Phoenix had easily taken out all three of us, I feared we knew less than we thought we did. I looked up at her. "I don't think we know what the hell we're doing."

Lynx chewed at her lip, staring beyond me.

I remembered the Phoenix' warning and it made the anger hiss inside me. "But no matter what it takes, we're going to get the bastard."

CHAPTER 30

*E*veryone took their place in the forest surrounding White Pine. The Silver Claws pack lined up at the front along with several witches, including Lynx, to hide the shifters' presence from the guards outside the building. Folas and Eddie were also with them. Folas had decided the two of them would be strong enough to create the illusion needed to block the guards on driving patrol.

I remained back with Teddy, almost a mile away. Mateo was even further back with Angel and several other Nocs. They would be our last line of defense should we run into trouble we couldn't get out of. I hated that I couldn't rush in first with the rest of them, but, if we didn't have to blow my cover with Korin, then we weren't going to.

Briar would message me the second she believed none of my old coven was there. It was still a risk, my showing up to fight Hydes, but, for me, it was worth it. I wanted to play a part in destroying anything of Korin's. So did Teddy.

"Kristina skipped town," Teddy said, breaking the silence.

I closed my eyes in relief. "When?"

"As soon as the sun set. She wanted to say goodbye to you, but Korin left suddenly, and she wanted to take advantage of his absence. She plans on being millions of miles away by the time the sun rises."

"Where was Korin going?" I hid the alarm from my voice. I didn't like sudden changes in routines.

"He said he was meeting with the Ministry. Not sure why."

This eased my mind a little. Those meetings could last a very long time, although it made me nervous he was meeting with them in the first place. He'd never had an interest in the group, especially in becoming a member. He wanted to live by his own rules and not those made by some group of nine, no matter how much their ideology aligned with his.

"Did Faithe go with him?"

"She didn't, which was strange."

I wanted to think she'd made the choice to stay back.

An explosion sounded, making the fangs in my mouth grow. "They've begun."

We listened closely. Every muscle in my body was flexed tight, anxiously waiting for my turn. The distinct sounds of fists crashing into bodies, heads smashing together, blades running through flesh excited all my senses. It was the beast inside me that craved the violence, and right now, I gave into that most basic instinct.

Teddy shifted his weight back and forth, feeling the same as me. "Let me go."

"Wait," I ordered.

The sounds of bullets firing echoed through the trees. More clashing of blades. Explosions. Screams from both sides. My heart beat erratically in my chest. It took all my strength to keep from rushing forward.

Metal scraped against metal. I glanced at Teddy. "They're inside."

A few seconds later, the phone in my hand buzzed. I glanced down at the lit-up screen. One word: *Hurry.*

I became the wind, lifting leaves and dirt as I raced across the forest floor with Teddy on my tail. Seconds later, I exploded from the forest. Chaos raged everywhere. Two Hydes were on fire and yet they still fought, oblivious to the flames consuming their flesh. A shifter shot one of them in the head.

Several bodies littered the ground. Near the front of the property,

Eddie and Folas stood with their hands stretched out toward the road. Their hands shook as they tried to maintain the illusion. With all the explosions and guns firing, it must take great effort to conceal this battle from the rest of the world.

Stepping over a body, I withdrew the blades from my back and engaged the nearest Hyde who caught my eye. My blades clashed with his. He spun and blinked behind me so fast I barely managed to stop his long sword before it pierced my back. This Hyde was also a vampire, a deadly combination.

Dropping, I swiped my foot low, knocking his legs out from under him. I swung my blade downward, but he rolled out of the way and jumped to his feet. He stabbed forward. I spun on my heel and slashed to the side. The tip of my blade sliced through his arm. He didn't flinch as he attacked me again. One jab to my left, another to my right.

Screams echoed from inside the warehouse. I was wasting time.

Giving myself a boost of power, I released a mere fraction of the Kiss's strength. As my movements sped up, his appeared in slow motion. I ducked to the side to avoid his blade and stabbed forward. My blade slid past his breast bone and into his chest. I withdrew it just as quickly and delivered another fatal blow to his brain. Before he hit the ground, I had already moved on to the next Hyde.

Four more died by my hands, each one as challenging as the next. Members of the Silver Claws were having a difficult time battling them unless they engaged them as partners. We may have had the numbers, but they had genetically-altered strength.

Teddy hadn't wasted any time to jump into the slaughter. He teamed up with Gerald and, together, they were a formidable force.

A gun fired and more bullets began to fill the air. I dodged them and searched for the gunman. I spotted the Hyde standing partially behind a van holding a SIG MPX tactical rifle. One bullet after another fired into the crowd with no regard as to who they hit. One of them grazed my shoulder.

To gain his attention, I leapt on top of the nearest parked vehicle and began to race toward him, leaping car to car. He fired at me, but I dodged most of them. On my last leap to him, a bullet pierced my left shoulder. Silver wouldn't harm me, but the bullet could limit my movements.

Before he could fire the weapon again, I slashed forward, severing his head from his body. Blood misted the air all around me. I wiped at my eyes and took in what was left of the fight. There appeared to be only a dozen or so Hydes left; each were being overwhelmed by the Silver Claws.

Confident the shifters had the fight under control, I ran toward the building and leapt into the back of an open bay. I stopped briefly to gain my bearings. Rows and rows of stocked shelves lay to my right. On my left, cages. Lots of them, all filled with people. At the end, I spotted Lynx and Roma. They had already begun to free people and were guiding them out a side entrance.

Further toward the back, I heard Briar shouting. It was laced with anger and yet, I also detected fear. I bolted toward her and came to a screeching halt, my heart stopping when I saw what Briar was yelling at. Luke and Loxley stood next to her.

Blocking the entrance to another section of the large building where even more supernaturals were being held captive, stood Faithe, a line of fire burning behind her.

"Faithe?"

Her head snapped my direction. "Hello, Mother. I wondered if I'd see you here."

"What are you doing?"

"She won't let us past to save everyone," Briar answered for her. "The bitch keeps trying to light us up." Her hand snapped to her mouth. "Sorry for calling your offspring a dirty name, but that's what she's being."

"Silence, wolf," Faithe growled and stretched out her hand. A sting of fire broke off from the main line and raced toward Briar. Briar dove out of the way.

"How are you doing this?" I asked, my mind reeling. She looked completely different than the last time I saw her. Her eyes seethed as she stared at me.

"Korin gave me some of his powers and sent me here to kill whoever tried to take what was his, including you."

"Can vampires do that?" Briar asked me. She wiped blood from a cut on her head that kept running into her eye.

"No. It would've taken great magic. Why are you doing this, Faithe?" My heart hurt, and it was hard to breathe. My chest was so tight, the pain almost unbearable.

"Because Korin has been the only person in my life who hasn't abandoned me."

"He's using you. Please—"

"Shut up!" she screamed, her long white hair lifting into the air. Whatever magic she'd been given, she looked like she could barely contain it. She pushed her hand forward, sending more fire racing toward us. We quickly dodged it but just barely.

"Incoming!" Luke yelled at something behind us. Briar and Loxley whirled around to fight several Hydes who'd just discovered us. They must've been hiding in the building.

I returned my attention back to Faithe, my eyes pleading.

"I'll give you one chance, Mother. Leave now. I don't want to hurt you." A pink tint mottled her white skin. I noted several blisters on her hands.

"You know I can't do that." I searched her eyes, trying to find a way past her blind devotion to Korin. "You say you want to be with Korin, but does he treat you with kindness?"

"Has anyone?"

"Was I not good to you? I loved you and still do. You're all that matters to me in this world."

"But you left me." She blinked her eyes rapidly, and that's when I noticed the emptiness in them. Korin had broken her. Whatever humanity she'd had all those years before had been depleted. Agony burst through me. Somehow I had to find the sliver of desperation she'd expressed the other night. It was a sign that she wanted something different, something better.

I reached out my hand. "I swear, I did it to protect you. I thought it was the only way to keep you safe from Korin. Clearly, I was wrong. Let me make up for it."

The Kiss's dark power I'd unleashed earlier turned its attention to my great fear and sorrow and began to devour it. I could feel it growing inside me. *Relax. Breathe.*

"I have to kill you. Kill all of them." Her chin quivered.

"You have a choice."

She laughed at this. "You of all people should know that I don't."

"What did Korin say would happen if you didn't kill us?" I glanced behind me. More Hydes were coming as if they'd been let out from somewhere deep within the building. Briar's eyes flashed a brilliant yellow as she released her Komira powers. I felt the strength of it rush through the room, and it nearly took my breath away. I glanced away just as Briar raged forward into the incoming Hydes.

Faithe's expression hardened. "Then I die. One thing I am is a survivor."

I searched her eyes and something came alive in them. Pain raw as an open wound reflected back. "Will killing me make you feel better?"

"It will make me alive."

I stepped forward, nearing the flames. "Then kill me, because your life is all that matters. But please, spare my friends."

Her gaze flickered behind me, and her hands shook. Doubt crept into her eyes.

"Do it, Faithe. Then live your life, but do it without existing in Korin's shadow. You were meant for more." I took another step, my face sincere. I knew this was the only way to save her, to give her back what I had taken from her. Her chance for hope.

"Stay back!" she cried. Flames roared to life in front of me.

Heat singed my hair, but I didn't flinch.

"I don't have a choice!" she screamed. Her eyes flooded with tears.

Behind me, I heard Lynx's voice call my name. If anyone could stop Faithe, it was Lynx using her magic. I held my hand backwards in a stopping gesture to make sure she didn't interfere. "Look at me, Faithe."

The edges of pink eyes bled red as she stared at me, desperation spilling from them. She didn't want to kill me. The tightness in my chest loosened.

"I swear to you, I will protect you. Korin will not lay another finger on you."

She hissed and bore her fangs. Fire licked at my feet and legs, burning my clothing. Blisters formed on my legs.

"You can't protect me from him!" She glanced behind me again, her face paling. She probably saw Lynx and felt Lynx's power.

"Let me try." I kept my voice calm, even though searing pain ripped through my flesh. But I could handle this. I would do it, for her.

Her gaze, pitiful and sad, slowly returned to mine. "I'm sorry."

Her hands shot forward and fire followed the motion, but before it could fully consume me and anyone behind me, a strong gust of wind reversed the flames' direction.

"No!" I cried and lunged directly through the fire to get at Faithe before she was engulfed by the inferno.

Pain lanced my whole body, and I gasped as I crashed into Faithe. We tumbled to the ground, my back on fire.

"Samira!" a deep voice yelled. Hope leapt in my heart at the sound. Mateo. Mateo was here. He came for me, even though I'd pushed him away.

Faithe pulled herself into a ball cradling her knees. Great tears spilled from her eyes. I crawled over to her even as I felt someone hitting at the flames at my back. I didn't care. Faithe was what mattered now.

"Hold still," Mateo begged.

He tried to keep me still, but I stumbled forward until I reached her. I looked into her eyes, filled with such pain and sadness. I cupped her face, even while Mateo attended to my wounds. But right now, in this moment, it was only her and me.

"I love you." I should've told her this the minute I saw her.

"I'm so sorry," she whimpered. Her whole body was covered in blisters, her hair singed and blackened, but she was already healing at a rapid rate.

"It's okay, Faithe." I lay next to her, pulling her into my arms. "I'll protect you," I said over and over.

Briar and Lynx hurried over to me, but I waved them away. "Save everyone."

I could still hear the sounds of fighting outside of the building, but they had mostly died down. The fight was over. We had won and yet, with Faithe lying next to me completely broken, I couldn't feel the victory. Her pain sunk into me like an anvil.

"Angel!" Mateo called. I winced when Mateo pulled back part of my shirt from my back.

"No, Mateo," I said. "He can't heal me here. Not in front of everyone. He's exposed his secret enough."

"But you're hurt. Terribly."

"I'll survive. We need to get Faithe far away from here."

"We will," he promised.

I gripped his chin, forcing him to focus on me. "You came for me."

His eyes darkened with anger. "Of course I came for you."

"But I ... I left you there."

His hand snapped to the nape of my neck, his eyes fierce. "When will you stop doubting me? I will always come for you, Samira." Then his eyes softened and he leaned forward, swiping his lips softly against mine. Energy buzzed through me. "I understand you more than you know, my love."

I closed my eyes, giving in to the moment, feeling the warmth of his love wash over me. I truly loved this man. Then I opened my eyes to look into his. "We have much to talk about, but we must wait until this is over. I need my wits about me to handle this, or the Kiss will take over me." My voice caught. "I can't let that happen."

He nodded. "I'm ready when you are." Then he kissed me again, softly, sweetly and my whole world lit up. It was a brief kiss, but hope rushed through my body, making me feel alive again.

"Help us to stand?" I asked, hoping he could see through my eyes how he affected me; somehow I think he did.

His lips turned down as he looked over me. "I don't know where to touch."

He carefully slipped his arm around me and lifted slowly. I pulled Faithe up with me, grinding my jaw together. I wanted to cry it hurt so much, but I steeled myself, bearing the pain.

Briar and the rest of them, including Roma and Lynx, were inside the other section of the building beginning to unlock cages. Most of them required magic. Lynx and Roma separated and hurried up and down the long rows to break them open.

"Let's get out of here," Mateo said.

"Faithe ... "

"I'll take her," Angel said. He gently took her from my arms. She barely made a sound.

Just as we turned to leave, a wave of intense power rolled through the building, making us stumble.

"What's that?" Mateo said, his voice alarmed.

I slowly turned around. The building began to shake. Bits of dust and light debris fell from the ceiling.

"Get her out of here," I said to Angel. "And don't leave her, no matter what."

He glanced at Briar in concern, but then obeyed.

Pressure in the air grew stronger, suffocating even.

"We have to leave!" Luke called.

"Not until we've saved everyone," Briar said. Only a dozen had managed to get out of their cages. I couldn't see Lynx or Roma. Loxley was at the end, her face pale. She fell to her knees almost as if she was in some kind of trance.

Eddie ran in just then, his eyes wide. "Something bad is coming!"

I slowly turned to him. "It's already here."

CHAPTER 31

a high-pitched wailing, louder than anything I'd ever heard, screamed through the building. Everyone covered their ears as the roaring shook right through us. Mateo and I looked at each other, centuries of pain and love in our eyes. I truly thought I'd die in that moment, especially when the lights exploded all around us, bathing us in darkness. We both felt the darkness coming.

And then all was quiet.

"Are we dead?" Lynx's voice asked from the darkness.

"We can't be," Briar whispered. "I don't see Chris Hemsworth."

"Chris Hemsworth?"

"A psychic promised me once he'd be waiting for me in the afterlife."

Luke snorted. "Everyone turn on your phones. We need light."

"Are you okay?" Mateo whispered to me.

Streams of light spread out all around. "I'll be okay."

"Where's Roma?" Lynx asked.

"Oh shit," Luke said. "Eddie's down."

My gaze followed Luke's light. Eddie lay on the ground, unconscious.

"So is Loxley!" Briar's light bounced in the darkness as Briar hurried over to her.

"Roma!" Lynx called. Her light hurried up and down the aisles. "Found her! She's down too!"

"That's not our only problem," Mateo said. He shined his own light into the cages. "They're gone. All of them."

All lights turned toward the cages. He was right. Not a single prisoner remained.

Eddie groaned on the floor next to me.

"Help me," I told Mateo.

Mateo slowly removed his arms from around me to see if I'd fall without his support. When he was sure I was okay, he lowered to the floor to Eddie, who was stirring.

"What happened?" Mateo asked him.

Eddie lifted up on his elbow and rubbed his head. "I'm not sure. One second I was in here warning you, and the next it felt like someone was sucking the light right out of me."

Briar called over to us, "Loxley's coming to. Lynx, how's Roma?"

"Still out!" she called back.

Luke began walking up and down the aisles and into the other side of the warehouse. "A lot of the crates are gone too."

My mind reeled at the power it must've taken to teleport everything. "We should go. It's not safe."

"Let's go back to Fire Ridge," Briar ordered. She assisted Loxley to her feet, while Luke carried Roma, Lynx fretting over her.

Mateo helped me exit the building. The burns on my legs had begun to heal, but it would take much longer for my back. Every slight movement sent shooting pain throughout my body. Angel was pacing just outside the entrance, glancing anxiously inside the darkened hole. Only when Briar arrived did he relax. Faithe was sitting on the ground staring into the distance.

"What the hell happened in there?" Briar asked to no one in particular.

"Powerful magic," Lynx answered as she walked past with Luke. Roma was beginning to regain consciousness in his arms.

Lynx rubbed at her arms. "I could feel it. Dark and suffocating. It tried to get inside my head."

At this, I snapped my head in her direction, then flickered my gaze to Eddie, Loxley, and Roma. "Just like the Phoenix the other day when Luke got hurt."

Briar frowned, her eyes shooting to Loxley, who was helping Gerald carry an injured shifter to a vehicle. Briar looked at me.

I raised my eyebrows as if to question, *"Could it be her?"*

Briar's gaze grew thoughtful, but she called out to everyone. "Load up!" Then she turned to Eddie, who had walked over to Folas. Folas still held his hands up, maintaining the illusion around the perimeter. "Give us a few more minutes to get out of here, then let it drop."

"Hurry," Folas growled, sweat dotting his forehead.

"Meet at Fire Ridge," Briar told us. "We'll try to sort through what exactly happened here."

I limped over to Faithe, trying to keep my heart intact. The despondent look in her eyes shattered everything hard and emotionless inside me. "Faithe?"

She didn't respond.

I tried a couple more times while the shifters gathered their wounded and loaded them into SUVs. From the looks of it, the Silver Claws had lost three members. Briar moaned when she realized it and punched the nearest tree followed by a string of profanities. I didn't envy her position as Alpha.

Roma finally regained consciousness and sat in a vehicle breathing heavily while Lynx guided the ones we had saved into the back of a van. There were ten. Ten out of maybe fifty? It made me ill. By the looks of them, the glazed look in their eyes, their hands shaking, they would need time to recover. We'd take them to the Blutel Estate where the Ames de la Terra would help them recover.

When I couldn't get Faithe to respond, I glanced over at Mateo who was speaking quietly with Angel. "Help me?"

He nodded. Together we led Faithe to my car that Teddy had driven over for me earlier and slowly helped her into the back. I still wasn't sure what to do with her, but I planned on keeping my promise. I would keep her safe.

Unable to lean into the seat, I slid on my side in the back, facing Faithe, while Mateo drove toward Fire Ridge. Angel sat in the passenger seat. I tried not to grimace over every bump in the road, but it was impossible.

"Sorry," Mateo mumbled, eyeing me in the rearview mirror. He drove slowly and carefully back to Fire Ridge, making us the last to arrive.

By the time we reached there, the immediate sting of burned flesh had passed, and I was able to move without grimacing as much. What I needed was loose clothing.

As soon as I exited, Briar found me and nodded her head toward the van Lynx had been driving. "Where should we take the supernaturals we saved? They look pretty messed up."

"Blutel Estate." I turned to Angel who had just opened his car door. "Will you take them?"

Over the last century, I'd seen him there a few times. He never stayed long, but he always came back. Just for a few days. Enough time to remind him that he wasn't a monster. Sometimes we needed that.

"You've been there?" Briar asked, surprised.

Pain lanced his eyes, but he didn't say anything. Only nodded his head. He walked toward the van. Briar stared after him, a puzzled look on her face.

I stuck my head back into the car. "Faithe. I need you to come in. You'll be safe here."

She didn't respond, but she did exit the car and follow after me.

As Alpha, Briar took control, ordering the injured upstairs to be cared for by the doctor and arranging for the dead. Families would need to be notified, funerals planned. Others may have not noticed, but as the night wore on, her shoulders sank further under the weight of leadership. She made all the hard decisions so the others wouldn't have to, and she had to do it under a mask of strength and confidence.

Luke and her friends helped where they could. Marge became the loud, doting, and often inappropriate mother figure, while Samantha played the role of a high school football coach, telling people to suck it up because during the next game they were going to smash balls and break spines.

I would've helped more, but I didn't dare leave Faithe, plus my back was still mending.

Mateo came to me and, noticing my shirt was badly damaged, yanked off his jacket. Then he removed his shirt and offered it to me. As it came over his head, I eyed the perfect lines of his muscled chest and the way they rippled as he moved. He moved behind me, giving me a smirk as if he knew I'd been gawking at him, and gently pulled my shirt over my head. Parts of the material had melted into my skin, and I gulped down the pain as he slowly, gently pulled it off me. His hands traced down my back, caressing my skin, and goosebumps broke out. I shivered and could've swore I heard him smile. Gently, he maneuvered his shirt over my head, and I inhaled a deep breath, reveling in his earthy smell.

Tucked away in Briar's office, Faithe had curled up on the love seat. Mateo and I checked on her, and I placed a blanket over her before settling into a chair next to her. Her eyes slowly closed. She would need lots of time to heal.

While she rested, I telephoned Sersi and explained what had happened. She already knew most of it from Angel, who had shown up thirty minutes earlier. But she didn't know about Faithe. And so I told her, speaking quietly and vaguely, unsure if Faithe was listening in, even though she appeared to be sleeping soundlessly, her chest rising and lowering slowly with each breath.

Sersi read between the lines. "I have the perfect place for her. No one but me will know about it, and you can join her just as soon as you can."

"Thank you." We spoke for a few more minutes about what to do if we found the other missing supernaturals who had disappeared. She recommended the facility in Wildemoor. My heart clenched at the mention. That's where my longtime friend Rebecca, also a wolf shifter, used to work. I missed her terribly.

When someone knocked on the door outside the office, I said goodbye and ended the call. Briar walked in with Luke, Eddie, Lynx, Roma, and Mateo behind her. The small office grew crowded fast.

Briar was shaking her head fiercely before Mateo was all the way inside. "Nope. No way. Too crowded. Everyone out before I lose my shit. We'll go downstairs."

I sometimes forgot Briar was claustrophobic. She mostly handled it well except for in cases like this. The night's events probably didn't help. Like the rest of us, her nerves had been pulled too tight.

Everyone filed out of the room. I was the last to leave, glancing down at Faithe. She was still sleeping. I left the door open a crack so I could hear her should she begin to stir.

Mateo was waiting for me in the hall. "How's she doing?"

"She's broken. But I have vowed to mend her."

He slipped his fingers into mine. "I'm here for you."

His honey eyes stared into mine. As much as he was in my heart, my veins, my very bones, this wasn't the time to rekindle anything between us. Too much had to happen before I could commit to him fully. Starting with knowing I wouldn't harm him if I gave in to my emotions. That might never happen.

I smiled gently and slowly let go of his hand to follow after the others into the training room. Roma was sitting on a chair speaking quietly with Lynx. Roma's face was pale, and she looked ten years older. Regret pained my heart. Maybe we shouldn't have gotten her involved. This may prove too much for her.

I shifted my gaze. Mats lined the floor, dried blood and sweat on most of them. Briar didn't care and collapsed onto her back in the middle of the room, arms outstretched. "This sucks. I can't keep asking the pack to fight for me. Too many deaths."

Luke stared down at her. "They're not just fighting for you. They are fighting for Rouen."

"It doesn't matter the reason. Lives are being lost because of what I'm asking them to do."

Eddie leaned into the wall, his gaze glued to his phone.

"Where's Folas?" I asked.

He looked up at me. "He had to report to the Queen. She's not going to be happy."

Briar lifted her head and frowned at him. "It's not our fault everything went poof."

"She won't see it that way. She risked me and Folas exposing our powers and for what? Korin probably knows fae are involved now and will seek retribution against our people. This is what we've been trying to avoid for decades."

Mateo tensed and glared at Eddie. His sudden hostility surprised me. "Your kind have always been silent players," he spat. "Don't pretend your King and Queen aren't secretly manipulating events and people. It's what fae do. They care more about power and money than any other group I know."

"Not all of us," Eddie said, not cowering in the least. "We know the Phoenix must be stopped. Every species on this planet depends upon it."

"The witches aren't going to be happy either," Roma added, shaking her head. She smoothed stray hairs away from her face. "From the captives we rescued only one was a witch, which means Korin still has a bunch of our kind."

"Then we get them back," I said, my voice firm and full of power. "They couldn't have just disappeared altogether. They've been moved. My guess is they are still in the city, in another building, perhaps. It would take too much power to transport them far away."

"Samira's right," Lynx said and paused, thinking. "You know, the magic that was used, maybe we can trace it back to the source."

"Can you do that?" Luke asked.

Lynx and Roma locked eyes, hesitating.

"We can," Roma said, "but we must be careful. If whoever performed that powerful spell discovers us, they could break the connection."

"Isn't it worth the risk?" Briar had propped herself onto her elbows.

"It's a mental connection," Lynx explained. "My mind would have to latch onto the other witch's power. If that gets cut prematurely, it could affect my mind. And not in a good way."

No one said anything. Physical injuries were one thing; they could heal. But injuries of the mind? Sometimes one could never recover. They become trapped in a world of nightmares, lost in an endless mental maze of torment. No amount of magic could bring them back. The mind was too big.

"Too risky," Briar said. "Let's try something else first."

Lynx was biting her lip, staring at the matted floor. I recognized the look in her eyes.

"Lynx," I warned, "don't even think about it. We'll find another way."

She looked up at me. "The magic that was used will only be there for forty-eight hours at most. This may be our only chance to locate the Phoenix."

"How do we know it was the Phoenix?" Luke asked. "Couldn't it have been Korin?"

Mateo scoffed. "Korin may be powerful, but he doesn't have the ability to wield that kind of magic."

"It was the Phoenix," I added. "The magic had the same feeling as when we were all attacked the last night by the bald man."

Lynx nodded in agreement.

Mateo looked at me, his brows furrowed. "You were attacked?"

"Look, Lynx," Briar interrupted. "It's too dangerous. Besides, Eddie will find him."

Eddie's eyes widened. "I will?" He shook his head. "No, the King will not want them knowing of our involvement."

"You will find a way to make him allow it." Her face grew serious and her Komira powers lit fire in her eyes. "It's time fae got more involved instead of relying on the rest of the supernatural community to do all of the heavy lifting. I lost three shifters tonight and you're worried about the Phoenix knowing fae are involved?" She asked him. "You're stronger than this. Now that I know you are fae, I can feel your strength, your power. You should let the Phoenix know you're involved and not to fuck with your kind."

He slowly nodded. "You're right."

"Of course I am. Besides, the fae need a dog in this fight. You will become united if you all have something on the line. And we need all the help we can get."

"Okay. I'll talk to him myself."

Mateo leaned over and whispered, "It will be sunrise soon."

Just as he said it, I felt the familiar tugging on all my senses.

Briar pulled herself off the floor and stood next to Luke. To us, she said, "I have a couple of coffins here."

I tilted my head. "Since when?"

"I ordered them a few weeks ago. I figured now that our pack is working with vampires, we should have some accommodations for them for cases like this. They're in that old boiler room. Do you remember where that is?"

I nodded.

"I can't stay here," Mateo said. "Korin can't find out I'm working with you all just yet."

No one disagreed. Korin believing all the vampires were on his side was the only advantage we had over him.

Mateo gave me a meaningful look before he exited the room. I ignored the part of me that wanted to rush after him and bury my soul into his.

Eddie pushed away from the wall. "I need to go, too. I'll let you know what I discover."

After he left the room, I turned to Briar. "What will you do?"

"First, I plan on sleeping for a few hours. Then I'll get up, put on my big girl panties, and play the role of Alpha for the funerals. I don't want to wait a few days to do them. We'll mourn now, then I plan on giving my pack a choice."

"A choice?" Luke asked.

"Yes. I'm going to give them the opportunity to run." When Luke opened his mouth to argue, Briar added, "My mind is made up. As Alpha, I order you not to say another word."

Sensing an argument brewing between them, I left them alone with Lynx and Roma on my heels. Before I slipped into Briar's office to get Faithe, I said to Lynx, "Please. Don't track the Phoenix. Just wait. See what Eddie comes up with."

She nodded slowly, but I caught the determined look in her eyes.

"I'll make sure she's good," Roma said, patting my shoulder. "Get some rest. You were on fire a few hours ago, after all. You deserve a break."

I rotated my shoulders, barely feeling pain anymore. Healing quickly was one of the greatest perks of being a vampire. Having the Kiss inside me also made the process much quicker.

After saying goodbye, I quietly opened the door to Briar's office. Faithe was sitting up, staring at the poster of a rockstar.

"Sun's coming up," she whispered.

"We are sleeping here. There are coffins downstairs."

Without blinking or breathing, she said, "I may just go outside and watch it. It's been so long since I've seen the sun."

My insides clenched, and I lowered in front of her. "That is not the answer. You're safe now. You can live a new life, free from Korin. I swear it!"

Her gaze tracked to mine. Those once vibrant light eyes held a deep-rooted darkness, the kind that might take years to unearth. But I wouldn't give up.

"I'll never be free of him, Mother," she whispered, tears filling her eyes.

I clasped her hands in mine. "I believed the same as you once, but I promise you, this is a new dawn! I won't leave you."

She didn't respond, only let her eyes drift back to the poster.

"Let's sleep. Tomorrow is a new night, one filled with promise."

I guided her downstairs and helped her into the coffin Briar had provided. It was better than I would've expected, made from Brazilian ebony, a dark chocolate color. The inside was lined with plush, dark purple velvet. It was nicer than my own. Part of me wondered if she had been thinking of Angel when she purchased them.

After closing the lid over her, I laid down in mine but I didn't close the top over me. Fire Ridge was alive with sounds. Luke and Briar had found their way upstairs. I could hear her calling the pack together to give an announcement. A short time later, she made good on her promise and offered all of them a way out. She said she'd even provide funds for them to leave the state.

By their silence, many of them had not expected this. Alphas didn't give choices; they gave orders. I admired Briar for doing something different, something better. When I'd first discovered she was the shifter mentioned in the prophecy, I'd been surprised. She had a temper coupled with a foul mouth and made stupid decisions. She still had the foul mouth, but she had grown in so many ways. I had hoped she wouldn't fulfill her part of the prophecy by killing three Alphas, and had almost told her about it, but how could I? She needed to become a full Komira. It was who she was, and I couldn't take that from her.

Instead, I would stop the prophecy by never giving up the Kiss of Eternal Night.

No matter what, it would be my curse for eternity.

CHAPTER 32

*N*ightmares plagued my sleep. Darkness crept along the whole earth, a black mist devouring everything it touched. Humans rotted into grotesque things with bloated stomachs, hair falling out and flesh melting. Supernaturals didn't fare much better, and yet, no one cared. Those who still lived roamed the lands, a vacant look in their eyes. Living zombies void of emotions. I didn't wake from the nightmares until I came face to face with one who looked exactly like me.

I sat up, gasping for breath. My coffin lid was still open. Faithe's was still covered. By the way my body felt, a deep ache squeezing my bones, the sun was still up. It was a pain I could tolerate, having learned to adjust to the sensation over the centuries.

Sounds echoed down from the floors above me. Lots of shifters, mostly quiet or speaking in hushed tones. More funerals. I didn't want to go up there to be a part of it. I hated funerals. They had a tendency to remind me of everyone I'd ever lost in my life. I'd lost too many.

In the end, I trudged my way upstairs, but only for Briar. She could use the support. I followed her scent until I found her near the patio door speaking to Luke. The last of the sun's rays highlighted the gold in her hair. Several shifters crowded the living room and kitchen. I remained in the shadows, waiting for her to notice me. It took her only a moment.

She kissed Luke on the cheek and crossed the room. "How's your back?"

"Healed. How's everyone here?"

She sighed, her gaze sweeping over the large room. "Numb." She looked back at me. "Is this ever going to end?"

"Having lived what feels like an eternity, I can tell you that it will end. Maybe not in the way we want or expect, but it will end."

She rubbed at the back of her shoulder. No doubt that's where she carried most of her stress. "That's good, I think."

"But then a new problem will arise."

Her hand lowered, and she scowled. "Why are you always shitting on my Oreos?"

"That's a stupid comparison and doesn't even make sense."

"Your mom doesn't make sense."

I didn't normally engage in her nonsensical banter, but I could sense she needed the release, something to lighten up the depressing mood in the room. My breaking character might give her just that. Besides, I had been funny once when I hadn't had to handle my emotions as if they were glass. Vulgar, too. I had spent more than fifty years with Russian warriors, after all.

And so I let it slip. "She sure made sense when she complained about your father's little dick last night. A real shame."

Her mouth fell open, her eyes just as wide. The pressure of being Alpha that had filled her eyes moments ago had been replaced with shock. Then laughter. It erupted from her so loud and sudden that everyone in the room turned to us. She quickly clamped both hands over her mouth and tried to stifle the laugher.

"Are you finished?"

Her hands slowly lowered. She still smiled big. "I fucking love you."

She chuckled quietly and leaned into the wall. I would've liked to have shared in Briar's laughter, to really let loose, but that kind of joy was for others.

"Is Lynx coming?" I asked.

"She'll be here soon. I talked to Roma. Roma practically had to restrain Lynx from going back to White Pine to track the Phoenix."

"Good. She shouldn't mess around with such dangerous magic."

"Briar!" Marge called from the kitchen. "We don't have enough beer to last the night."

"Emergency?" I asked.

"Definitely. I'll catch up with you later."

Briar left me alone while she ordered someone to go out and get more alcohol. Everyone wanted or needed something from her. She handled their requests like a true leader. Not a single one had chosen to leave her last night when she'd given them a chance to flee Rouen. Understandable. They looked up to her. Trusted her. Just like I did.

The ceremony was about to start when Lynx showed up at sunset. Though she looked freshly showered, her outfit undoubtedly a cut of the latest fashion, the fire in her jade eyes could've exploded the house. I'd never seen her so agitated before.

Briar and I glanced at each other. Most of the pack was outside already. I could hear Gerald's voice organizing everyone. Fires had already been lit.

"You okay, Lynx?" Briar asked.

"No, I'm not. We could be storming the Phoenix's castle or his trailer park right now and end this once and for all."

Her aggression worried me. "You saw what he did. That was powerful magic he used."

"I have powerful magic," she snapped, then cleared her throat. "I mean all of us do. Together, the witches, fae, shifters, vampires, can defeat him if we act quickly. Let's go on the offensive for once."

Briar was rubbing at her shoulders again. "Look, I love rushing into an unknown situation as much as the next mentally unstable person, but I have people I'm in charge of. I won't risk their lives until I know what I'm up against."

"Briar's right," I added. "We need to know more."

Lynx sighed and walked past us. "We'll see."

A gong sounded. Briar hurried outside to take part of the festivities. I tilted my head to listen below. Faithe was just getting up.

Before heading downstairs, I grabbed a few blood bags Briar kept in the fridge and drank one as I brought the other two to Faithe. She still had that lifeless look in her eyes, but at least she accepted and drank the blood I gave her, which meant she wasn't thinking about dying anymore.

"How long are we going to be here for?" she asked and wiped her mouth with the back of her hand.

"We'll leave after the funerals. Maybe a few hours?"

She thought about this as she began drinking the next bag.

"What do you know about the Phoenix?" I asked.

The blood bag nearly slipped from her grasp. "He, she, it … is a monster. Worse than a monster. I've seen it shift forms so many times, I fear to trust anyone. It once pretended to be Korin and came to my bed." She visibly shivered. "As cold as Korin's touch is, the Phoenix's is much colder and crueler too. I knew right away something was wrong. I yelled for Korin. Actually called *him* for help." She paused, her face paling.

"What happened?"

"It's the only fight I ever saw between them. Korin wasn't upset that the Phoenix had touched me. He was angry because the Phoenix had tried to be him."

I could imagine. "Do you know where we can find the Phoenix?"

She shook her head. "I wish I did. I want him gone as much as everyone else. He gave Korin all these new powers that made him even more dangerous."

"Do you know their plans?"

"Some. Korin didn't talk much about them with me, but he did say something big was going to happen on a special day in the late fall. It wasn't Halloween …"

A sinking feeling burned my insides. "Was it Diablos Nocte?"

"That's it. What does it mean?"

"It means Night of the Devil. It's an ancient holiday that hasn't been celebrated in centuries."

She lowered the empty bag. "Something terrible is going to happen on that day."

"Not if we stop them."

At this, she stilled, the vacant look in her eyes returning. I wish she would allow herself to believe me. I would protect her. "Come on. Let's go upstairs and honor the dead who have fallen for our cause."

She didn't say anything but followed after me. The funeral had already begun. Luke, Gerald and several others carried in three coffins. Lynx, Faithe, and I stayed back by the house, as was our place for such a ceremony.

Within an hour, it ended and the celebration of life for those lost commenced. Stories were shared and alcohol was consumed. Briar made sure to visit with each and every pack member. They used to be divided between Greybacks and Silver Claws, but now you couldn't tell who had once belonged to which pack. A sign of great leadership.

The midnight hour called. Lynx had had her fair share of alcohol and was currently dancing with a younger shifter with grabby paws. I might've interfered, but Lynx didn't seem to have any qualms. Maybe this was her way to release pent-up rage. I preferred to kill. She may prefer to mate. Briar? I glanced at her sitting on Luke's lap, holding a blade playfully to his throat. She liked to do both.

I would've left a while ago, but Faithe hadn't wanted to. We'd even gone as far as the front door, but night's darkness had stopped her.

"Not yet," she said, her eyes fearful. "He's out there."

"No one's there." I knew because I'd patrolled it myself. I also knew Gerald and his men were taking shifts running the perimeter of the property.

She sat in the corner on a recliner, her arms curled around her bent knees, rocking gently. A few shifters had tried to interact with her earlier, but now everyone left her alone. Lynx, however, tried multiple times to connect with her, even managing a short conversation at one point, but Faithe's fear prevented her from warming to anyone.

I needed to get her out of here. Once I had her safely behind the walls of the Blutel Estate with the Ames de la Terra, she would feel much better. I hoped.

"You look like you're ready to bolt," Briar said.

I whirled around. Briar set a wine bottle on the counter. Lynx appeared and picked it up.

"I really should be leaving with Faithe to the Blutel Estate."

Lynx lowered the bottle of wine from her lips. "Can I go, too? I've always wanted to, but my mother forbade it."

Briar looked from me to Lynx. "If she's going, I'm coming too. I picture it like some fancy resort spa with mani-pedis for monsters."

I opened my mouth to counter her when a wave of dark and powerful energy slammed into me. I gripped the nearby counter for support, my head spinning. I slowly looked up at Briar and Lynx. By their pale faces and fearful eyes, they were feeling the same thing.

An eerie quiet blanketed the room.

Faithe's soft voice broke the silence. "He's here."

CHAPTER 33

"Sober up!" Briar called, blanketing the order with a wave of Alpha strength. "We have company. Bring everyone inside!"

Luke was the first to respond, followed by Gerald who had just returned from patrol. Gerald rushed outside the backyard to gather shifters into the mansion, while Luke sprinted up the stairs to find any stragglers.

Lynx and I moved to the front window and peered into the darkness. Smoke crept toward the mansion in great billowing waves. I stared in amazement as it broke off into several pieces, then began to take shape into massive beasts. They resembled enormous hyenas with long, sharp teeth and six-inch claws on furred feet. Two horns protruded from their red scaled heads, and glowing red eyes watched me intently.

They all wore thick, unyielding rhinoceros armor and their misty forms faded in and out, only to reappear a moment later in a different location.

The Hellhounds of the First Hierarchy.

Ice filled my veins and fear like I'd never known before gripped me.

"What the hell is that?" Briar asked over her shoulder.

I'd seen these beasts one other time, and what had followed had killed hundreds if not thousands of people. I straightened, thinking hard. There wasn't enough time to ask the Witches of Rouen to come help or even Eddie and his kind. And as strong as Mateo and his coven were, vampires couldn't fight this. No reason to expose their true allegiances prematurely.

"Get everyone downstairs," I said. "Tell them to lock themselves inside. It might save them."

Briar gripped my arm. "From what?"

"From the Legions of Hell."

She didn't ask any more questions. She raced around the room, rushing everyone into the basement. Several asked to stay with her and fight but she wouldn't hear of it. At one point, she had to call upon her Komira powers to give orders. None of them could disobey those. The only two she didn't order to the basement were Gerald and Luke, but she did give them a choice. They both chose to stay with us.

I lowered next to Faithe, who was rocking even more erratically. "I need you to go downstairs with the others."

She shook her head frantically. "I'm staying with you."

I almost tossed her over my shoulder to make her go, but stopped myself. She'd had enough of people telling her what to do. I'd keep her by my side and somehow find a way to keep her safe.

"Something's happening," Lynx whispered.

Returning to the window, I stood side by side with her. Briar joined me on the other side just as the fog began to part. Emerging from within, two forms strolled out, their strides long and purposeful. With every footfall, I felt myself and all those I cared about come one step closer to death.

I sucked in a breath at the two men coming toward us, the dark mist flanking each side of them. "Korin and the Phoenix."

The Phoenix, tall and thin, held an indifferent, stony expression, but Korin, his face pinched and eyes seething with rage, looked ready to kill anything that moved.

They stopped at the end of the long, brick walkway leading to the front doors. The mist separated behind them and began to circle the mansion. The two men stared forward, eying everything about the huge home as if searching for weaknesses.

"I'm going to watch the back doors," Gerald said, fear unmistakable in his voice.

Luke rested his hand on Briar's shoulder. "What do you want me to do?"

"Get me a fresh pair of panties," she whispered.

Lynx pressed her palm to the window. "What are they doing?"

I stepped back. "I'm going to talk to them."

Briar and Lynx both turned to me in horror.

"I'm just going to see what they want," I said. "Maybe they can be reasoned with."

Briar pulled her shoulders back. "This is my home. I'll talk to them."

"We'll go together," I said.

Lynx gripped both our hands. "We'll all go."

Luke opened his mouth to probably say he was going to come too, but Briar stopped him. "Stay with Faithe."

He nodded.

While Lynx and Briar slowly walked toward the door, I glanced at Faithe. Her already pale face had turned pasty white. Words appeared in my mind: *She's already gone. A ghost.* I shook my head, tossing them away. She was going to be fine. I would make sure of it.

"I'll be right back," I said. "I promise."

She didn't answer.

Briar and Lynx waited for me to reach them before they opened the front door. We inhaled a collective breath then stepped outside. Shoulder to shoulder, we walked toward the two most powerful beings I'd ever encountered, who were backed by the Legions of Hell. To say I was scared shitless, to use Briar's expression, would be an understatement.

At the sight of us, Korin smiled. "I thought I was going to have to come in after you, Samira. How very brave of you to join me." His gaze flickered to Lynx and Briar. "And look, you brought some friends equally as stupid."

"What do you want?" I snapped. I kept a watchful on the Phoenix. His unnatural stillness had me on edge.

"You took something of mine. Return Faithe to me."

"She's not here," Briar said. "So turn your vampire ass around and leave. Take slender man with you. He's scaring the children."

A line of fire materialized from nowhere and rushed toward us. Lynx's hands shot up and blocked it with an invisible wall.

Korin's hands lowered, and he chuckled at Lynx. "Do you feel strong, young witch? If you keep using baby magic with the grownups, you're going to get killed. Run back to your mama's tit. We're not here for you."

"I'm not going anywhere," she growled.

Briar moved a protective hand in front of Lynx, more to protect Lynx from herself. Looks like I wasn't the only one worried Lynx might do something foolish. She was in over her head with these two. We all were.

Briar kept her voice even and controlled when she said, "You need to leave. This is Silver Claws property."

Korin's nostrils flared. "Give me back Faithe!"

I stepped forward. "Take me instead. I'll do whatever you want."

Korin's eyes narrowed, as he considered my offer. "Come here."

"Samira, don't—"

I held a hand up to Briar to silence her. If my leaving with Korin would save the others, I'd do it. My body numbed as I walked toward him. With every step, I mentally buried all the emotions I had been feeling during the last few days. Fear, anger, sorrow? Gone. And love? I added an extra layer of will and determination over that one, too.

By the time I reached Korin, I felt nothing. This was how it had to be. Otherwise I feared he would somehow manipulate me into using the Kiss of Eternal Night. That was what he wanted from me, for nefarious purposes I didn't want to uncover.

I stopped in front of him. He grabbed my chin with a vulture-like grip and stared into my eyes, searching for something he wouldn't find.

"I'm here," I said. "Take me. Wherever you want to go. I'm ready."

He pretended he didn't hear me and stepped back. The Phoenix took his place and lifted his long arm. He caressed my face with the back of his hand. I flinched as the contact left an ice burn across my skin in its wake.

I peered into his eyes. Dark, endless pits that bled misery, pain, and suffering. Every part of me screamed to look away, but I refused to let him see any sign of weakness. An invisible, cold finger touched my mind, trying to gain access, but I mentally pushed back at the intrusion.

The Phoenix tore his gaze away and said to Korin, "She's not ready."

Korin groaned while the Phoenix flicked his wrist in my direction. An invisible force slammed into me. My arms windmilled through the air as I flew backwards. Briar tried to catch me, but the momentum was too great. She crashed to the ground, with me landing on top of her.

"Give me Faithe," Korin repeated, "or I'll kill every last one of you."

Lynx began to mumble, whispering foreign words. A sudden gust of wind swirled at her feet and twirled around her, rising higher and higher and gaining strength. The sound of it grew louder, a storm of epic proportions. It snatched small rocks, leaves, and dirt and spun them through the air. Lynx's red hair lifted and whipped violently around her face.

"Lynx, don't!" I cried.

But she couldn't hear me over the roaring of wind and debris crashing together in the raging tempest. She shoved her hands forward. The storm raging around her exploded outward toward Korin and the Phoenix. Just before the debris crashed into them, it parted and sped past them, leaving them completely unscathed. The fog behind them absorbed the blow. More monstrous shapes appeared, holding their corporeal forms longer than before. Her magic only seemed to strengthen them, like they had the ability to siphon it.

Lynx continued her momentum pushing as hard as she could, but the two men weren't fazed by what I thought was a big show of power. Korin glanced lazily at the Phoenix. The Phoenix lifted his arm and opened his hand, palm up. His fingers slowly curled inward. The storm followed the motion and sucked itself into his large hand. Dirt, pebbles, grass. He absorbed it all and then some.

When nothing was left, Lynx gasped, her arms dropping to her sides. Her wide eyes stared in horror. She realized she was no match for him.

The Phoenix opened his hand and raised it to his lips. He blew in Lynx's direction.

"No!" Briar and I shouted at the same time.

We lunged for her, but were too late. Her body lifted several feet from the ground and flew through the large front window. Glass shattered everywhere. I rushed to help her, but found my body frozen in place. Briar, too, stood motionless next to me.

Korin strolled toward us, his gaze flickering towards Briar. "The witch must die now, and it will be by the Alpha's hand."

CHAPTER 34

*B*riar began to panic, thrashing against her invisible restraints. I had to end this. If Briar killed Lynx, she'd never come back from that. It would mentally shatter her.

Korin was almost to her, when a figure emerged from the broken window. Faithe, her bare feet bleeding from broken glass, glided toward us. Her long white hair hung lifelessly on each side of her face. Again, the image of a ghost entered my mind.

"Go back, Faithe!" Where was Luke? He should've stopped her.

She opened her mouth and barely whispered the words in my direction, "Thank you for trying, Mother, but I can't be responsible for any more deaths."

Her eyes, full of sadness and defeat, met mine before the emotions were replaced with bored indifference. Exactly how Korin liked her.

"I'm here, Master," she said, her voice deep and throaty, not a hint of the terror she had been feeling moments ago.

Korin's back stiffened at the sight of her. "You're bleeding, pet. This is what happens when you leave me. You know you can't take care of yourself."

She lowered her head. "You're right. Please forgive my insolence. I had a moment of weakness."

"Don't touch her!" I snapped at Korin. "I swear, if you do, I'll kill you."

His head jerked my direction. "I'd like to see you try. In fact, I encourage you to."

"It's time," the Phoenix said. He glanced to each side of him as if giving a silent command. The hordes of beasts hidden within the fog began to retreat.

Korin grabbed Faithe's arm, squeezing tightly until she flinched. "Let's go home. You'll need to be punished for a very long time. I'm thinking I'll make it a coven punishment. Lots of fire. Weapons. Whatever they wish. It will last for days."

"Whatever you wish," she said, her voice flat.

"Please, Korin," I begged. The mental wall containing my emotions cracked. Rage leaked through the opening, a dark, inky creature slithering inside my heart and mind.

Korin turned on his heel with Faithe on his arm. The Phoenix stared at me, the corner of his mouth twitching upward as if it could see this new thing worming its way through me. He spun around and joined Korin and Faithe. The heavy mist surrounded them, then quickly sucked into itself until it disappeared altogether, taking the three of them with it.

The invisible grip on my body disappeared. I sprinted down the brick path and onto the driveway, my head on a swivel. Where were they? Using my super speed, I darted all along the property, desperate to find them. But they had vanished.

I glanced back at the mansion. I could hear Briar inside, attending to Lynx. I recognized Lynx's voice when she moaned. She was alive, thank goodness.

I returned to the mansion, breathing heavily. It took great effort to hold back the growing darkness inside me. Instead of fighting against the rage, desperation took its place. I had to get Faithe back. If Korin did to her what he said he would, she would not mentally recover. It would break her so thoroughly she would never return to her old self.

I ran back to the house, determined to find a way to get Faithe back, but the sight of my friends gave me pause. Lynx was hurt. She had cuts all over her body. Luke leaned against the wall, rubbing his head as if someone had hit it with something.

Briar's hands shook as she helped Lynx, and she was abnormally quiet. It had probably terrified her to have such power come this close to her pack. Had the Phoenix decided to use the Legions of Hell, we wouldn't have stood a chance. Not as we were now.

"Are you okay?" Briar asked me, her voice quivering.

"I have to save her."

Briar straightened, her expression darkening. "You're not going near either one of them!"

"I will save Faithe."

"Sure. When the time is right." She walked over to me, studying me closely. "Your eyes. They're doing that scary color thing again. Knock that shit off!" She looked around and pointed to a chair. "Sit down right there and wait. We need you with us. You can't go off the rails now."

I inhaled a long slow breath, barely containing the rage simmering inside me.

"Mateo and Angel are on their way here. Together, we'll figure out what to do."

Mateo. I nearly stumbled at the sound of his name, barely making it to the chair. I needed him, needed his strong hands to steady me, his heart next to mine to calm its erratic beat, and his mind to burrow inside me and take away these dark thoughts threatening to take over.

I wanted to help Briar with Lynx and the others, but I found myself doing what she said. I sat in the chair, staring at the wall, struggling to contain the Kiss.

Korin had Faithe. I had promised her she was safe with me. I was going to free her. And now her life was made even worse. I tried not to think about all the horrible things he was doing to her right now because of me.

On and on my thoughts cut through me, the crack leading to the heart of the Kiss of Eternal Night widening. More of it leaked out. I gripped the edges of the arm chair until my nails dug into it and ripped apart the upholstery.

Voices were behind me, muted and dull. I couldn't decipher their words over the ringing in my ears. I had to get Faithe back! Why was I just sitting here? I moved to do just that when a shadow stepped in front of me, large and powerful.

"Samira." I sucked in a shaky breath. Mateo pulled me to my feet and crushed me to his chest. He hurried me out of the room, down the darkened hallway and into Briar's office. The door closed behind us. His back to the door, he held me tightly and whispered into my ear with breath that warmed the coldness inside me.

"Briar told me what happened. I swear to you, we'll get her back. I will do everything in my power."

He smoothed my hair all the way down my back, as if to swipe away the darkness inside me. Over and over, his hand caressed me while his calming voice grounded me to him.

I focused on the rise and fall of his chest. On the steady beat of his heart. On his scent, musky and earthy. After a while, I began to calm down and my body relaxed into his.

"Good," he said. "Keep coming back to me."

I inhaled and exhaled slowly, quivering inside.

He leaned away from me and searched my eyes. "Better, but not where I'd like it to be." He leaned closer. "I think I know what you need."

His breath washed over me, a slight hesitation, and when I did not stop him, he lightly brushed his lips over mine. A soft kiss.

My lips tingled, and my chest opened; I hadn't realized the crushing feeling inside me until it was released. I breathed him in and slid my hands up to cup his face. I needed more. He sealed his lips over mine, groaning as he claimed me with his lips, his tongue sweeping into my mouth. I sucked on it, oblivious to my fangs growing long.

"Take it," he whispered through my kiss.

I pricked the soft flesh with my fangs and lapped at his tongue with my own. His warm blood flowed into me, a taste so sweet and invigorating I moaned in ecstasy and pulled him closer until our bodies were flush against each other.

His blood, laced with strength and power, slid down the back of my throat and raced through my veins. It pushed back the dark tendrils that had begun to dig its claws into my heart and mind, until I felt like myself again.

I pulled back, sucking in a great breath. I'd forgotten how potent and healing Mateo's blood was to mine. It was as if it knew what my soul needed in the moment and gave it freely. Whether it was comfort, courage, or even to heighten my sexual pleasure, his blood was my antidote to everything.

Mateo wiped at his mouth. "Look at me."

"I'm better. Thank you." I avoided eye contact, embarrassed I'd taken his blood, something usually only done between lovers.

He latched onto my chin and gently guided my face forward. His golden eyes held the power of the sun. "Every last drop of my blood belongs to you. It always has."

I nodded. "Thank you."

"Don't thank me, Samira."

A small smile tickled my lips. He hated it when I thanked him for his strength. His bond to me was reason enough, he'd always said. I traced his lips and he nipped at my finger, but my smile slipped off my lips. "How do we get her back?"

"I've been thinking about that." He led me to the couch, and we eased into the cushions. "It's too risky for you to return to Winter's Cove, but I can with my men."

"You can't risk Korin discovering—"

He held up a finger to silence me. "Once I'm inside, I will create a distraction. Maybe I'll start the house on fire. Something to get everyone out of the house. Once she's out, you'll grab her."

"Korin will compel every last one of you into telling the truth. It's too risky. Even having this conversation is dangerous."

"It is time for me to get involved, Samira. I've stood by for too long." His eyes searched mine. "I know what Faithe means to you. I will take this risk. It is worth it to me." His golden amber eyes turned to steel. "I will leave it to you to find her once the fire has started and to take her to safety. In the meantime, I have decided I will kill him." I gasped, surprised. "I let him control me for far too long. It's time I take my power back and destroy him, while his compulsion has no power over me."

I sucked in a deep breath. "But—"

"I will do it swiftly. I'll wait until he goes into his office, and then I'll start the fire just outside. As soon as he runs out, I'll be waiting for him. This can work. I know it."

I was quiet for a moment, thinking. Korin may be so distracted with the fire that he wouldn't notice Mateo just outside his door. "It could work. As soon as I get Faithe out safely, I will find you and help if you need it."

He nodded, and the bond between us strengthened. We would do this, together. He searched my eyes and raised his hand to my face, caressing it gently. His gaze dropped to my lips, and he moved toward me. A knock at the door interrupted the moment.

"Sorry to bug you." Briar opened the door, her eyes puffy and red. "But I just wanted to let you know, Mateo, you're welcome to stay. Sun's coming up soon."

"How's Lynx?" I asked.

"She has some nasty cuts, but she'll survive. Roma's coming over with Owen. They'll help heal her."

"I should go to her."

Briar lifted her hand in a stopping gesture. "She doesn't want to see anyone. I had to force my way into the bedroom just to talk to her."

My muscles tightened. "Why?"

Briar sighed and raked her fingers through her hair. "I think her pride was hurt more than her body. Like the rest of us, she realized just how out of our league we are. I mean, seriously? Did you see those monsters in the fog? How do we fight that shit?"

I nodded, biting my lip. We were out of our league, but not because of the Legions of Hell. I'd fought them once before. The Phoenix was the unknown variable.

"We'll figure this out," Mateo answered for me. "I know people. All is not lost." For whatever reason, he didn't mention our plans to her about killing Korin.

Angel appeared in the doorway behind Briar, his green eyes hard and angry. Every muscle in his body stretched tight. "Mateo, I'm staying here for the night."

Briar whirled around. "I thought you said you were leaving?"

His eyes found hers. He hesitated briefly, then said, "I can't."

Her breath hitched and shoulders dropped. "Thank you. There's a coffin downstairs." She glanced back at us. "You two don't mind sharing one, do you? Assuming you're staying, Mateo?"

His hand tightened on me. "I'm staying."

I didn't dare look at him, afraid he'd see how relieved I was at his words. Rarely did I need a man, even Mateo, but I needed him tonight more than ever.

We left Briar's office and hung back while she assured the pack they were safe. She managed to keep an air of strength to her voice for the pack's sake, but I knew the truth. She had no idea how to keep them safe. Neither did I. Maybe it was time to call upon old friends. I thought specifically of Aris Crow and his unique abilities. They could help. Detrand, too.

Mateo tugged on my hand. "Let's go."

I nodded, feeling the sun's rays tugging on me, just barely. My body was too numb to feel much of anything.

I showed Mateo to the basement. Angel wouldn't be too far behind us. He had been hovering on the edge of the living room, anxiously waiting for Briar to finish her speech.

"It might be a little tight," I said, staring down at the coffin I'd slept in the night before.

"Good." He climbed inside and held out his arms to me.

I crawled in after him and closed the lid, sighing when his arms folded around me. We lay in silence for a long while, our thoughts our own, before the sun tugged our minds into darkness. But reposing there with him, his strong and steady presence calming the storm of my rage, planted a tiny, hopeful seed inside me. We would get Faithe back and destroy Korin. The last time we'd separated, allowing Korin to control us, we were weak. But this time, together, we could make it work.

We had to.

CHAPTER 35

The sound of Angel's coffin lid opening made my eyes open. Darkness greeted me as well as Mateo's body warming my back side. I hadn't slept that well in centuries. My mind felt crisp, my body strengthened. Somehow, tonight I was going to get Faithe back, then Mateo and I would fight Korin. Just how it should've been all those years ago.

I moved to exit our casket, but Mateo's arms tightened around me. He breathed in my ear, "Just a moment longer."

Settling into him, I allowed his hands to trace my stomach, his lips to move down the back of my neck, his warm breath igniting a fire within me. I would use it as fuel to fight harder, strategize better, do whatever I had to do to get us safely away from Rouen with Faithe.

As if sensing my new determination, he said, "It's time."

I lifted the lid to find my blades by the coffin. I slid them into place at my back, and without another word we headed upstairs. Angel was already there in the shadows, leaning a shoulder on the living room wall while his gaze took in everything and everyone.

Eddie was on a sofa with Folas and a few other fae, speaking in hushed voices. Opposite them on another couch sat Owen and two witches I recognized from the Apex. I didn't spot Roma or Lynx.

The rest of the living room was packed with shifters. Briar saluted me in passing as she hurried around the room, giving out orders. Add more security around the property border. Find more weapons. Guns, knives, bows. At one point, she asked someone for a cannon.

Mateo left me, his fingers grazing my hips as he headed toward Angel. He was probably going to tell him about our new plans. They would work. We just had to make sure Winter's Cove caught on fire long enough to get vampires outside.

Luke caught my eye from the kitchen and nodded me over. I moved to join him when the front door flew open. Roma stood in the entry, gasping for breath with wide eyes. I glanced behind her into the darkness, half expecting to see the Legions of Hell, but no one was there.

At the same time, Briar and I hurried over to her.

"What's wrong?" I asked.

"Lynx. She's gone! I told her not to."

Briar grabbed her arm. "Not to what?"

"She went back to White Pine to try and track the Phoenix with magic. She had this scary look in her eyes, like she's trying to prove something. I tried to stop her, but she did some voodoo shit on me and knocked me out."

Briar and I looked at each other at the same time. We didn't have to say anything. We knew we would go after her.

I stepped out the door first, followed by Briar. Luke, Mateo, and Angel joined us.

Roma called out, "Hurry! It's going to destroy her mind if she tries to track such strong magic."

Briar jumped onto the back of Luke's motorcycle. Angel slid onto his own. Mateo gave me a look. If we super sped and cut through the mountainous hills, we could beat them. I nodded once.

Together we darted behind the house and sliced through the woods. A blur of trees and darkness whipped by me. The scents of earth, water, and chemicals filled my nostrils all at once. I rarely traveled this fast. It could be disorienting for the first few minutes after I stopped, but I wasn't racing into battle. I was racing to stop a friend from doing something that could destroy her.

We came to a screeching halt half a mile before reaching White Pine. I inhaled several slow breaths to calm the swimming sensation in my head and stomach, then listened closely. I couldn't detect voices or movement, not like I could last time I was here.

"Go slowly," Mateo whispered.

We separated about a hundred yards apart and cautiously approached the area. Within a short time, I knew the place had been abandoned. We emerged from the forest and came together. All the garage bay doors were open, spilling darkness into the moon's full light.

"Lynx!" I called out. In the distance, I heard the familiar roaring of motorcycles approaching.

"I'll go inside." Mateo jumped into one of the openings.

I circled the building. Near the rear, I caught her scent. Just barely.

Luke, Briar, and Angel arrived just then, their bikes leaving angry marks along the ground.

I jogged over to Briar and pointed the way I just came. "She was here. I can smell her over there."

"Everyone split up. She's probably in the forest."

We split ways, each of us trying to track her scent. I thought I could smell her, but the next second I couldn't, only to pick it up again several yards further. The way she kept breaking up worried me.

It wasn't long before I sensed I was far away from the others. I thought about returning to White Pine when my phone vibrated in my pocket. I fully expected it to be Briar calling me back, but it was from a number I didn't recognize.

I hit the answer button. "Yes?"

"Thank God it's you!"

My pulse raced. "Faithe? What are you doing?"

"I snuck away. Come get me right now. I only have a few minutes before he finds out."

"Where are you?"

"It's a butcher shop. Korin took me here once before. It's the only place I knew to go."

"I'll be right there." I knew exactly where it was. It was Mateo's building. I'd met him there once with Briar.

I moved to super speed there but paused. What if it was a trap? What if Korin was waiting for me? I glanced back, thinking about calling for the others to help. But if I took them, then there would be no one to look for Lynx. Plus, if it really was a trap, would I want any of them near Korin? He could compel them to do anything.

I exhaled a large breath. I had to do this on my own. Faithe had sounded truly terrified. What if this was my only chance to save her?

Once again, the world transformed into a blended mess of grays and blacks as I raced along the forest floor, moonlight warming the blades on my back. The landscape changed to darkened buildings, parked cars, and street lamps. I kept to the shadows as much as I could until I reached my destination. I stopped on the sidewalk of Chuck's Butchery Shop and stared ahead, wishing I could see through the cinderblock walls. No sounds echoed from within.

I opened the door, glancing at an annoying jingle of a bell above me. The tangy smell of fresh blood punched me in the gut. I'd forgotten to eat when I'd woken for the night, and the pain was sharp. I shoved the sensation aside and proceeded forward down a hall that led to the back. I pressed my ear to a closed door. On the other side, a cold storage room held fresh meat. The only sound I could hear was the barely squeaking sounds of metal hooks holding up slabs of beef from the ceiling.

Soundlessly, I pushed open the door and slipped inside. Using my night vision, I maneuvered my way through the skinned pigs and cows. There were so many more hanging compared to last time. The scent of all their blood made me dizzy. I backed up into one and jumped, my nerves on edge. Something didn't feel right.

Taking a quick moment to calm myself, I proceeded forward. Within the aroma of the animal blood filling the air, a whiff of something unexpected stung my nostrils, and I froze. *Vampire blood.*

My heart slammed against my ribcage. "Faithe!"

I stumbled forward around a large pork carcass and sucked in a breath. Kristina hung upside down by her feet, her arms outstretched. The tips of her still fingers rested in a puddle of dark crimson blood.

I covered my hand with my mouth to keep from screaming. What was she doing here? Teddy said she left! Crouching down, I quickly felt for a pulse. My eyes slid over her slit throat. Kristina was dead. Too much blood loss. I lightly touched her face, regret and guilt swelling within me. But in my next breath, pure rage surged to the surface, ripping open recently patched wounds.

"I knew you would come."

I stood slowly and turned around.

Korin detached from the shadows at his back and snapped his fingers. Small fires ignited around the room. I didn't see Faithe.

"Where is she?"

"She's here." He glanced back into the darkness. "Come, child. Your Mother wants to see you."

I heard the shuffling of feet in the room behind him before I saw her. Hell's fire cast dancing shadows across her lithe frame as she emerged into the light. The orangish glow reached her face. I gasped in horror. One of her eyes was swollen shut, and she had dozens of cuts all over her body. None of them had healed which meant Korin had used a rare Saranton knife.

"What have you done?" I growled.

"I gave her what she deserved." He paused. "Things changed after you left. I couldn't be so soft on everyone."

He smoothed the back of Faithe's hair. Faithe stared straight ahead, her eyes lifeless.

"Faithe?" I asked, my voice gentle.

She didn't respond.

Korin eyed her curiously. "I think we broke her. Naburus especially. He was particularly cruel." Korin's eyes dropped to the lower half of Faithe's white dress that was now stained red.

A wave of raw rage crashed through me so suddenly I sucked in a breath. "I'm going to kill you, Korin."

He chuckled. "Impossible."

In a split second, I had my sword in my hand and was swinging it to Korin's throat. He caught it just as quickly and twisted it from my grip. He tossed it to the ground. The clanking sound echoed against the concrete floor.

I spun on my heel to round-kick him, but he darted out of the way and drove his palm into my chest. My sternum shattered as I flew backwards into a pork carcass, pain lancing every inch of my body. I collapsed to the floor, my body quivering.

"You can't save her." His voice held a note of regret. He turned to Faithe and ran his fingers through her hair. "I did enjoy you some of the time."

"Please, Korin," I begged. "Don't hurt her. I'll do whatever you want."

I pulled myself to all fours.

"I wish I could, but I simply cannot trust you. And you need to stretch yourself, Samira. It's the only way. Sacrifices must be made."

My eyes dropped to my sword a few feet away from him.

He followed my gaze. "You'll never make it in time, but I'd like to see you try."

Latching onto the dark tendrils that had begun to crawl out of my fragile heart, I leapt forward, driven only by rage and anger. My fingers grazed the handle of the sword just as Korin's elbow crashed into my spine. The sound of my back cracking hurt less than the pain that followed. For I knew in that moment, I had lost the one thing that mattered most to me in life.

"Faithe," Korin began, his voice sticky sweet, "Please pick up Samira's blade."

She did as he asked, not casting me a single look. I couldn't tell if she was compelled or not, but one thing was certain. The Faithe I knew was gone.

Faithe stopped in front of him, the sword hanging limply at her side. Korin smoothed back her hair and kissed her as tenderly as a lover would. "My beautiful, sweet pet."

His grip on her chin slowly tightened until she yelped. He stared into her eyes and gave one last order. "Cut your head off. I am no longer in need of it."

"No!" I cried and attempted to move but the bottom half of my body wouldn't respond. Panic surged through me. If I could just stall for sixty seconds, maybe a little more, I might heal. "Look at me, Faithe!"

With both hands, she inched the blade upward and outward, her hands beginning to shake.

"Faithe!" I used my palms to pull me along the cold and filthy floor. Pain lit every nerve ending in white-hot fire, threatening to overwhelm my mind with sheer agony. Sweat broke from my pores.

"That's a good girl," Korin cooed. "Keep going."

Tears filled her eyes and spilled onto her cheeks. The tip of the sword began to turn toward her throat.

"Stop! I order you!" I cried, but any parental bond I might've had with her had shattered centuries ago.

"Do it!" Korin yelled, spittle flying from his mouth and landing on her upper lip.

"No! Listen to me!" I was almost to her. I reached out to grab her leg; my fingers skimmed the sheer material of her skirt.

Faithe was silently crying now, her hands shaking uncontrollably as she fought against his compulsion, trying to survive just one more day.

Just as I was to grab her, Korin kicked me in the face. My vision exploded into an array of colors, and I dropped to the ground.

He returned his deadly gaze to Faithe. "Cut. Your. Head. Off."

She swung the tip of the blade to the side of her, her desperate gaze flickering to mine.

"Mother," she whimpered. A flash of silver sliced through the air, followed by a spray of blood all around me. The crimson droplets stung my face.

I moaned in agony as her body decomposed right in front of me, until all that remained of my precious daughter was a mess of tangled hair and bubbling fat mixed with the ashes from her bones. I touched the remains as if I could still gather her to me, but she slipped through my fingers.

The shell around my heart crumbled into a thousand charred pieces with sharp, deadly edges. And as it fell away, a new dark and ugly beast took its place. This time, I eagerly welcomed the power that came with it. The fire of hell and the breath of a thousand demons raced through my veins.

Without bending my body even a little, I rose to my feet as if lifted by the ghosts of the animals around me who had been slaughtered not long ago.

A slow smile spread across Korin's face. He stared deeply into my eyes, pleased by what he saw. "There you are."

I snapped my hand forward to crush his larynx but just as I reached him, his body dematerialized, leaving me grasping at empty air.

His laughter echoed against the walls. "See you soon, Samira."

CHAPTER 36

The Eternal Night's Kiss flowed through me, licking at my veins and whispering words of death and destruction. I didn't bridle it, for if I did, I would feel all the crippling emotions: sorrow, guilt, regret, sadness. I didn't want any of that weakness right now. I needed strength, rage, raw power. The Kiss gave me all of that.

I strode down the sidewalk toward Briar's house, aware of everything around me. A dog whining in a house the next block over, a conversation between lovers, the way each pebble depressed the soles of my feet, wind carrying the scent of a textile plant across town. I missed nothing.

My steps slowed the closer I came to home. Briar was speaking to Luke, her voice pained. They'd found Lynx unconscious a mile out from White Pine. Roma was with her upstairs, trying to bring her out of it. Mateo was there, too. I couldn't hear him, but I could smell him and feel him. The darkness inside me craved his body and drove me forward to screw him. This urge alone I stifled. The rest, I unleashed.

Before I reached the back door, it flung open and Mateo's body filled the space.

"Where have you been?" he demanded.

I brushed past him and entered the kitchen to drink from my

thermos until it was empty. I licked my lips, needing more. The pangs of hunger still burned my stomach.

"Hey!" Briar said from behind me. "Mateo asked you a question. Where were you? You disappeared."

"I had something to do." I left them to go into the basement to get more blood bags, but when I opened my small fridge, I groaned. I can't believe I'd forgotten; I only had one left. I drank it and returned to the kitchen to grab a bottle of Vodka from on top of the fridge. Alcohol would temporarily numb the pain.

Briar gripped my arm before I could take a swig. "What is going on with you? You're more," she searched for a word, "bitchy than usual. You haven't even asked about Lynx."

"Roma's taking care of her." I shook off her grip and swallowed the alcohol. I relished its burn all the way to my stomach.

"Listening in and asking about her are two very different things. And you still haven't told us where you were."

I stared in her eyes, barely able to contain the power within me. "Because it's none of your business."

"Samira," Mateo warned.

Briar's left eye twitched, and her nostrils flared.

Looking from Briar to him, I stepped back. I needed to get out of here before I did something terrible. I didn't belong in this house anymore, not how I was.

"I have to go, but I'll be back to check on Lynx."

"Go?" Briar's eyes bulged from her head. "What the hell is going on? Something happened, I know it!"

A pang of guilt and sadness swelled within me, but the Kiss devoured it and buried it with the rest of my emotions.

Mateo reached for me but I moved away from him, closer to the back door. "Don't touch me."

"Talk to us. Please," he urged.

I placed my hand on the doorknob. "The Phoenix has come for blood. We need to prepare."

"What does that mean, Samira?" Briar snapped. "Or whoever you are right now."

"And we will." Mateo's voice was soft and gentle. I didn't let my gaze linger on the worry bleeding from his eyes. "Just stay with me."

A breath caught in my lungs. "You don't want to be anywhere near me."

Before either of them could disagree, I bolted out the door and into the darkness, super speeding like lightning across the city, away from everything I'd come to love. My friends, Mateo. They couldn't be a part of what came next. Yes, I would use them to help me take down Korin and the Phoenix, but beyond that, I must keep them at arm's reach. Eternal Night's poisonous kiss would destroy them otherwise.

I came to an abrupt stop in the seedy part of Rouen where drugs and crime flourished. *Hell's Peak.* The filthy streets and run-down buildings pulled darkness to it like an addict to his fix. Light didn't exist in this place. Those who ran the Hell's Peak wouldn't allow it. The Ames de la Terra had attempted to remove the supernaturals and humans in control, but their strangling hold ran deep through many political circles. Even Dominic hadn't managed to gain control over this area.

Predatory instincts burned deep within my bones, honing all my senses. All around me, night life was very much alive. Prostitutes strutted freely, exchanging money and sex in the shallowest of shadows. Drugs were as abundant as the clubs and bars, drug dealers and their thugs outnumbering the police ten to one. And what officers dared to brave the streets this time of night only did so that they might participate in all that Hell's Peak had to offer.

I zeroed in on a tall man with tan skin and long hair. Scabs marked his face and arms. He stood across the street speaking in harsh tones to two prostitutes. By the looks of the women, halter tops, short skirts and long stockings, they had seen better days. One of them had her arm bandaged, and the other reeked of alcohol and urine.

Crossing the street to him, I removed my jacket and pulled my tank top down to reveal the swell of my breasts. The man spotted me approaching and shooed the women away. He stared at my breasts only looking up at me when I stopped in front of him.

He licked his chapped lips. "How may I have the pleasure of serving you?"

I twisted the front of his shirt and brought him close to me, staring deep into his eyes. My powers of compulsion flowed into him. "Follow me."

His dark pupils dilated, then returned to normal. I let him go and sauntered toward an alley blacker than night, my heart thundering in my chest and heat burning between my legs. His footsteps echoed behind me, adding to my pleasure. I'd forgotten how much I loved to be obeyed.

I turned around and smiled at him as I stepped backwards into the darkness, fingering him to come with me. The beat of his heart stuttered and fear flashed in his eyes, but his body followed after me. It didn't have a choice.

Darkness swallowed us, its cool breath whispering across my flesh. Fangs grew long in my mouth, and I parted my lips to make room for them. The man must've seen a glint of them in the darkness because he moved to bolt, but I appeared in front of him, making him stumble back. He reached into his jacket pocket and fumbled with something inside. A gun appeared in my face, shaking within his grip.

"What the hell are you?" he gasped.

My hand struck forward and knocked the weapon from his hand. It clattered to the cracked pavement. "I am Samira Chevoky, barer of the Kiss of Eternal Night. And your time running these streets with the rest of the filth is over. I'm going to give you all the Kiss of death."

I jerked his head to the side and plunged my fangs into his weathered skin. Warm blood coated my tongue and ran down the back of my throat. I moaned in ecstasy. It had been too long since I'd indulged.

But not anymore.

I gave into the Kiss and let its power consume me. I stoked its raging fire further, whispering words to the darkness, promising blood and violence. Vowing revenge. With it, I might just stand a chance against Korin. And right now, that's all that mattered.

The final beat of the man's heart echoed through my veins. I unlatched before death could claim me, too. I sucked in a great breath and stared toward the night sky, blood running down my chin.

Lingering thoughts of my friends, Mateo, and even my daughter were all gone. Only my hatred for Korin remained.

Before all of this was over, one of us was going to die. And if fate chose me, then I'd be damn sure to go down destroying everything that belonged to him.

The night was young, after all.

A VAMPIRE'S BANE

Download the next book in the series, *A Vampire's Fury*

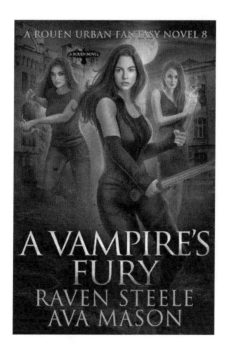

"The monster isn't under my bed. It's screaming inside my head."

Cursed by the Kiss of Eternal Night, Samira lives her life as an ancient and powerful vampire, guarding her emotions carefully. One slip up and the darkness inside her could send her on a rage-filled, bloodlust path of death and destruction. It's happened once before, and it could easily happen again.

For over a century, she's managed to keep the beast inside her at bay, but when someone from her past shows up unexpectedly, her emotions hang by a thread. Especially when she finds out they are working with the Phoenix, the source of the growing evil in Rouen.

Maybe it's time she stops controlling the monster inside her. It may be the only way she can save those she loves.

Continue this dark and hilarious journey with a SNARKY shifter, BADASS Vampire, and POWERFUL witch TODAY!

Coming soon!
Pre-order TODAY

* * *

While you are waiting for Samira's story to continue, read more about Samira's other friends in Coast City, including the infamous Aris Crow Vampire Legend who is coming to Rouen soon! Download A Monster's Death, book 5 in the Rouen Chronicles.

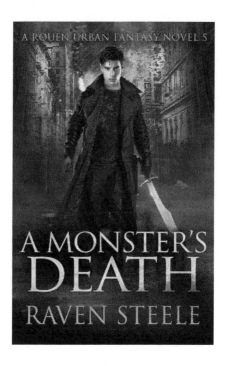

"The city doesn't need another hero. It needs a monster."

Aris has lived beneath the streets all his life while a growing evil overtook the city he loved. He's watched the people suffer, smelled their fear, and heard their cries for mercy. All while living under the control of the ruthless man who murdered his parents.

But the time has come for Aris to rise from the darkness. He's trained his whole life for this moment and, unlike the justice system, he will not fail the people of Coast City, or the woman he fell in love with as a child, the woman who believes him dead.

But no one told him that sometimes heroes aren't enough. Sometimes people need a monster.

NEWSLETTER SIGN UP

Dear Reader,

Thank you for taking the time to read this novel. We hope you enjoyed it! Please consider leaving an honest review, as they not only impact other readers' purchasing decisions, but also help determine the success of my novels. Plus your opinion matters to me as well. I want to give you the best reading experience possible!

To sign up for release notifications for future releases, please visit our personal webpages at www.RavenSteele.net.

OTHER BOOKS BY RAVEN STEELE:

Raven Steele is a coauthor pen name for Rachel McClellan. You can find her other books on her website at RachelMcClellan.com.

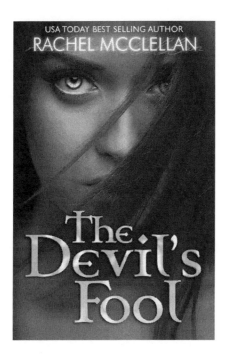

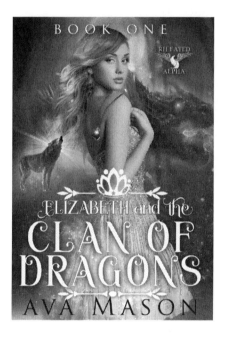

A female Wolf in danger. Four Sexy Dragons determined to protect her.

A reverse harem paranormal romance